Farhill Farm

By

Rick J. Barrett

Tracey & Dr.
To good friends.

Rick Barrett

This book is a work of fiction. Places, events, and situations in this story are purely fictional. Any resemblance to actual persons, living or dead, is coincidental.

ISBN: 1-4107-7560-7 (e-book)
ISBN: 1-4107-7559-3 (Paperback)

Library of Congress Control Number: 2003095250

This book is printed on acid free paper.

Printed in the United States of America
Bloomington, IN

1stBooks - rev. 09/23/03

Chapter 1

"You ever have to shoot a smuggler, Uncle Sean?" Kate asked.

The hard frost reflected the moonlight in the clear as glass pre-dawn sky making it almost as bright as day in southeast Michigan.

The Taurus roared to life as Sean Ferguson threw the car into gear on Interstate 75 near Monroe. Although it appeared generic, the car with the cop package could run with the fastest wheels on the road. He felt the vibration from the engine in the steering wheel like a wild stallion straining to be free of a rope. Tires screeched as they roared out into traffic.

He smiled. "Nervous, Kate?" Ferguson asked.

She flicked him a quick tight smile. "Yeah, guess I am."

He shrugged. "Don't worry about it. If it makes you feel any better I've never had to shoot anything more than paper targets on the range."

"That helps. Thanks," Kate said, visibly relieved.

Ferguson removed the ever-present Michigan State baseball cap from his head and glanced at the rearview mirror to see the royal blue state police cruiser right behind them. He motioned for the officer to pass and take the point. Ferguson pulled the victory cigar from his breast pocket and set it in the ashtray on the console. The plastic tube that held the tobacco had a price label of $9.99 unlike one of the cheap Swisher Sweets he smoked daily.

"Have you always smoked a victory cigar after a bust, Uncle Sean?" Kate asked. "I'm surprised Aunt Joanne hasn't stopped that."

Ferguson looked sheepishly at his niece. "It wasn't because she hasn't tried, Katie. Anyway, don't worry about the bust. I've been stopping cigarette smugglers for twenty-five years and I'm always careful."

Had it really been twenty-five years? Ferguson took a mental inventory. He still carried 147 pounds soaking wet on his six-foot-two frame, just as he had back in 1978. He still had the strawberry blond brush cut, albeit a little longer these days because of his teenage daughters' prodding. The radio crackled to life. "Hey, Music Man! Give our congrats on her first bust to Red." Ferguson shook his head at the transmission from Mother Hen as he snatched the microphone from its mooring on the dashboard. Jessica Cooper, alias Mother Hen, worked the other tax fraud car with Hound Dog. She looked nothing like a mother hen, though. Her thrice-weekly six-mile runs probably had something to do with it. No one ever guessed she had stepped over that magical forty threshold. Looking more like a college student than some veteran Treasury agent, Jessica had a youthful appearance due in part to the blond ponytail that bobbed up and down as she scurried about.

Ferguson pulled a worn cassette tape from the visor above his seat and shoved it into the player in the dashboard. Turning to Kate, he cranked up the volume as the wahoo, wahoo sound intensified before the whump whump sound like a helicopter took over.

"Sounds like an air raid warning," Kate screamed over the music.

But then the booming bass shook the inside of the car as the singer began- I like to dream. Yes, Yes. Right between the...Ferguson sang to the music like the raspy voice on the tape. About a minute into the rendition he turned it down to reasonable levels and picked up the microphone.

"We are now good to go, team."

The radio hissed. "Sorry, Red. Forgot to tell ya 'bout our fearless leader. Did he play the Steppenwolf tune or the Who's Pinball Wizard at top volume?" Hound Dog asked.

Kate grabbed the microphone. "Steppenwolf. And my ears will never be the same."

"You tell the man he don't know what good music is. Listen and name this tune, Music." The microphone remained open as the drums started.

After four seconds the music was gone and Ferguson spoke. "In the Midnight Hour."

"Artist?" Hound Dog asked.

"Wilson Pickett."

"Year?"

"1965.

Ferguson heard a sigh over the radio. "Label?" Hound Dog said almost apologetically.

"Atlantic Records. Give it up, Dog."

They heard a sound from the microphone like there was a struggle in the other fraud car. Mother Hen came on, "Will you two just grow up. Why is it we have to listen to this competitive bullshit all the time?"

"Sorry, Ma," Ferguson said into the microphone, "but tell him not to send a boy to try and stump me on a song." Ferguson grinned at his niece. He and Hound Dog had jousted too many times to count over music and it gave him great pleasure that his friend with the

3

bodybuilder physique and stoic personality could not throw out a song and the particulars that Ferguson did not know.

Reaching mile marker eighteen on Interstate Seventy-five, Ferguson's Taurus and Mother Hen's Camaro made their move, drivers tromping on the gas pedals of the high performance machines. They closed in on the suspect's battered blue Oldsmobile in a matter of seconds. Ferguson's breathing became shallow and his left leg twitched. The first police car rushed past with red lights flashing as if pursuing an unseen speeder ahead of them but slowed to let the other cars catch him after only a quarter mile. The other tax fraud car pulled along side the suspect on the left. A second police cruiser approached from behind as Ferguson pulled up along side the suspect on the right to complete the box of the smuggler's car. Boxing the suspect vehicle with other cars usually prevented a chase. They had used the technique successfully for years without incident.

"Subject is dark complexion, black hair, slight build," Ferguson said into the microphone. Most of the smugglers the team saw these days were of middle-eastern descent so it didn't surprise him. He saw the suspect glance at them and then snap his head forward to look into the rear view mirror.

"He made us, Ma," Ferguson said into the microphone. "Just close the box and don't make it too loose. We're gonna slow him down easy. I don't want him getting' antsy and ramming our rides." The cars ground to a stop like rush hour on a Detroit freeway. "Gotcha!" Ferguson said, clearly relieved. The smuggler raised his right hand as if to

4

surrender but he clutched something in it. For a split second Ferguson couldn't see what it was. When he saw the glint of light reflect from it his eyes went wild. The man was waving a handgun.

"Gun! Get down!" Ferguson screamed as smoke and fire erupted from the barrel of the weapon. He saw the shooter's hand pitch upward as he tried to control the recoil. A bullet exploded through the side window of the Taurus and zipped past Ferguson's right ear. He heard the buzz of it. Before he could move another shot split the air as a maniacal grin spread across the face of the shooter. Ferguson put his hands up to ward off any other bullets while trying to shrink down in his seat. Peering over the door of the Taurus, he saw the shooter turn to his left and point the Smith and Wesson at Mother Hen just as a round from the state trooper's nine millimeter Glock pierced the windshield and hit him in the shoulder. Jerking to his right from the force of the bullet, the suspect stared with crazed eyes at Ferguson, his contorted face showing brown stained teeth. A second bullet pierced the windshield and hit the man in the chest. He jumped like a marionette on a string. A third bullet hit him in the face and exited the back of his head, splattering pieces of brain and bone onto the rear window of the car.

Closing his eyes, Ferguson collapsed against the wheel gulping for air as his chest heaved spasmodically. "Oh shit! Oh shit! You okay, Kate?" he said. "That was too close." Everything was silent. "Kate?" The monotonous hum from the radio suddenly seemed deafening to Ferguson- louder than the gun

5

blasts. He sat stunned, strangling the
steering wheel with both hands.

     Moochy Lancona sat in the distribution
center- not a true warehouse really but a
converted barn that from the outside looked
like any other weathered farm building and
inside was a modern industrial structure. He
and Abdul, one of the runners, waited for a
load of illegal cigarettes to come in from
North Carolina, one of five they expected in
the next twenty-four hours. Stepping outside,
Lancona squinted at the early morning sun as
he lit a smoke. He thought about his wife and
little boy. They would love to live out here.
And why not? This was everything a family
could want- lots of land, space, and clear
air. Too bad things never worked out for him
to buy something like this for his son.
     Abdul stood next to Moochy fidgeting and
glancing down the quarter of a mile drive that
led to the main road. He was not used to a
rural setting like this- hundreds of acres now
stripped of its bounty. He yearned to be an
hour east in Detroit. His life growing up had
been on the streets of Beirut in Lebanon and
he felt comfortable in a city.
     "Once we get the cigarettes from tonight
unloaded we'll put the order together for the
Flint stores and you can make the deliveries
tomorrow," Lancona said.
     "How many stores?" Abdul asked.
     "Six." He looked at his watch again.
"Where the hell is Faisal? Shoulda been here
an hour ago," Lancona asked.
     "He will be here. He is always on time
so something must have delayed him," Abdul
said.

"Maybe, a flat tire," Lancona returned. "Try him on the cell phone."

After listening to the cell phone ring, Abdul flipped it and turned to Lancona. "No answer," he said, his brow furrowing.

"You're sure it was charged when he went out last night, right?"

"Yes, I am sure," Abdul said.

"Turn on the police scanners in case he had an accident or was stopped."

Abdul froze. "If we lose a car, Bat will kill us. He is a crazy man," Abdul said.

Chapter 2

Billy Johnston tossed Fred Tompkins the case of Salems from the top shelf at S&S Distributing in Greensboro, North Carolina. The industrial shelves held case upon case of cigarettes, many brands Johnston had never even heard of. The majority of the shelves held the staples of the industry- Winston, Kools, and Marlboro. Thousands of dollars in cigarettes came and went every day here in what was the state of the art warehousing. Computer terminals, strategically mounted like sentries, waited to access records and print invoices. The overhead doors with loading docks gave them a view of an acre of concrete pad for moving trucks in and out.

The palate was nearly full and Johnston stood up and flexed his back.

"Damn," he said, I must be getting' old or somethin' 'cause these cigarettes sure seem to be getting' heavier." The movement only exaggerated the distended belly grown with too many beers and too few workouts.

"Order's complete, Billy," Tompkins said as he ticked off the line on the order slip and shoved it in his pocket.

After wrapping the palate with clear plastic like some huge sandwich for a box lunch, Johnson pulled a permanent marker to write the name and address of the recipient for delivery.

"Who's it for?" he asked wearily.

"Another one for F," Tompkins said.

Johnson pushed his Lansing Lugnuts baseball hat, a remembrance from his days in Michigan, up on his head and scratched his temple. "Now, who in the hell is F and where

8

is he? We been puttin' together twenty or
thirty orders for them every week and no one
knows where or how they get delivered. Every
other order comes through here we mark it with
name and address for delivery. Why are these
so different? We hilo'em down aisle one at
night and the next morning they're gone."

"Just keep your mouth shut Billy,"
Tompkins said, looking around nervously.
"Remember how much trouble that Barber kid got
himself in with that Arab guy for spoutin' off
in here. One day he was workin' and the next
he was gone and no one ever saw him again.
Angie told me he never even came in for his
last paycheck and rumor has it he ended up
swimmin' at the bottom of the river. I tell
ya, these guys don't screw around."

"Yeah, yeah," Johnston said trying to
rotate his upper body to get the kinks out.

The manager of the business, Vincent
Scarponi, turned the corner and came down the
aisle as Johnson stepped onto the concrete
floor.

"Hey, Vinnie, how's it hangin'" Johnston
said, his hat now sitting cockeyed on his
head.

"The name is Vince, you stupid ass,"
Scarponi said.

Tompkins lowered his head and tried to
suppress a laugh as his hand went to his
mouth.

"Yeah, I know, but I love the name
Vinnie. You ever see that movie, My Cousin
Vinnie. Man, what a riot that was. Remember
that scene when Vinnie was in front of the
judge, who was that again- oh yeah Herman
Munster, talkin' about the two youtes and..."

"For cripe sake, Johnston, if I had a
nickel for every time you've told that story

I'd be a rich man. Now, can it," Scarponi said. "You guys got the orders filled?"

"Yeah and would you please tell us who the hell F is?" Johnston asked as all the color drained from Tompkins face.

"None of your fucking business Johnston and let it drop, now," Scarponi said, clearly irritated. "These people are very private and they buy a lot of cigarettes from us." Scarponi turned and walked quickly away shaking his head.

"He's gotta learn to relax," Johnson said, "Life's too short to be wound up like a rubber band airplane all the time."

Billy Johnston was the epitome of a good old boy redneck once removed. Until he came to work at S&S a few months ago, his previous thirty years had been occupied throwing together Oldsmobiles at the auto plant in Lansing, Michigan after a stint in the Army fighting in Vietnam. He had moved home to the Carolinas after retirement beckoned but the rewards for his labor had not been enough to see him through each month, mostly because of his beer drinking expense and generous nature for anyone who wanted to listen to his stories at the bar.

"All these guys should stop to smell the roses. You see all them cameras all over. It's a wonder we can even take a dump in privacy around here," Johnston continued. "And with all the fence and razor wire it's more like a state penitentiary than a business."

"I heard Scarponi telling one of those ATF guys last year that at any given time we could have fifteen or twenty million dollars in cigarettes in here. I guess I'd be careful for that kinda money," Tompkins said.

"Well, I'll tell ya, it just seems odd that all these northern boys come down here all the time and it doesn't seem like we ever see'em pulling out with loads for stores here. And then there's some A-rab guy who's as mean as a mad rattler. Explain that," Johnston countered.

"Chill, man, will ya," Tompkins said. "They could be listening to us in here right now," he whispered.

"Something ain't right here, Fred, you know that," Johnston said scratching his three-day growth of whiskers.

"Kahlil!" Ali said in his native Arabic tongue. "What of Faris? He did not call."

"He did not get back to Detroit, my brother. Abdul called and said this," Kahlil said. "Where are you?"

"I am home in Dearborn. The authorities are everywhere. The FBI has many ears. Should we flee?"

"Don't be concerned. If they knew something we would have been picked up, already." Kahlil said. He did wonder how close the FBI was to them. Others had been contacted and picked up for questioning in Dearborn but he had remained cool when interviewed by them after September 11. He had stopped looking out the windows and over his shoulder months ago. They would not find them. God protected them.

"What are we to do? If the authorities find the telephone numbers and pictures Faris has, we are finished," Ali said nervously.

Kahlil thought about the company that supplied people in the old country with money to fight the Americans. He had come over to

America as a student six years ago and fell into this smuggling business through his cousin Abdul. Finding it lucrative he watched and learned and soon he and his friends would take control of the business and the millions of dollars it made. The Bat man would be the first to die.

"We will wait. The authorities may not find anything that would lead them to us. Are you sure the photos are with Faris?"

"I don't know but he always carries the book of phone numbers. If he does have them the authorities will be at our doors," Ali said. "When do you go to Carolina again?"

"I am supposed to go tomorrow and pick up a load tomorrow night," Kahlil said. "I have friends there who may help us. They live in Florida and will do whatever needs to be done."

"Don't underestimate this Bat man. He seems to know everything we all do and he is brutal."

"God will protect us, my brother. Our cause is just," Kahlil said.

Chapter 3

Cursing the smuggling suspect's vehicle of death, Ferguson stared blankly at the white plastic sheet covering the shooter as state police technicians took pictures and measurements. Standing in the middle of Interstate 75 in the early morning haze, he would never forget this scene. Lifting the Michigan State hat from his head, Ferguson wiped his eyes. Empty shell casings lay on the ground as detectives started their investigation. The fraud agents commandeered an officer and cruiser to follow Kate to the hospital.

Arriving at the emergency room a short drive away in Monroe, Ferguson dashed to the reception counter. "Agent brought in little while ago with a gunshot. Where is she?" he snapped at the receptionist.

"She was taken directly to surgery. Do you know how to reach her family?" the receptionist asked.

"How is she? Who can I talk to?" Ferguson asked.

"I'm sure they'll come out and talk to you when they're finished in the operating room sir," the receptionist said.

"I want to talk to someone now, dammit!" Ferguson growled.

The receptionist looked alarmed as she picked up the phone to call someone. "I-I'll find someone right away, sir."

Ferguson realized he had stepped over the line. Lifting the hat from his head, he ran his hand stiffly through his hair. "Sorry ma'am. She's my niece."

Rick J. Barrett

Snatching the cell phone from his breast
pocket, Ferguson punched in the number to his
home. His wife, Joanne, answered on the
second ring. He never called and if she knew
of a bust it kept her awake, even if it was in
the middle of the night.
"Joanne!"
"Sean? Is that you? What's the matter?"
Joanne asked.
"It's Katie. She's been shot," he
managed.
Silence preceded the barrage. "Oh, my
God, Sean. Is she all right? Where is she?
How could you do this?" Joanne cried.
The words stung him. He tried to answer
but the words would not come. Even if he'd
found them, what could he say to make
everything all right.
"I couldn't know, Joanne. We've never
had anyone shoot at us on a stop like this.
Oh, God why her?" Ferguson murmured, more to
himself than his wife.
"How long ago, Sean?" Joanne asked.
His hand touched the ornate gold chain
clipped to a belt loop and followed it down to
the timepiece attached to it. It had been his
strength since the death of his father thirty-
two years before. That also was the last time
he had been in a hospital with someone near
death.
Ferguson remembered his dad's voice,
raspy from the ventilator. "Sean, you're now
the man of the family. I'm sorry to put you
in this position, son, but I just can't help
anymore. All I can do is tell you I'll always
be with you. Hand me my watch."
Sean slowly opened the drawer of the
cabinet and clenched his fist before removing
the timepiece. With shaking hands, Sean took

14

it and gingerly put it in his father's wizened hand. He remembered saying nothing as he struggled to maintain composure.

With Herculean effort his father slid the watch up his torso to his lips, kissed it, and slowly handed it to his son. His chest heaved spasmodically and in a final effort he clenched his son's hand, the watch now part of them together.

"Sean," Thomas had whispered. "Remember your heritage and be true to yourself. I love you." Those were the last words Thomas Michael Ferguson ever said as he lapsed into a coma before passing away the next day.

Sean then became the keeper of the family heirloom handed down through the generations of Fergusons since their coming to America in the 1870s.

Holding the watch, Ferguson pushed the release and the cover popped open revealing the face. "Maybe an hour and a half ago, Joanne."

"I'll call Karen." Before he could respond the phone clicked dead.

Steve Wellston would be in his office. Ferguson called his boss before settling in to wait. Wandering to the counter for the third time in the last hour, Ferguson saw the receptionist eye him nervously as he approached so he steered clear.

Returning to the waiting room, Ferguson walked over to where fraud investigators Orlando Pena, alias Hound Dog, and Jessica Cooper stood. Pena held his right hand to his forehead as if meditating, the crown of his black bald head gleaming. Comforting Jessica, Hound Dog draped his muscular left arm over her shoulder. The streaks of mascara, the only hint of make-up on her pale puffy face,

told the story. He looked at the blue down
filled vest she wore over the baggy Fort
Lauderdale sweatshirt. On her wrist was an
elegant gold watch with a dainty chain
attached. Not that it didn't fit her trim,
athletic body but she rarely wore jewelry at
work and certainly never what must be an
expensive watch. Jessica looked up at
Ferguson, her deep blue eyes asking for
answers he didn't have.

"Oh, Sean," she cried. "There's so much
we have to do. We need to water Kate's
plants. Feed her cat. Stop the paper for a
week or so 'til she gets home. We'll have to
pick up her mail." She stopped short and
sobbed. Kate and Jessica were as close as
sisters. Even though fifteen years in age
separated them, they had bonded.

"Why would anyone do this? What's a few
thousand stinkin' bucks in cigarettes? It's a
lousy minor felony. Hell, they don't even get
jail time very often," Jessica wailed.

"I don't have a clue, Jess."

Hound Dog sat quietly with his elbows on
his knees. Moving to sit up, he stroked his
curly beard. Looking at his comrades,
Ferguson saw only despair. This is as bad as
it gets, thought Ferguson, or so he hoped.

A nurse in mauve scrubs with her surgical
mask pulled down silently appeared in the door
of the room and moved to them, the rustling of
the surgical footies sliding across the floor
the only sound in the room.

"She's holding her own," the nurse said.
"Her pressure is better and her heart has good
sinus rhythm. The surgeon is having a little
trouble locating all the bleeders but he's a
good doc."

The three leaned back in their chairs and exhaled. "Red's tough. She'll make it, man. Ain't no smuggler gonna take her out," Hound Dog said. The atmosphere in the room turned hopeful as the agents continued the vigil. Red, thought Ferguson. Kate had hated that radio handle when the team had bestowed it on her just three weeks ago. Her crimson flowing hair and fiery personality made her handle appropriate. It was meant to guarantee her anonymity, to protect her if any of the perpetrators were listening on police scanners, so no one knew her real name. The handle had not saved her from a gunshot by some yahoo, however.

Even when the team did pick up a smuggler, he'd see bars only until he was arraigned before a magistrate, usually within a few hours. Hell, the only ones who showed remorse were the citizens who had some uncle or brother send them four or five cartons of cigarettes into Michigan to save a few bucks. The thought of a felony record scared them to death. As Ferguson struggled with his own fear, the Administrator of the Fraud Division, Steve Wellston hurried into the waiting room. "Sean, this is terrible, just terrible," Wellston said reaching to shake hands with Ferguson. He nodded to acknowledge Jessica and Pena. "Any news?"

"She's in surgery, Steve. We don't know any more than that."

"How long?"

Ferguson pulled out the much worn pocket watch and popped the cap open. He fumbled with the winding mechanism on top and glanced at the time.

"About two hours. Kate would..." Ferguson stopped in mid-sentence as a doctor, bathed in sweat and blood, came into the waiting room. He looked haggard and his face wore no expression.

"Is there any family of Katherine Burnham here?" he asked, surveying the room.

"I'm her uncle," Ferguson said. The doctor cleared his throat. "Katherine is in critical condition but we have her stabilized. We believe we've found all the bleeders. The bullet fragments are isolated in her body and pose no threat. She was lucky in that respect but she has a collapsed lung from the bullet bouncing around in there. The next forty-eight hours will determine her fate. It would be presumptuous of me to comment any further, but I stress that she is stable right now and has a chance if she remains that way."

Everyone breathed as the tension in the room lifted and a few smiles emerged. But Ferguson did not smile because someone very dear to him was lying in a hospital with a gunshot wound. Not that kids today didn't get shot for trivial reasons. They did. But he had never experienced life-threatening violence in his tenure with the department and to have it strike Katie was unthinkable. He moved away from the group and walked down the hall, afraid he would vomit. He would do whatever it took to put these people away; the smugglers who had changed the rules and started the shooting. In his experience the smugglers worked in groups like packs of dogs and he was sure he was dealing with a ring this time. He had cultivated more snitches in his tenure with fraud than anyone and he was about to make a lot of noise on the street. Someone out there would give the bastards up, he just had to find who.

Chapter 4

Bat woke with a ring of the telephone next to the bed in his East Lansing home. Squinting to see, he groused to himself. Heavy velvet drapes covered the massive windows, keeping the sun at bay. Scanning the darkened room, his gaze fell on the source of the ringing. The phone creating the intrusion was the black one, which rarely rang. Adrenaline surged, bringing him alert.

He slid out of bed and padded across the carpet into the bathroom. Bat knew the caller would be one of four people who had the number and that he would not hang up. Splashing water on his face and rinsing the night taste from his mouth, he went to the phone and picked up after pushing a button on a hidden panel under the nightstand. In another room of the house, behind the walls of a hidden safe, the recording equipment clicked on.

Bat hoped the thousands of dollars he had spent on the electronics to guarantee a totally secure line, phone-tracing capabilities to any caller, and the ability to tape conversations were well spent.

"Yes," he said in his high-pitched voice.

"We, ah, we lost a runner, sir," Moochy Lancona said. "He was stopped near the border and shot it out with state police. He lost."

"What happened to the product and the car?" Bat asked.

"State police have it," Lancona answered.

"Unfortunate. And who was the driver?" Bat asked. He almost seemed disinterested in the conversation. Bat already knew the answers to the questions but he wanted Lancona to tell him.

Lancona cleared his throat. "His name was Faisal, Faris Faisal. He, ah, came over from Lebanon about a year ago. I started him with cleaning and unloading and thought he was good," Lancona said. "I told him no guns, boss. I swear I did." Bat heard Lancona swallow hard. "Moussa was there," Lancona went on. "He made sure the man understood there were to be no guns."

"But, you were responsible for him, Mr. Lancona, weren't you?" Bat said. Bat loved to play mind games with his people. He tried not to show any emotion to them. He found it had an unsettling effect. But there was emotion-rage that some imbecilic Arab runner would jeopardize his business.

"Yes, sir, but we told him no guns; I swear we did." Lancona pleaded.

"I'm sure you did. And what about the car, Mr. Lancona?"

"The car is at the state police impound. There's no way to get it back," he said. Bat heard the quick breaths over the line and knew he had made his point.

"Mr. Lancona, I suggest you find a way to get it back. Do I make myself clear?"

"But sir..."

"Do I make myself clear?" Bat raised his voice almost imperceptibly. Bat knew there was no way to get the car back but he would squirm at this and maybe think twice about who he hired to work for them. Bat's right eye twitched as he clenched and unclenched his hand into a fist. His voice sounded monotone after years of learning to control his anger. The discipline would definitely come. The only question was whether Lancona would survive the session and even Bat didn't know the answer to that question now.

"Yes, sir," Lancona said.

"Good. Think about it and I want to see you next week." Bat hung up the phone and switched off the electronics. He cursed Lancona. He had put the stupid, stupid immigrant in one of Bat's cars- a car that made him thousands of dollars every week. And Lancona had trusted this valuable piece of equipment to a man who probably could speak little English and had little respect for life. He cursed the runner. A man had died and Bat felt only a loss for the car. Hungry immigrants were a dime a dozen but the car took time to replace. "Damn him," Bat said through clenched teeth. He hurled the phone across the room, breaking it into a hundred pieces when it hit the ornate papered wall. "No one takes my money and no one jeopardizes my business."

If discovered, Bat stood to lose millions of dollars from smuggling cigarettes. It wasn't only the money, of course, but the pure joy of beating the system. All of this with little risk of discovery and virtually no risk of jail time for any of his people.

After showering and dressing, Bat went to the study on the first floor of his huge Tudor home. Imported walnut paneling hand oiled and buffed to a soft sheen covered the walls of the room with built-in floor to ceiling bookshelves. The books lining the shelves, mostly first editions worth more than Bat understood, had been owned by his father. Bat had never read most of them and had no use for them except to put on a facade. Pressing a switch hidden under a section of ornate wainscoting on the wall, a four foot section of the wall silently rose into the ceiling of the room revealing a three-foot wide by six-

foot high safe. Bat twirled the tumbler back
and forth until an almost inaudible click let
him know he had opened it. He struggled a bit
to pull open the massive steel door.

Bat peered at the contents and a slight
smile tugged at his face. Had his parents
ever accumulated over $2 million in tax free
cash like this in the safe of their mansion in
Grosse Pointe Woods before they died? Bat had
contemplated a life of luxury when his
parents, rich from working for the lucrative
auto industry, died in a plane crash. Gee,
too bad.

He never really knew them. His father
always worked and his mother was too busy
climbing the social ladder to give him any
time. The only person he knew from his
childhood was Tammy Littleton, his nanny. She
was proper and formal about everything she
did, never ever letting her hair down to play
with a love starved boy of seven. As he grew
and matured his parents had sent him away to
prep school and when he graduated from Harvard
he thought he had finally pleased his parents,
even though he had struggled between studies
and trying awkwardly to socialize. It wasn't
about grade point anyway, he had reasoned. It
was the piece of paper that opened all the
doors- except with his parents.

They scorned him again. Bat could still
remember his father's first comment after
commencement, "Well, son, let's hope all the
money we've spent on preparing you for life
pays off."

Bat felt like a commodity that his
parents had invested their resources in
instead of a son. There had been few words
between them since that day and when the plane
went down seven years ago. Bat felt

vindicated. Their death validated his deep-
seeded hatred of these people who called
themselves his parents. He had never met
their expectations- nor they his.

   To his shock and amazement their will
left him virtually penniless by his standards.
They had the final word again! Of an estate
worth in excess of $32 million he received
only a paltry $300,000 and their home on which
to make his way while charities he had never
even heard of received millions. Everyone had
spoken so well of his parents and nearly
talked of sainthood because of their
generosity. Bat, on the other hand, sold the
house because there were no wonderful
childhood memories and he needed the money it
would bring. After sulking and exploring
every avenue to break the will, Bat had to
face the fact that he had lost the inheritance
and attorney fees had relieved him of $100,000
of his nest egg. To make ends meet he started
his enterprise after a casual conversation
with one of his prep school acquaintances, Tad
Hanson. Hanson, who worked for Immigration
and Naturalization, told Bat about the Arab
immigrants who were entering the country on
visas and being deported for smuggling
cigarettes and anything else that could make
them a buck. That simple conversation had
been the impetus for a business that now
netted him millions every year. All it took
was one screw-up like Faisal to bring the
whole thing down. At least the loser now had
a name for Bat to curse. What a pity Lancona
had not hired good people. He liked Moochy
but discipline was the foundation for
everything in this world.

   He stabbed at the phone with his index
finger. "Mr. Moussa," Bat said, "I'll be back

in town on Thursday. Bring Mr. Lancona to me
at the warehouse at 6:00 p.m. Oh, and I want
someone watching him twenty-four hours a day
to make sure he doesn't do anything we'll
regret. Call security at the farm. Have them
take a long coffee break Thursday evening.
Understood?"

"Yeah, boss, I'm on him like stink on
shit," Moussa said.

Bat winced. "Crude but you have the
idea. Just make sure he doesn't do anything
that might jeopardize the operation."

"Do I punch his ticket if I see anything
or just call?" Moussa asked, wanting to be
clear.

"The business cannot be compromised. If
you suspect something and can't reach me, do
what you have to do," Bat said.

Bat trusted Moussa. He had found him in
Chicago, a gang member who did terrible things
to people with no shred of conscience. He had
beaten other boys to within an inch of his
life and a few times beyond. After hearing a
few of the stories, Bat knew that Moussa
wasn't just ferocious but mean- just plain
mean. Over the course of the last ten years
Moussa had done everything that Bat asked of
him and he would continue to do so because
they understood each other.

The phone rang at the home near Jackson,
Michigan at three in the morning. Ferguson,
still awake, snatched the receiver from its
cradle on the first ring.

"Hello," he said.

"Uncle Sean? This is Alan."

Ferguson sat upright, sucking air in
anticipation.

"I knew you'd want to know." Alan
paused. "The doctors said Kate is having

problems. Her blood pressure is dropping and she's not stable."

"I thought she was out of the woods? We hit forty-eight hours yesterday. He said that was the critical time," Ferguson protested. He knew better than to trust the doctors. His own father was supposed to come home years ago but never did.

"I don't know what happened. My folks just went to talk to the doctor on duty."

"I'll be there in an hour, Alan. Tell your dad," Ferguson said.

He stood in front of the bathroom mirror combing his hair, noting his red, puffy eyes. Finishing, he hesitated near his wife who slept before rushing to his Jeep for the trip to Monroe.

As Ferguson took hesitant steps toward Kate's room in the critical care unit of the hospital, the lack of noise seemed odd. Ferguson's steps quickened. He could not hear the constant push and pull of the respirator Kate had been hooked up to, or the beep of the EKG and pulse monitoring equipment. Oh, no, please let her be alive. Rounding the corner in her room he saw that the lifelines and tubes that had been part of her for the last three days were gone. His hands went to his face. The bed, instead of a messy mass of sheets and blankets, was now neatly made and tucked up under Kate's folded hands. There was nothing to indicate her ordeal except some adhesive and redness along her chin from the respirator and the tape where the IV's had punctured the veins in her arms. He moved to her, ran the back of his hand across her face. Cold- she was cold. They should give her another blanket.

She looked so peaceful. So calm. The muted light cast soft shadows on her face. Ferguson knew in his heart she was gone. When his mind accepted it, he wept- the same way he had as a teen at his father's death in 1968. The Burnham family moved to his side. Jim and Karen could only sob convulsively with him as they tried to comfort each other.

"I'm so sorry, Karen. I would gladly have given my own life to save her. You must believe that."

Karen put her hand on Ferguson's face trying to wipe away the tears. "Sean, don't blame yourself. You didn't cause it. It was God's will." She broke down again and Jim held her tightly in his arms.

He looked up at Ferguson. "Sean, we know you loved her like your own daughter. Please don't blame yourself."

"Need to call Joanne," Ferguson said, moving out of the room. He patted Alan on the arm as he moved past him.

The telephone at his home rang before Ferguson realized he had called. Joanne picked up before the first ring finished.

"Sean?" she said.

"Yes," he said exhaling.

"W-what's the matter?" she asked.

"It's Katie." A pause. "Joanne, she died about thirty minutes..." It was all he got out before sobbing uncontrollably.

Ferguson answered the telephone on the third ring at his home the night after Katie's death, immediately recognizing Billy Johnston's voice.

"Hey, Music Man, how ya doin'?" Johnston said.

Even one of his oldest friends called him by his handle. Ferguson remembered the first

time they had called him by that handle. The
fraud unit then was four men with three ten
pound walkie-talkies, a blue Ford Econoline
van, an orange Plymouth Duster, a white Ford
Galaxie and Walter "Buzzard" Ranson. Ranson
had joined the Treasury after a stint in the
European theatre during World War II. He fell
into the job in 1948 while rattling around
Detroit after his discharge from the Marines.
The division was new then and even the
bureaucrats upstairs didn't know what the hell
field agents should be doing so they made it
up as they went. Ranson, a tough old codger
with a temper, looked like a short weathered
linebacker for the Lions. He always loved a
fight and if a fellow agent could hold his own
in a brawl Buzzard might even talk to him from
time to time. By the time the 1970s rolled
around Ranson's methods were outdated and he
was on his way to a pension and sparring with
his wife, who reportedly could clean his clock
if they got into it. Ferguson never met her
but thought she must have been one big, mean
woman if she could really take him.

Ferguson never really knew why- unless it
was a joke- but he was partnered with Ranson
right out of the chute. He quickly learned
why the man's nickname fit so well.

"Okay, listen, kid," Ranson said as they
prepared to go into a warehouse reportedly
filled with illegal booze and cigarettes.
"I'll say this once. Stay the hell outta my
way when we go in and if you see something you
don't wanna know about walk away as fast as
those skinny legs will carry ya."

"Yes sir, Mr. Ranson," Ferguson said as
he saw him open the trunk and remove what
looked like a chunk of tree trunk about four
foot long.

"The name is Buzzard and if I ever hear
you call me Mr. Ranson or Walter or anything
else we won't have to worry about being
partners. Got it." He noticed Ferguson's
look at the piece of lumber. "Winda
dressing."

Ferguson nodded as the five agents lined
up with Ranson at point- their crisp white
shirts and wide paisley ties announcing to the
world who they were if the nylon jackets with
Treasury printed across the back didn't. As
Buzzard kicked in the door they rushed en
masse into the building but it was over almost
before it started. Ranson waved the log and
while one of the smugglers stood entranced by
it, threw a looping right hook that put the
man in lala land. Another man charged
Ferguson but a few simple moves and he was
down for the count.

After securing the scene and hauling out
the trash Buzzard walked over to Ferguson,
"Where'd you learn them moves?"

Ferguson immediately rolled up his left
sleeve, displaying the tattoo of the Marine
Corp emblem. "Semper fi." "Where?" Ranson
asked.

"'Nam."

"Bad shit, there?"

"Bad as it gets, Buzzard. You ever hit
anyone with that club."

"Naw, just winda dressing, like I said.
It scares the hell outta them so I get a clear
shot at their chins when they wanna duke it
out." After watching and teaching Ferguson for
a month, Ranson called him over to the rest of
the team as he leaned on the tree trunk.
"Time you got to use one of the radios when
we're doin' surveillance. Before you get on a
radio, though, you got to have a handle so

somebody don't come lookin' for your skinny
ass one night." Buzzard sat there trying to
build suspense. He cleared his throat.
"Because of your vast knowledge and love of
this rock n' roll crap, and because we don't
wanna get your ass kicked by some low life
smuggler who listens to our transmissions, I
hereby name you The Music Man." Buzzard held
the tree at arms length and tapped Ferguson
first on the right shoulder and then on the
left. He was accepted as an equal from that
moment forward. Ferguson smiled.

"How'd you hear, B.J.?" Ferguson asked.

"Called this morning and talked to
Joanne. I'm really sorry, Sean. That's
pretty tough. Anything I can do? Ya want me
to fly up for a few days?"

Ferguson took a deep breath and exhaled.
"I'd really like to see your redneck ass but
you don't need to come up now. Maybe, I can
take a few days off in a couple a weeks. I
haven't seen your place since you moved back
to North Carolina."

"You talk to anyone about Kate, Sean?"

"Whaddya mean, B.J.?"

"Remember when we were in 'Nam and the
shrinks talked to us about seeing all those
guys gettin' killed? I just thought maybe
there was somebody you could talk to, that's
all."

"I haven't talked to anyone, Billy. I
still can't believe she's gone." Ferguson
paused to compose himself. "I tried to talk
to Joanne but she blames me for Kate's death
and even if she doesn't, I do."

"Sean, it's not your fault. You blame
yourself for the guys in 'Nam too? Drop the
baggage," Johnston said.

Ferguson buried his head in his left hand while holding the phone to his ear. He was silent.

"Sean? Sean!"

"Y-yeah, I'm here."

"Look man. This was no more your fault than that day when our patrol was ambushed in '71. You weren't responsible for Pinelli's death then and you're not responsible for Kate's now."

"I was in charge then and I was in charge the other day, Billy. In my book it was my fault."

"You were a fuckin' nineteen year old corporal, scared shitless 'cause we lost our sergeant and you had to make a decision. We all backed you. You couldn't know them V.C. was there."

"I know, I know but Kate was so young and she was blood."

"I ain't sayin' it don't hurt, Sean. I'm just sayin' it wasn't your fault. We worked through it back then and we'll work through it now. You know I'm there for ya. Now, you want my sorry ass on a plane to you or not?"

"I'll be okay. May need a few more phone calls, though."

"Phone calls is cheap enough. You just call anytime. I'm working at a cigarette wholesaler down here and Margaret knows my hangouts. If I'm not here, she'll find me. Hell, she finds me whether I want her to or not."

"Thanks B.J., I owe you."

"Just remember that the next time I ask you to come down for a visit to see our mansion."

Ferguson hung up the phone, staring blankly at the wall.

Chapter 5

Standing outside the funeral home in Ann Arbor, Ferguson felt the cell phone in his pocket vibrate. The service for Kate was scheduled to begin in thirty minutes and he had come outside with his family to get some fresh air.

"Ferguson," he answered.

"F-Ferguson, I-I don't know if you remember me. My name is Moochy Lancona. I got into a jam with you about three years ago and I remembered you were pretty fair with me." He paused for a few seconds. "I've got information on the shooting of that agent."

Ferguson's heart threatened to jump from his chest. "What do you know? Tell me?" Ferguson said through clenched teeth.

"Not now, not over the phone. H-he's got eyes in the back of his head. He knows people everywhere," Lancona said.

"Who? I'll protect you. I can get the police to you in twenty minutes. Just talk to me," Ferguson said.

"You can't protect me." Lancona said.

"Tell me what you know!" Ferguson screamed. He looked around and saw his daughters and wife staring at him.

"I-I can't. I'll meet you in an hour at the rest area on U.S. 23 north of Ann Arbor," Lancona said.

"No, I'm at the agent's funeral. I can't come now, dammit. Give me a break," Ferguson whispered.

"You come now or you'll never see me. I'm outta here for good and if you want the information it's now or never," Lancona said.

"I'm tellin' you, he'll find me if I stay here."

"Come on, we're about to bury her. She's my niece," Ferguson pleaded. "For God sake, haven't you got any compassion?"

"Never mind Ferguson. I'm go...," Lancona said.

"No, don't hang up! Please, please help me," Ferguson shouted. For a moment he thought Lancona had broken the connection.

"Now or never, Ferguson," Lancona repeated. "And you come alone."

"I'll be there, but if you're lying to me I'll hunt you like a dog. You'll wish you were dead when I catch you," Ferguson said.

"If he catches me Ferguson, I'll be dead by five," Lancona said. He sounded resigned to his fate.

Ferguson went to his wife. "I have to go, Joanne."

Her mouth dropped open. "You can't be serious, Sean. What about the funeral? She was your niece. Doesn't that mean anything to you?"

"A man just called and said he has information on those responsible for her death. I have to talk to him. He's scared," Ferguson said.

"Let someone else go, Sean. So help me, if you leave I-I don't know what I'll do but..." Crimson crept into her face as her words trailed off.

"I have to go, Joanne. There's no choice," Ferguson said. "I've got to catch these people." He wiped a tear from his eye.

"And what about Jim and Karen? What do I say to them, Sean?" Joanne said. "Better yet, what do you say to them?" His wife turned and walked briskly toward their daughters, shaking her head.

Stepping inside, Ferguson found it difficult to even look at Jim and Karen Burnham as they hovered over the casket containing their daughter. After speaking to Jessica, Ferguson trudged to his car and drove off. Tears flooded his eyes, blinding him as he drove. Ferguson reasoned that his niece would understand, but the guilt threatened to consume him.

Arriving at the rest stop, Ferguson pulled into a parking spot farthest away from the restrooms so that he could watch all the cars driving into the parking areas. Lighting a Swisher, he checked his watch when Lancona failed to show at the appointed time. He tapped his fingers on the steering wheel as if that would make the man appear. What had he said? Ferguson gnawed on the Swisher.

When Lancona was thirty minutes late Ferguson knew he wasn't coming. "You son of a bitch. I will find you wherever you go," he screamed as he beat the steering wheel with his hands repeatedly until his chest heaved from the exertion. He collapsed, his head in his hands. Sobbing, he finally calmed enough to turn the key to start the engine. A song wafted through his head- Only the Strong Survive by Jerry Butler. Sweat permeated all the fibers of his dress shirt as he loosened the tie around his neck. Ferguson drove slowly around the parking lot three times hoping he had missed something. He realized Lancona was his key- the only link he had to the people he hunted. He would leave no stone unturned to find him. Lancona had robbed him of the final good-bye to Kate.

Bat drove up the quarter mile winding drive to the farm, his base of operations. The proximity to the border and freeways in southeast Michigan made it an attractive choice as the distribution center for the cigarettes. He ran a stable of twelve cars to supply his customers. Each car carried three sets of license plates, North Carolina, New York, and Michigan- all good forgeries and unknown to authorities. Pulling off U.S.23, Bat picked up one of the three cell phones from the leather passenger seat of his Lexus and dialed the number to Moussa's phone.

"Mr. Moussa, do we have an appointment?"

"Yeah boss, I'm on the road," Moussa said.

Bat stepped on the accelerator sending gravel pinging off the mailbox with Farhill Farm hand-painted on the side. Dozens of naked maple trees lining the drive thrashed in the wind as if in anticipation of what was to come. The freshly painted white farmhouse on the right, with gingerbread at the eaves and porch, looked as though it was the model for Little House on the Prairie. To the casual observer, the house appeared to be a lived-in family abode.

Bat picked up his Louisville Slugger baseball bat from the seat, got out of his car, and looked around. He flipped the bat in the air and caught it on the way down. Who would ever guess this was a multi-million dollar operation? He felt a little guilty for using the only place he really had enjoyed for his enterprise but had to admit it was perfect. Walking to the fifty by eighty-foot barn, Bat disarmed the security system and unlocked the door.

"Can't be too careful," he muttered.
"Never know when someone might want to rob
you." Stepping into the barn it was clear no
animals had been housed inside for a long
time. The only horses were the 400 that lay
under the hood of the Lincoln in the first
stall.

The interior walls no longer were of
weathered planking but paneling and drywall.
There were few cigarettes left in the
warehouse- only six or seven cases. He made a
mental note to step up the runs to bring in
more stock. After all, it took a lot of
cigarettes to service sixty convenience
stores. Twelve florescent light fixtures cast
a sterile white light over the interior of the
barn.

A panel on the communication desk blinked
to life and beeped letting Bat know Moussa and
Lancona had arrived. It was time. A few
moments later the two men stepped into the
barn. Lancona's hands were handcuffed behind
his back, his head down.

"Mr. Lancona! How are you doing? I had
Mr. Moussa bring you in so we could discuss
our little problem and find a solution," Bat
said.

"Oh, my God," Lancona said under his
breath. He buckled at the sight of Bat with
the Al Kaline Louisville Slugger and would
have fallen if Moussa hadn't grabbed his arm.
"I'm sorry boss. I-I've been working on our
problem." He swallowed hard. "I think I know
how to get the car back."

"Don't worry about it, Moochy. I've
already taken care of the car. The little
problem I alluded to was the need to look more
closely at the people we hire. I know you
must have told Mr. Faisal about my cardinal

35

rule, didn't you? You said you did." He
continued without waiting for an answer. "No
guns. Never. So, Moochy, have you talked to
anyone since our little conversation last
week?" The high-pitched voice rose as he
talked to Lancona but there was calmness to
it. "Like maybe an agent or the police?" Bat
moved toward the communications desk.

"N-no, I didn't talk to nobody. Honest,
boss!" Lancona said.

"Well, I'm glad to hear that, Moochy,
because I think I've been very generous with
you, haven't I?"

"Yes, sir, more than generous," Lancona
said, a little more confident. He turned
toward the few cases of contraband cigarettes,
visibly relieved.

"Moochy, I don't believe you're being
truthful with me," Bat said. Redness crept
into his face.

The instant recognition of those words on
Lancona's face was all Bat needed to see. He
had been leery of hiring him but had done so
on Moussa's recommendation.

The first blow struck Lancona squarely on
the right knee. Just before he fell,
screaming in agony, Bat saw the knee move in
the opposite way a knee normally does. He
thought, now, what kind a bird was it that has
knees that bend backward? Was it a flamingo?
He couldn't remember.

"Well, what do you know, Mr. Moussa. A
double!" Bat screeched as he prepared to swing
again. Bat loved to run play-by-play
description of the game. Lancona's screams
rang through the barn. Bat looked into his
eyes, a smile no longer visible on his face.
Whomp. The Louisville Slugger struck the
man's lower leg. Bat stopped for a minute,

took out a handkerchief, and wiped his brow.
He was actually working up a sweat. As
Lancona turned his body away in an attempt to
protect himself, a vicious shot struck him in
the wrist. Lancona's hand hung at an odd
angle just above the handcuffs, now a useless
appendage.

"Mr. Lancona, I'm sorry we have to go
through this but discipline is important.
Surely, you understand that, don't you?"
Bat's voice rose like the fury raging in his
head.

Lancona stared in terror unable to utter
a word because of the pain. He watched the
little man circle him. Bat just poked him
with the bat, grinning as Lancona flinched at
each touch. "You miserable bastard," Bat said
to Lancona. You were going to meet that
agent, weren't you? You were going to spill
your guts to the Treasury agents." Bat swung
the bat again as the crunch of bone resounded.

"Mr. Moussa, have you made arrangements
for all our people?" Bat said, out of breath.
"Mr. Lancona looks like he may need a few days
off." Whomp. He no longer screamed. Bat
checked to see if the man had died on him.
"Just passed out," Bat said sounding pleased.

"Two are out now and I called the other
two." Moussa said. Even Moussa grimaced at
the beating that was being administered and he
was a veteran of such events.

"Good," Bat said. "And distribution has
been notified?"

"Sure boss," Moussa said, eyeing Bat
warily.

Bat was sure that the incident on the
freeway would create a storm. He just had to
stay one step ahead of the government agents
and police.

"Mr. Moussa, the police will check Immigration and be on our partner's doorstep shortly. I know how they work. Also, they'll have detectives everywhere checking on the car and its contents. Make sure they don't have any trail."

"Yes sir, boss," Moussa said.

"And I want you to give Mrs. Lancona severance pay. It's not fair she suffer because she married a traitor."

Chapter 6

The beep of his Treasury pager came just after Ferguson arrived at his rural home south of Lansing. The sound, usually exciting to Ferguson, grated on his nerves. Lancona's failure to show yesterday had left Ferguson enraged and the last thing he wanted was another case.

"Sean, please don't call them," Joanne pleaded, putting her hand on his arm. "Get some rest and go in tomorrow." He never ignored a page, never had, and never would. They both knew it. "You missed the funeral, and for what? The man never showed up, did he?" she asked. "For God sake, she was like a daughter to you- to us!" Joanne shook almost imperceptibly as she spit the words.

Ferguson knew Joanne loved him for the very qualities she questioned now. How many times had she talked about his dedication and loyalty- qualities she now hated. She had endured his long working hours because she had Emily and Annie to raise- many times by herself.

"You know I can't do that," he said, trying to control his anger and grief. He removed the MSU hat, running a hand up his brow and through his hair.

"No, I know you won't do that," she taunted. The words hit him like acid, burning deep into his soul. He walked away before his wife could make any other remarks. After calling the number on the pager he slowly hung up the phone and prepared to leave.

Dragging himself from the car at the state police post outside Monroe, Michigan, Ferguson saw Jessica and Hound Dog standing

near the door. He was sure no one wanted to
chase smugglers today. It had been the
longest day he could remember but the
criminals never stopped, not even to mourn.

"I'm sorry, Jess," Ferguson said. "I
didn't want to go out today." The three
strolled into a meeting room, none of them
looking forward to a stop.

She shrugged her shoulders. "It's what
we do." She Paused, staring at her boss.
"You know, Sean, you look like shit."

"Thanks for the complement. I remember a
time when you were a lot more subtle, like
when you cold cocked the perp with a blackjack
when he got the drop on Sal Bandetto just
after you started. Remember that? He was
your biggest fan after that. Hell, I didn't
find out you saved his bacon until after he
retired."

"Yeah, I remember and do you remember how
all the guys treated me?" Jessica asked
shaking her head. "They wouldn't even talk to
me. Gave me all the shit assignments. Being
the first woman agent wasn't very much fun. I
had to be just as tough if not tougher then
they were. They got a kick outta the fact
that I talked like one of the guys." She
paused. "I suppose I oughta watch my tongue
sometimes. Remember how Bandetto made it real
clear he thought I should be in the kitchen
before I saved his fat Italian ass."

Ferguson nodded. "Long time ago. Times
sure have changed. Let's get the briefing
goin'. Dog, you got all the information,
right?" Ferguson changed gears, forcing
himself to put aside his grief and pain.
Catching a smuggler didn't seem important but
if kept busy he wouldn't think about Kate.
The driving force was Ferguson's desire to put

the smugglers responsible for her death out of business. He knew that sooner or later he would find them and hopefully it was sooner-like now.

"Got it," Hound Dog said. "Call didn't go through central office. It come directly to my voice mail. Jerry Avalon at Central Tobacco down in Ashboro said they sent a pick-up truck out with a load at about 8:00 this morning. The guy driving said something about getting to Detroit by 7:00 tonight and then sounded nervous. He was from the north."

"So, we don't know how he's coming. Have you got a license plate and a description?" Ferguson asked as he took notes.

"Yeah, the vehicle is a black 1989 Ford pick-up with Michigan tag Zebra, Charley 65662. The guy has a black cap over the bed. ATF in Ohio was notified and has a tail on the truck. The captain here told me they thought the suspect was gonna cruise straight in on US-23."

"Good, let's get this set up," Ferguson said.

"Hound Dog, I want you to set up on the entrance ramp to US-23 at exit six with one of the troopers. I understand he's on road patrol but should be in shortly."

"No problem, Music," Hound Dog rumbled.

"Jess, you come with me. I want to sit on the overpass at M-223. We'll put two uniforms outta sight off the exit. We'll tail him to his crib and make the bust. Let's roll."

"No Steppenwolf!" Jessica said.

Ferguson nodded as a grin spread across his face. "Pinball Wizards turn anyway."

"Not with me in the car," Jessica said.

Thirty minutes later the trap was set and everyone was in position. The radio hissed to life. "Radio check. Music, you read, man?"

"Loud and clear, Dog. What's your twenty?" Ferguson asked.

"I'm in position," Hound Dog said.

The less said in the field the better. A bust could go bad with too much chatter.

"Roger that," Ferguson replied.

Ferguson popped open the gold case of the watch and looked at the face. The case held only a hint of the detail which once adorned it but he was unable to part with it even for repairs. He wondered if they were doing the right thing with surveillance. Staring blankly at the dashboard of the car, self doubt seeped into his brain.

"You doing okay, Jess?"

Jessica put the microphone down on the dashboard and smiled. "I guess I'm okay but I'm worried about you."

Ferguson shook his head slightly to acknowledge the comment. He yanked a Swisher cigar from his pocket and struck a kitchen match on the dashboard of the car. The sweet cherry aroma filled the car as he exhaled long and slow after a huge pull. He offered one to Jessica but she shook her head no.

"I'll wait for the victory smoke," she said.

By 6:30 p.m. no black pick-up had appeared. "Music," crackled the radio, "No sign of him. How long?"

Ferguson had been on surveillance dozens of times. Sometimes, they didn't pan out. Today, though, his gut told him it would. Investigators followed the smuggler onto U.S.23 north in Ohio and to the Michigan border. There was only a rest stop and one

42

exit between him and Hound Dog and a county
deputy sheriff was at the exit. The truck was
out there somewhere.

"Hold tight, Hound Dog. Give him a few
more minutes," Ferguson said. The sun was low
in the west and it would be dark within thirty
or forty minutes- too dark for surveillance.

Ferguson barely said his last word when
Hound Dog piped up, "He's on his way. Got a
visual." Ferguson felt the excitement. It
still made his heart race. His fingertips
tingled and twitched. He threatened to
hyperventilate from his shallow breathing.

"Short dark brown hair, thin build,
glasses," crackled Hound Dog through the
radio. Ferguson thought about Kate's killer.
Small build, dark hair. The hunt was on.
Ferguson looked at the state police cruiser
ahead. The royal blue cars with the markings
would hang back until the go signal was given
by Ferguson. The specially equipped cars were
fast. With the high performance V-8 engines,
the cars could run at 100 miles per hour all
day long. They would be tough to elude.

Ferguson started his pumped up Buick
LaSabre and pulled onto the northbound
entrance ramp to US-23. The pickup truck
passed the ramp and Ferguson punched the
accelerator. A throaty roar erupted from the
engine compartment as the car squealed onto
the freeway. In two minutes Ferguson had
caught Hound Dog.

"Hound Dog," he said in a tight higher
pitched voice, "I want you to accelerate past
him and pull out in front about a quarter of a
mile. I'll hang back to keep the police
cruisers company. Is that clear? We gotta
find out where this guy works from," Ferguson

said. He realized he was talking in a tight fast dialogue but couldn't help himself.

"Copy that," Hound Dog said. "Don't want him to get hinky." The adrenaline flowed. Ferguson's mouth tasted like cotton. His palms began to sweat. He took a deep breath and exhaled. Fuzz one and Fuzz two ran right behind him. The engines snarled at the touch of the accelerator, fuel injection pouring gasoline into the hungry iron beasts. The radios crackled as if electrically charged. The pursuit cars stayed back as Hound Dog accelerated toward their prey.

Before Hound Dog reached his position in front of the truck, however, it surged forward and moved away as if shot from a cannon. "Dammit! He must have made us. How?" Ferguson said, as he reached for the microphone. "Let's take him. This is a go. Take him. Take him." The game, however, was not over. The two marked police cars hit their sirens and sped off in pursuit.

"Holy shit!" Jessica said. "Did you see that thing move? I can't believe it. That truck looks like it's ready for the junkyard."

Ferguson lifted the microphone to his mouth. "Do not, I repeat, do not pursue. Let the marked cars do their job. Follow at a safe speed. Is that clear Hound Dog? Without lights, we can't risk an accident."

"Copy, Music. Will follow at safe speed."

The safe speed for these cars was ninety miles per hour. Ferguson monitored the radio chatter from the state police. Jessica looked frantically at exits ahead to advise Ferguson. The police patrolled the roads all over the area and knew them intimately. At 110 miles per hour, however, those roads came up quick.

The radio crackled to life and a trooper shouted over the roar of his engine. "Suspect exited at twelve! I repeat, exit twelve. Eastbound on Lakeland road. Call in the county. We can't catch him. This guy drives like Mario Andretti!"

Ferguson and Jessica arrived at exit twelve when the radio squawked again. "We've lost the suspect in Chamberlain. Will pursue to the north on Main."

Ferguson snatched the microphone from its mooring. "Hound dog, meet me at Tac 3," Ferguson ordered, changing the frequency on his radio to that setting. No sense in screwing up state police radio traffic, thought Ferguson. He did, however, switch on another radio hidden under the seat of his car to monitor progress of the police. "Hound Dog, meet at Chamberlain and Lewis. Out." The element of surprise lost; there was no need for further radio silence.

When the three agents and trooper met, Hound Dog shook his head. "Man, that was the fastest set of wheels I ever tailed. What the hell did they do to it?"

"I don't wanna get paranoid but this vehicle makes me think our shooter and this guy were related somehow," Jessica said.

The telephone rang four times before Abdul answered. Located in a million dollar home in Northville, Michigan, the phone sat in the library of solid walnut paneling. The brick two-story home which boasted six bedrooms with as many bathrooms sat in a neighborhood where the homes weren't bunched on 60x150 foot lots. Parked in the three-car attached garage sat a new Lincoln Towncar, a

Navigator sport utility vehicle, and a
Mercedes-Benz. It was a far cry from the
small bungalow he had once owned in Dearborn,
Michigan and even farther from the two rooms
in Lebanon he lived in until fifteen years
ago.

"How are you this evening?" Bat said.
"Everything is fine, I trust?"

Bat knew Abdul had been waiting for the
call to find exactly what price he might pay
for the indiscretion of the newest runner he
had brought to America. He heard Abdul clear
his throat while waiting for an answer.
Sufficient time had passed for everyone in the
organization to learn of Lancona's
disciplinary hearing a few nights ago.

"I am fine, sir," Abdul mumbled.

"I am very happy to hear you say that and
I'm also sure you want my opinion of the
events of last week, so I'll give you the
short story. I told you a hundred times there
were to be no, I repeat, no guns but someone
chose not to listen and now we have a dead
runner and a lot of heat from the authorities
that will hinder our operation for months,
maybe longer. And what have I told you about
the government?" Bat waited for an answer but
only the silence of the open line came back to
him. Bat decided to let the words soak into
Abdul's brain for a few seconds before going
on.

"I will tell you. They have nothing but
money to spend and can afford an expensive
long-term investigation. We cannot."

While Bat was sure he had Abdul's
attention, he decided insurance would help
keep the man focused.

"Let me ask you a question. How many
relatives and friends of yours have come over

to this great country of ours in the last
three or four years?"

"I do not know, sir," Abdul said quietly.

"Let me see. Maybe I can help you." A
silence ensued for what seemed to last at
least a minute. Hearing the bong of what
sounded like a grandfather's clock in the
background, Bat wondered what the man's house
looked like. With the money he made from
their business, the man must live like a king
compared to Lebanon. Bat sowed the seed of
fear in the man, the most compelling emotion
Bat knew.

"I believe we helped three brothers and a
sister immigrate to this country, didn't we?"

Abdul sighed. "Yes, sir, that is
correct." He had heard this before usually
when something threatened the cartel. Abdul
needed Bat though for a source of cigarettes.
Bat had the warehouse in North Carolina.
Abdul had tried his own cigarette import
business in the past without success,
especially on the scale that he needed to
supply dozens of stores. So here he was. He
endured the calls but one day he would kill
Bat and take it all. He promised himself.

"And how many of your extended family
came over? Let's see. I think it was five
cousins if my memory serves," Bat said. Bat
played now and the man didn't even feel the
blade of the knife at his neck. "And how many
of them are United States citizens? Can you
tell me?"

Silence again greeted Bat.

"Again, I believe that number is none,
isn't it?"

The breathing in the phone became heavier
as Abdul attempted to maintain composure.

"I certainly am glad my memory is so good," Bat said. "I don't like to forget any of my employees."

"How can you do this to me? You know my family is important to me and you call to make veiled threats? I understand, all right? I know you have the power to have my family deported or killed so you can stop now," Abdul said, fear in his voice. He sounded as if he might lose it.

"That is right," Bat said. "Just remember that and let me do the thinking. If I want you or your people to do something, I will tell you."

Bat paused for a moment, collecting himself. Knowing the message rolled around in the brain of the man, he knew there would be no further problems. He played one last card that would remain in the back of the man's brain for a long time.

"Mr. Hanson was the immigration supervisor all of you saw when you came to this country, right?" Bat could almost feel Abdul's grip tighten on the phone piece. He hadn't heard cursing yet but he was sure there would be words that would not reach his ears.

"I want to make it very clear to you and your people that you need to work hard to make sure nothing prevents us from doing business. You must admit, it is nice to live here, especially when you don't have to worry that your people back home will ostracize you for living a blasphemers life with all of us sinners. Would they hurt you if you went back?"

Bat knew very well that the last thing Abdul wanted was to be shipped back to Lebanon. He would do anything to make sure that didn't happen.

"You have a good life here and I would hate to see you leave. Just watch your step and I'll guarantee you won't have to work the rest of your life. Understood?"

"Yes," Abdul choked.

"Now, clean everything up at your stores," Bat said. "Oh, and have a nice evening."

Bat knew that the glue that held the enterprise together was fear; fear of losing what one had gained in life. A person's mind always did a better job of keeping people focused than any words Bat could say. Giving the man a taste of the good life was all that was necessary to gain loyalty and devotion.

Of course, Bat needed the man as much or more than the man needed him but it was a good fit. The distribution of the cigarettes would never have been so easy to establish without the blind obedience of the man to his family. Bat understood this and that is why there would be no recrimination. Thugs, like Moussa, were important but Abdul was supplying the retail outlets- the most important element of the operation.

Chapter 7

On the morning following the chase near
Chamberlain, the phone at the Ferguson house
rang just after 7:00 a.m. He answered
cautiously, knowing the calls were usually for
one of his teenage girls even though it was
impossible that any teenage boy would call
this early. "Hello."

"Sean, this is Jess. I'm down here at
the state police impound taking inventory of
the shooter's car. The lab guys finished
takin' evidence and photos yesterday. You
need to get down here to see this. This car
is different than anything I've ever seen."

A twinge of panic poked at Ferguson. He
had not seen the car that brought the shooter
since that night on the freeway.

Ferguson looked up at the wall clock. "I
can be there in an hour. Just hang loose
until I get there."

At 8:15 a.m. Ferguson arrived at the
state police impound outside of Detroit. An
eight-foot fence with a canopy of razor wire
stood as sentry around the buildings.
Ferguson pulled through the electric gate and
up to the guard shack. An M-16 rifle, visible
through an open door provided ample firepower
should anyone try to crash the facility.
Ferguson recognized the trooper posted at the
guardhouse. "Hi Ted," Ferguson said.

The guard gave Ferguson a slight wave.
"Hi Sean. Jess is in back at bay number two.
She's been waiting on you. Nervous as a
chicken at KFC. When I was back there on
break she said she found something odd about
the car."

"Guess I better get back there. Thanks."

Ferguson looked at the nondescript building. Pulling into a parking space, he felt safe. How many people knew that this facility was the state police forensics lab? Not many. The numerous cameras tipped the observant that this was no ordinary industrial business. Ferguson looked at the building as a sweat bead formed on his upper lip. Gripping the steering wheel with both hands, he found himself unable to move. Sitting in a trance, he did not see Jessica walk up to the car.

"Sean, what's wrong?" Jessica said as she tapped on the window but the trance would not be broken. "Sean!"

Jessica's shouts wrestled Ferguson from his secret place. He slowly turned his head toward her, without recognition at first. Shaking his head, Ferguson fumbled to roll down the side window. "Sorry, Jess," he said quickly wiping his face with the back of his hand.

Jessica walked around the car and sat in the passenger seat. "What's going on, Sean? You've been so preoccupied ever since Kate was shot. Let me help, please. It'll do us both good." Jessica took Ferguson's limp hand as tears welled up in her own eyes.

"Jess, this goes a lot deeper than you know," Ferguson said. He sighed long and deep.

"Help me to understand. You guys don't call me Mother Hen for nothin'," Jessica said, smiling at him.

They sat in silence for what seemed an eternity. Ferguson played with a paper clip he found on the seat, bending in different ways so that it resembled some abstract piece of art. He never looked up.

"You know, Jess, I remember when Joanne and I first got married thinkin' we'd have a son and how I'd do all kinds a things with him. I thought I'd teach him to hunt and fish, play baseball with him. And then we had Emily. She was a beautiful baby and we were so proud."

"She sure was," Jessica said. "I often think that when I see that picture on your desk from her first birthday."

"I love that picture. It brings back such sweet memories from when we were startin' out." Ferguson paused. "Those early years were our best, I think. We didn't have much, just a couple of old raggedy cars, and a small bungalow on the east side of Flint but it was a home. And then Annie popped on the scene like Tigger on Winnie the Pooh, always bouncin' around. Even today I see that in her." Ferguson chuckled and then became somber. "We decided we didn't want any more kids and even though I didn't have a son I was happy. They both loved soccer but had little use for baseball. That game is my passion. Then my sister shipped Katie up here for a month visit one summer to visit and I discovered she loved baseball. We became very close. Played catch, listened to the Tiger's games. She visited every summer. Got along great with the other kids even though she was older." Ferguson sat immersed in his thoughts for a moment as a smile crept onto his face. "What a great kid- hell they're all great kids. And now I have mine and Karen's is gone."

"So how did she end up stayin' in Michigan, Sean?" Jessica asked.

"She was a lost soul for a year or so after graduating from high school. Always

runnin' off here or there. Gave my brother
fits. And then one day she came to visit me
and asked if I could get her a job in my
office. It just worked out."

"It's great to think you were such a
positive influence on her, Sean," Jessica
said.

Ferguson pushed out a chuckle. "Yeah,
and got her killed," he said sarcastically.

"Don't blame yourself for what happened,"
she commanded. "She was up here because she
wanted to be. She admired and loved you so
don't you ever blame yourself."

"And just who should I blame, Jess?"
Ferguson asked quietly.

"How about the bastards who are running
the smuggling operation?" she said.

"That's only half of it," he said. He
sat looking at the floor of the car.

"There are only two people in the world
I've ever told about this, Joanne and my mom,
and that was years ago." Ferguson paused to
collect himself. "Y-you ever notice the watch
I carry, Jess?"

"You mean the gold pocket watch?"

Ferguson nodded. "My dad gave me that
watch the day he died. He was everything to
me. He taught me baseball. I was pretty good
back then. I remember playin' catch and
shaggin' fly balls 'til dark many nights
during the summer. The crickets would start
their music, the heat would start to dissipate
and I'd be runnin' and catching and throwin'.
Did it for hours after he had worked the
fields all day. He'd coach me if I made a
mistake. Waving me in, he'd put one of his
huge muscular arms around my shoulder and
start his banter- always makin' sure I
understood what I did wrong. Then when I was

sixteen, he was gone. Lung cancer from
smokin'. You know I used to stand out there
in that field for hours after he died watchin'
the waves of heat rise from the ground as the
sun was almost down waiting for that next fly
ball. It never came."

"Oh, Sean," Jessica said grasping his arm
while she buried her head in his shoulder.
"We'll get them," she whispered.

"You can bet on it," Ferguson said.
Clearing his throat, he shook himself awake.
"So what've you got here?"

They stepped from the car and walked to
the building in silence.

"This car is state of the art for
smugglers," Jessica said.

Ferguson looked at the battered blue
Delta 88 with the crime scene tape around it.
Bullet holes riddled the windshield where the
troopers had fired at the shooter. Blood
splattered upholstery told the rest of the
story. Ferguson stuck his head inside and
instantly noted the mixed smells of copper,
cordite, and fast food. Remnants of a
hamburger and french fries lay on the floor,
no doubt left over from the guy's last meal.
A lone shell casing lay on the front passenger
seat marked by an index card folded and
numbered. Ferguson wondered if that casing
could have held the bullet that took Kate's
life. Clenching his hand, Ferguson shook his
head. The rear seat of the full size car was
gone. A hole had been cut into the trunk of
the vehicle. Underneath fabric that matched
the interior of the car lay dozens of cartons
of illegal cigarettes. Jessica had not
removed them because she wanted Ferguson to
see what they were dealing with.

Jessica grabbed Ferguson's arm. "And look here," She said dragging him to a workbench. Picking up the two sets of license plates found inside the vehicle- New York, Michigan and North Carolina, she fanned them like a deck of cards. "We ran these and they're bogus."

"These guys went to a lot of trouble, didn't they?" Ferguson said.

"You ain't seen nothin' yet, Sean," she blurted. Ferguson loved the enthusiasm he saw in Jessica. He still enjoyed the job and knew directed emotion could make the difference in solving a tough case and he felt this might be the toughest. Jessica moved to the car, reached across the front seat and took a panel from the dashboard, revealing a police scanner, a high tech camera of some sort, and two cell phones mounted on chargers. The front panel actually had the fake face of an AM/FM radio with knobs glued on and air conditioning vents mounted on a board that snapped into place. It looked like the original dashboard.

"Look under the hood of this puppy." Jessica talked fast.

Crammed under the hood of the beat-up family four door was a 454 engine much like the police cruisers with a few goodies added: like the dual quads, enough carburetor to dump gallons of gas into the engine for speed. Ferguson didn't know much about cars but it was obvious this car was built to run, like the car they had chased yesterday. No small smuggling operations would build cars specifically to bring illegal cigarettes into the state unless this was for the long haul. Ferguson feared this case. Were these

smugglers as well connected as they appeared?
He hoped not.

"Did you run the vehicle identification
number? Have the auto theft guys been over
it? Any prints?" Ferguson rattled off.

"Yeah, we ran the VIN. Fake. There are
no prints other than the shooters, and the car
theft unit hasn't been here yet." Jessica
returned the volley. Ferguson raised an
eyebrow and smiled.

"Okay, Jess, let's check the cell phones
origin and see if we can get phone records.
Also, pull the scanner and see if we can find
where it was purchased and when."

"One other thing, Sean," Jessica said,
now somber. She stepped to a workbench and
picked up an evidence bag holding what looked
like cards. Carefully opening the bag, she
pulled out a photograph by the edges.

Ferguson's mouth fell open. "Are the
rest like this?" Jessica nodded, "All ten
of'em. Four different men in various poses."

"F.B.I. notified?"

"They're on the way."

The photograph showed Kate's killer
dressed in camouflage holding an AK-47 rifle.
In the background a mural of a cleric on a
wall that appeared to be in a middle-east
location. The bullet- pocked wall around the
mural sent a shudder through Ferguson.

"The F.B.I. agent said they have evidence
of terrorist funding through cigarette
smuggling," Jessica said.

"Heard about it but I haven't seen any
evidence until now," Ferguson said, his brow
furrowing.

After making phone calls to Lansing to
inform Wellston about what they had found,
Ferguson and Jessica started the inventory

task. By the time they had finished, the tally was 846 cartons of cigarettes for a profit of over $8,000 on the street—double that, if they had distribution. They had cigarettes hidden in every nook and cranny of the vehicle.

"This is a cash cow," Ferguson said. His breath stuck in his throat. He had seen U-haul trucks down to Volkswagens, but he had never seen a full size car modified for the single purpose of smuggling cigarettes.

"If these guys make even a run or two a week that's almost a half a million bucks a year in profit even taking Christmas week off. If this car is related to the truck we lost last night we might have a huge operation bringing in cigarettes. At a mill per vehicle per year someone could get very rich in one helluva hurry," Jessica said. "But where are they selling all these cigarettes?" Ferguson asked. Many retailers were buying cigarettes outside the system. Convenience store owners might purchase illegal cigarettes, if the price was right. Ferguson knew these smugglers were not amateurs, and the thought of the magnitude of this operation sent a chill through him. If the truck and the car were part of the operation, how many other vehicles were they running? Five, ten, maybe even twenty. These cars might belong to the big boys and his boss, Wellston, needed to know. More resources than usual might be needed for this one and he would use anything he had to use to catch these people.

Ferguson looked at Jessica, remembering how much he relied on her intuition and dedication over the years. Ferguson felt guilt when Jessica's marriage had failed a few years ago but she intuitively knew his thoughts and reassured him many times that it

was destined to fail. Kate's death had worn
him out mentally until today. Ferguson knew
he had the juice to go the distance but not
without an investigation using every skill he
had acquired over the years and a little luck.

Ferguson flipped open his cell phone and
called their boss. When told of the
specialized car the smuggler had been driving,
Wellston seemed distant. "I'll let Treasurer
Shapiro know immediately, Sean. He'll
probably want to see you if he knows this may
be a major case."

Why didn't Wellston get excited about the
car? Sean Had never seen anything as big as
he thought this smuggling operation might be
and he knew Wellston hadn't either. Who could
have bankrolled something of this size? This
was big dollars. Could it be mob related?
The money certainly was big enough but the
overhead seemed too high for them. Questions
only brought more questions that swirled
around his brain.

Kenneth Shapiro, Treasurer for the State
of Michigan rose from his massive walnut desk
at the Treasury Building in Lansing and
reached out to shake Ferguson's hand. "Sean,
what the hell's going on with the Kate Burnham
investigation? I hear you think there's a
major player out there. Why? What do you
have to substantiate that? I want to know
before the press gets a hold of it." Shapiro
motioned to Ferguson to sit in one of two
chairs in front of the desk while he sat in
the other.

Ferguson liked Shapiro. You always knew
where you stood with the man and he always
backed his people. Ferguson glanced at the

desk, seeing a walnut gavel from the man's tenure as chair of the powerful taxation committee in the house.

"We have the car the shooter drove and it's set up to do nothing but smuggle cigarettes. We found a police scanner, two cell phones, and the inside chopped to make more room for cigarettes. The engine was souped up to run like a NASCAR racer. I also have a gut feeling this is no small player," Ferguson said.

"That all you've got, Sean?"

"No, sir. Last night we were tailing another vehicle, a truck and he got away by outrunning us and the state police cruisers. It was the fastest truck I've ever chased. I think the vehicles are related," Ferguson said.

Shapiro stood while loosening his tie. He pulled two cold drinks from a small refrigerator under a credenza in his office. He didn't speak for a minute. Finally he exhaled and said, "I don't buy it, Sean. You don't have enough evidence for me to accept that. You know I think you're the best, Sean, and I hope you realize that's why I want you on it. Anybody else and I would have pulled them because of the relationship with Kate."

Ferguson shook his head slowly. "Thank you but I don't understand, sir. I'm just putting out a theory. I believe we'll prove this is a major operation."

"And I tend to agree, but talk to me when you get more, Sean. You know I'll do anything to support you but I need more. When you get it- and I'm sure you will-I'll get you a whole task force if we need it. For now, I've got a name for you to check out. He's tied to the shooter according to Immigration. Name's Paul

Hamood. He owns two convenience stores, one
in Canton and one in Plymouth. Evidently
Hamood sponsored the shooter's move to
Michigan from Lebanon."

Ferguson wrote the name on a small pad of
paper he always carried, ripped it off and
stuffed it in his pocket.

"I don't mean to sound unsupportive,
Sean. I'm under a lot of pressure from the
Governor to close this case and catch the
bastards. Privately, he's hinting at calling
this an isolated incident and sweeping it
under the rug. You need to make sure that
doesn't happen."

Ferguson ran his hand through his hair.
"It would help if you could run interference
for me with ATF. I need their information and
clout."

The Bureau of Alcohol, Tobacco, and
Firearms, a branch of the Federal government
had access to information all over the United
States and Ferguson could use the help to
bolster his limited resources.

"Okay, Sean, I'll see what I can do,"
Shapiro said. He thought for a moment. "I
attended a seminar last year in Maryland.
Maybe I can pull a few strings."

"I need the time to find the
perpetrators," Ferguson reasoned. "Kate was
murdered and there are more people responsible
than the shooter."

Shapiro stood, letting Ferguson know that
this meeting had ended. Walking to the door,
Shapiro put a hand on Ferguson's shoulder. He
pulled a business card from his pocket.

"Oops, another meeting," Shapiro said, as
he looked at his watch. "Sean, I'll do
everything I can. Take my card. I've put my
private phone number on the back. Call me

anytime, especially when you get any evidence
to support your position. Understood?"
Shapiro said, putting the card in Ferguson's
shirt pocket and hustling him to the door.

Chapter 8

The fifteen Fraud Division field agents met for a briefing at their offices five miles southwest of downtown Lansing where the State Police facilities were located. The academy and offices, serving as the training ground for all new recruits, was surrounded by an eight-foot fence where surveillance cameras mounted on poles prowled the grounds. Built in the 1970's the facility was stark and utilitarian even though creature comforts like air conditioning had been added. The eighty-acre complex allowed for something not available downtown- room to roam and expand.

Steve Wellston was waiting for Ferguson when he arrived at the building, surprising since his office was in the Treasury Building downtown. Ferguson knew his boss was a publicity junky and loved the limelight. Dressing in designer suits, he seemed to have an unlimited clothing allowance. If asked to describe his boss, Ferguson would probably say the man reminded him of Emily's Ken doll, Barbie's friend. Kate's case was high profile and Wellston had said he wanted it closed quickly with a big splash. Wellston knew between the State Police and Fraud division informants, something would turn up and he pushed hard.

"I want everyone to keep their eyes and ears open," Ferguson said, starting the briefing. "I'll be the point man for the department. For your information we have a lead on a man named Paul Hamood. If anyone has anything or finds anything on this man, talk to me A.S.A.P. Clear?" Ferguson paused before continuing. He was quieter now.

Clearing his throat, he looked down at his table. "On a personal note, most of you know Kate was my niece. I want to thank those of you who have offered condolences and I want to tell everyone that I won't rest until I bring this organization down. Kate will not have died in vain. Thanks again. Any questions?" Ted Simmons a long-time agent raised his hand. "How long we gonna be tied up on this, anyway? I got investigations close to indictments and don't want them to get stale."

Ferguson raised an eyebrow. Ted Simmons looked like some macho extra out of a Steven Seagal movie who was long on muscles and short on brains. Indeed, Simmons had worked for him for two years and was wily and closed cases at all costs- even if he had to squeeze the evidence a bit. Ferguson hated the way Simmons cut corners to get a case closed but the results were all anyone at the top saw and his numbers were good. Ferguson had lobbied hard to get rid of him but he had wriggled free of documented inequities and saved his job, albeit on another team. Simmons had made no secret that he blamed Ferguson for derailing his career with marginal evaluations and innuendos. "We hope this will be done in a few days, Simmons," he said. Maybe his timetable was optimistic but he hoped something or someone would give them the smugglers very soon.

Ferguson's team met at a McDonald's off Interstate 275 in Plymouth at 6:30 a.m. the next morning. Hound Dog was already downing his third cup of coffee as Ferguson strolled over to Jessicas not there yet in the back of the parking lot.

Hound Dog, looked up as Ferguson approached, nodding to acknowledge his boss's arrival. He lifted his sunglasses, propping them on top of his shiny bald head and stood. He looked like Mr. Clean from the detergent bottles. "H'lo, Music Man" he said in his deep baritone voice which made rooms reverberate. A man of few words, he was a stable factor on the team with fifteen years experience. As formidable as he appeared, he was a quiet, efficient agent who melted into the landscape but always there if any trouble started. Army Special Forces had given him the background for the job.

"Mornin'," Ferguson said. "How ya doin'today? You ready for an easy shift of doin' nothing but sittin' on your butt watching a store? Hound Dog, even you can smile."

"I smile when I'm happy," Hound Dog said. There was no intonation in his voice.

"And?" said Ferguson, rolling his arm to encourage a reply.

"And I guess I'm not that happy right now."

Ferguson grinned for the first time since Kate's death. "Where's Ma?" As the words left his mouth, Ferguson saw Jessica Cooper pull into the parking lot.

As she stepped into the restaurant she looked at Ferguson, "Sorry Sean. Had to take Edith in to get a remote start."

Edith was Jessica's 1996 Corvette, a trophy from the divorce proceedings of 2000 and the one thing both combatants wanted. Because there were no children, this was her baby.

"A remote start! Whaddya need that for?" Ferguson asked.

"Baby, it's cold outside in the winter. Or are you too old to know that?"

Ferguson rolled his eyes and stepped to an unoccupied corner of the restaurant near the door to the giant hamster tubes and slides the kids played in. As they settled in, Ferguson started the briefing. The smile faded from his face.

"The scum who caused Kate's death are still out there smuggling their cigarettes and rakin' in the big bucks. I won't rest 'til they're caught. The place we're watching today belongs to Paul Hamood." Ferguson handed printouts to his people. "These are the locations of his stores. He was Immigration's sponsor for our alien shooter, and I believe he's smuggling cigarettes. We need to prove it. It's that simple."

The team looked over the computer prints and pictures of the suspect.

"How do we handle this guy?" Jessica said as she looked at the driver's license photo.

"I have his cigarette purchases from the wholesalers. I've had other fraud people tailing him and I think we have something. Once he brings in a shipment of cigarettes, we'll go in with the state police and a search warrant to take a look at records and cigarettes. Hamood's store is in a commercial area off Windemere Road." Ferguson handed out a map and assignments for the team. "We can set up across the street at a self-storage facility. The other car will be in the parking lot of the shopping mall behind the store. Any questions?"

The team sat on the convenience store for most of the day on Tuesday and at 3:00 p.m. a full size white Ford cargo van pulled up with a load of cigarettes. Even without the

binoculars Ferguson knew it was Hamood. He
looked like a castoff from the Saturday Night
Fever crowd.

"Hound Dog, this is Music. That's the
vehicle, just like the snitch said. Go on in
and check it out."

Hound Dog pulled up to the store in the
Camaro and went inside to purchase a can of
soda pop and a pack of cigarettes. Five
minutes later he emerged from the store and
drove east out of the parking lot.

The next day the fraud investigators,
state police and county sheriff's deputies
assembled at the State Police Post to execute
a search warrant. Ferguson addressed the task
force. "Ladies and gentlemen, we are looking
for anything that will tie the owner of this
business to cigarette smuggling.
Specifically, we want any cigarettes having
decals or tax stamps from other states,
accounting records which include invoices for
the purchase of cigarettes from wholesalers,
and sales records. We intend to seize these
records and any illegal contraband we find on
the premises. Is that clear?" Ferguson had
delivered this speech so many times in the
past, he could give it in his sleep. He had
anticipated this day, hoping he could tie
Hamood to the operation they searched for.
The delivery this day came at 1:00 p.m. and as
the van was unloaded, the agents and officers
swarmed onto the premises and served Paul
Hamood with the paper authorizing them to
search the store. Ferguson and Jessica took
him aside for an interview. "Mr. Hamood, we
have a warrant to search your business
premises today. We will be taking records and

any illegal cigarettes we find. If you have
any questions, please talk to me. I would
like to ask a few questions after you call
your attorney, if you deem that necessary. Do
you understand what's happening?"

Paul Hamood appeared calm and nonchalant.
"I have nothing to hide. I do resent your
tactics, though, and my attorney will hear of
this." He smiled at the agents.

The slight man, 5'8" and 130 pounds, wore
a silk shirt unbuttoned to his chest to show
three pounds of gold chains and enough hair to
stuff a mattress. Judging from the scent
wafting about the man, it was obvious he had
been to the cologne counter at Marshall
Fields. It was also evident he had not come
into the store to put in an eight- hour shift.
The man turned and walked to his office in the
rear of the store as Ferguson did a slow burn.
He knew they would find nothing incriminating
this day. Hamood was too sure of himself.
Ferguson threw his clipboard down on a
counter. Pulling Jessica aside, Ferguson
looked at her. "We got nothing, Jess. This
son of a bitch knew we were coming. I want to
know how."

The group did a cursory sweep of Hamood's
building before getting down to a thorough
search. The store was typical of large liquor
stores in Michigan: it carried some food
items, a lot of beer and soda pop, and a huge
inventory of liquor and cigarettes. Three
hours of searching netted the agents six boxes
of records and no contraband. There was
absolutely no evidence of smuggling or illegal
cigarettes. Ferguson wanted to know who had
tipped this bastard off. The cocky man would
go down, maybe not now, but Ferguson would
make it his business to bust him.

As Ferguson stood there Jessica hurried over and put a hand on his arm. "Sean, you gotta come upstairs. We found something that just might trip this shit for brains. Don't know what it is yet."

Ferguson bounded up the stairs to the loft. Hamood followed close behind. The office measured only ten-foot by twelve-foot. Hound Dog leaned casually against one wall, no hint of excitement on his face. Moving to the center of the room, Ferguson turned to look at every wall in the room. Behind a wall of floor to ceiling utility shelves that had been pulled out from the wall agents found a steel door sealed with two chrome American padlocks that boasted half-inch shanks. It was like a hidden vault.

Ferguson turned grinning at Hamood. "Mr. Hamood, you can unlock it for us or we will unlock it. Be aware that if we open it; you probably won't be able to secure it again without a carpenter," Ferguson said.

With a look that could kill, Hamood unlocked the door. Ferguson's eyes got as big as saucers as the door opened. He could not believe what greeted his eyes.

The phone rang in a house in West Bloomfield near Interstate six ninety-six northwest of Detroit. Hermiz answered it. "Hermiz, you have talked to our cousin, Paul?" Abdul said in his native Arabic tongue.

"Speak in English," Hermiz said. "I received a call from him an hour ago. Agents from the Treasury are at the store with the police. They are searching everywhere."

"But there is nothing to find. We removed all cigarettes and papers for them the other night and the authorities do not have any of the other names and addresses of our people in the old country."

"The Bat man was right when he told us the agents would come," Hermiz said. "Somehow he knows."

"Unfortunately he did not know the agents would shoot Faris. My brother is dead and I must provide for his wife and child in Lebanon until I can bring them to America," Abdul said.

Hermiz sighed into the phone. "We will help you. They will come soon. You know we take care of our own."

"That does not comfort me," Abdul said.

"Then think about this. Do you have your own store? And where would you be without the money this man gives us to buy the stores? I think you should be grateful for what you have gotten," Hermiz said.

"Grateful that we had to bring these cigarettes here from that other state and take all the risks? Grateful that this Bat man threatens to send us back to the old country unless we are loyal to him? I am grateful that our God has allowed me to survive in this country," Abdul said. "This man is not our friend."

Chapter 9

"Holy cow," Ferguson exclaimed, as he stared at the hidden room in Hamood's store. "That's exactly what I said- well, holy something," Jessica said trying to suppress a grin. Ferguson had no doubt Jessica would have said something a little more colorful.

"Whaddya know," Ferguson said. "Looks like we got something, doesn't it."

"Yep, I'd say we do," Jessica said under her breath. "Still got that victory cigar?"

Ferguson smirked. The hidden closet in Hamood's store held electronic gear and a lot of it. It looked like something out of a spy movie. Ferguson knew most of the miniature equipment from ATF training in Maryland. Looking at the specialized eavesdropping electronics, Ferguson put the tab for everything at well over $30,000. There were cameras the size of a pen, laser activated electronic bugs that could track anyone, and listening devices that could pick up a whisper hundreds of yards away. Twelve ten inch monitors and digital recorders were stacked on three shelves toward the top of the closet.

"What the hell is all this stuff?" Hound Dog asked, manhandling a sensitive listening bug.

Ferguson stood too stunned to answer right away. He knew this could be a major break as his heart thumped against his ribcage.

"Some of the newest, most sophisticated electronics on the market today, I'd say," Ferguson said, picking up a catalog called the Spy Supply from a shelf.

"You mean anyone can buy this stuff without a license?" Jessica asked.

"Shoot, ain't free enterprise great?" Hound Dog said dragging out the words.

Ferguson picked up a tiny camera. Turning to Jessica he whispered, "Ever see a camera like this Jess?"

Jessica's eyes brightened. "Damn! In the car," she whispered.

"You got it," Ferguson said, a furrow growing on his brow.

Because the search warrant did not specify electronic gear, there was nothing the team could do except leave it, but they now knew Hamood was a man to watch. In Ferguson's mind Hamood was the enemy and he knew the smugglers would stop at nothing to protect their operation. He would not underestimate them again.

"Mr. Hamood, can you tell me why you have all these electronics?" Ferguson asked.

"It's a hobby, Mr. Ferguson, that's all," Hamood said.

"Expensive hobby, isn't it, Hamood?" Ferguson returned.

"We all have our vices," Hamood said.

Ferguson's hands shook almost imperceptibly. He stepped to Hamood and standing inches away whispered to the man. "I am putting you on notice, Hamood. You are going down. It may not be today or tomorrow but you are mine." Then Ferguson saw it. Standing there toe to toe he saw Hamood's cheek twitch. Not much of a twitch but Ferguson knew the man understood. A small smile pierced his lips.

Jessica squeezed in between the two men. "Okay gentlemen, no dancing on my time." She pulled Ferguson away from Hamood.

"Okay, Jess, okay," Ferguson said, finally breaking his stare.

"C'mon Sean, don't jeopardize the case if he's the hot shot in all this," Jessica whispered to her boss.

Searching the closet, agents found nothing else listed on the search warrant but they now had another scrap of evidence. They sealed the boxes of records, noting where they had been found and numbering the boxes consecutively so none were lost. The videotape from the security system went into an evidence envelope and the agents loaded everything into a truck to be taken to secure storage. Jessica and Ferguson walked to their car and prepared to follow the records to their office.

"Sean, this guy is so dirty," Jessica said. She shook her head. "I don't get it. Why no records or illegal cigarettes?"

"He knew we were comin', Jess. Oh, and thanks for stepping in. I was havin' trouble keeping quiet," Ferguson said sheepishly. After a pensive few seconds he said, "The man's wired, Jess."

Ferguson had seen it before- a self-storage place with a major stash of cigarettes four years ago. Treasury agents and police had stepped into a storage locker only hours after learning it held $1 million in illegal cigarettes. Cutting the lock after service of the warrant to seize the cache, agents stopped short when they found all the cigarettes gone. An electronic bug was found in one of the fraud cars. The smugglers had listened to every radio transmission made including one that tipped them of the impending raid. What Ferguson had to know is where Hamood's devices were and how much they had learned about the Treasury case, if anything.

Bat dialed the cell phone number almost automatically.

"How was your visit from the Treasury agents, Mr. Hamood?" Bat asked, smiling.

"They just left. They know I am involved. I know they do," Hamood said. "The one called Ferguson told me he would get me. He picked up a camera and smiled at me."

"A camera. What kind of camera?" Bat asked.

"I told you about my interest in surveillance and spy equipment. You told me you might be able to use my expertise," Hamood said.

"So where does the camera come in, Hamood?"

"I-I have some surveillance equipment in the store. It was well hidden behind a wall but they found it when they searched."

"How much is some, you fool?" Bat asked through clenched teeth.

"About $25,000 worth," Hamood said quietly.

"You jeopardize our whole business because you like to spy on people? I should call immigration myself and have you sent..."

"No, you can't do that. I have done everything you have asked," Hamood said.

Bat calmed. He could not afford to lose Hamood and his connections but he also didn't want to be a sitting duck because of another stupid mistake. He sighed loudly and closed his eyes while trying to maintain control of his anger.

"Just relax and leave Ferguson to me," Bat said. "Just think about our little conversation the other night if you need some backbone. I can do you much more harm than Ferguson and you would be well advised to remember that."

Bat slammed the receiver down, annoyed with Hamood and the agent's blind luck at finding the surveillance equipment. He could control Hamood and his family and friends if it came down to it but he didn't know what the Treasury fraud agents would do. As much as he hated the thought of it, Bat recognized that he might have to eliminate others to protect himself and the operation. He ran his hand through thinning hair, breathing more shallow now. Could it be that all these current problems were the result of some plot from beyond the grave by his long dead parents? They had taken everything from him once and now it appeared invisible forces were at work trying to take his little empire away again. He would not go quietly like last time when his parents pulled the rug from underneath him. His naiveté was gone and he had learned to land on his feet; no matter the obstacle placed in his way.

On the day following the execution of the search warrant, agents started the mundane task of going through the boxes of records, piece by piece. Invoices from three different years were stuffed into bags here and there. Since Hamood used only cash and money orders to pay all bills, bank statements only reflected what the owner wanted them to portray- nothing. A cash analysis, comparing the amount of cash taken in versus the bills paid by a taxpayer, might show they had thousands of dollars to spend but tax returns

reflected they lived on little or nothing.
When questioned about that fact, they always
said they borrowed from a relative to live.
It never failed to amuse Ferguson that a
family of five could live on $10,000 a year
when the mortgage payments alone were $9,000.
A better trick was how frugal a convenience
store owner could be when he paid cash for a
new Lexus or even the building his store
operated from. After a week of pouring over
business records, Hamood was given a clean
bill of health- officially that is. Ferguson
phoned his boss. "Steve, this is Sean. Got
some information for you."

"What can I do for you, Sean?" Wellston
asked.

"We've gone over the records we took from
Hamood and haven't come up with a thing. I
still think he's a player. We'd like to use
surveillance."

"I just don't know about that, Sean.
What basis do we have for that? I've got to
justify it upstairs."

"Twenty-five years in the field is the
basis. The guy also spends money like it's
water. He had at least $30,000 in
surveillance and monitoring equipment in that
store and you don't buy that quality stuff
unless you're gonna use it for something- like
smuggling. We found a miniature camera in the
smuggler's car and in the store as well. I
know this guy is into it up to his eyeballs.
C'mon Steve. I think with some time we can
nail the smart ass."

"We didn't find any evidence of smuggling
with a surprise search warrant and I don't
think we have the time or the manpower to sit
on this guy for weeks," Wellston said. "I'll
check upstairs and get back to you tomorrow."

Ferguson knew, however, that tomorrow would never come. As he put the receiver down, Jessica knocked on the frame of the open door.

"Have a seat, Jess," Ferguson said.

"What's the matter, Sean? You look like you just lost your best friend."

"Wellston told me to drop Hamood. If I didn't know better I'd say he was in on..."

"He can't do that! Go upstairs on the sonofabitch if he wants to fold."

Ferguson had to smile at his agent's grit. She had always been his staunchest ally and confidant. She had not really changed over the years. Usually up in a ponytail, her auburn hair was always damp from a shower in the morning. She wore little or no makeup and it suited her fine. Not that she was plain by any means. A down home elegance seemed to follow her- not anything you could put your finger on but you felt it even after she opened her mouth. Ferguson thought she reminded him of Liza Doolittle from that Broadway show, My Fair Lady, a bit. "Listen Sean, I've got something on the security tape we seized. Maybe it'll turn Wellston." Jessica pulled a cart with a television and video recorder into the office. Turning it on, she grinned as the security tape showed a familiar face walk onto the screen. "Is that who I think it is?" Ferguson said. "One of our people?"

"Sure is," Jessica said.

"I don't believe it. What the hell's he doin'?" Ferguson asked.

Chapter 10

Ferguson and Jessica sat alone in his office watching the security surveillance tape for any other signs of familiar faces, hoping they would not find any. Friday morning moved into afternoon as they rewound the tape to scrutinize the portion of the tape where fraud agent, Ted Simmons, stood at the counter of Hamood's store. Ferguson pushed slow motion mode on the video recorder watching in particular any exchange between Simmons and the clerk.

The clerk produced a small paper bag from under the counter and seemed to shove something into it. He then picked up the Baby Ruth candy bar that lie on the counter and put it into the bag. Simmons' hand movements indicated he was saying something but there was no sound to hear. According to the tape counter Simmons was there for over five minutes.

"Seems like a long time to buy a candy bar, wouldn't you say, Sean?" Jessica asked.

"Yeah, and if you just bought a candy bar, why put it in a bag?" Ferguson countered.

"I wouldn't say he's dirty without a lot more evidence but it looks odd," Ferguson said.

"Yeah, but Simmons has never been a good fit here," Jessica said. "He sure didn't like workin' under you."

Ferguson remembered the day two years ago when the team raided a store on Flint's west side and found contraband cigarettes on one of Simmons' cases. Finding cigarettes from the Indian reservations in New York and cigarettes from North Carolina, Ferguson had thought it odd because they didn't get that many seizures where contraband came in from two different places by one smuggler.

"Seems odd this guy would bring cigarettes in from both places, doesn't it, Simmons?" Ferguson asked.

Simmons had shrugged his shoulders and kept on working on documenting the seizure.

Ferguson kept an eye on his agent and especially the seized contraband. Upon returning to the office, he checked the inventory of seized tobacco and found a discrepancy in the count. Those few cartons of cigarettes had shown up mysteriously at the store they had just raided.

"What the hell's going on, Simmons? Are those reservation cigarettes from our lockup?"

A sly smile crept onto Simmons' face. "No way, Sean. That would be illegal. And anyway we found dozens of cartons from down south. This Arab is as dirty as they come."

Ferguson cornered Simmons and when he could see Simmons twitch he spoke. "You don't belong on my team and you certainly don't belong on this job. You have one month to find other employment or I'll have your ass tacked on this wall. Clear?" Ferguson turned and walked away without listening to another word.

A week later Ferguson had been called into Steve Wellston's office and told that Simmons would be transferred to another team and that anything that had happened in the past would be left there. Simmons had cleaned his desk and moved on within an hour of that conversation.

"He cut too many corners," Ferguson said.
"So how do we handle him?" Jessica asked.

"I'm not sure, yet," Ferguson said. "I'll get back to you."

The doorbell rang at 9:00 a.m. on Saturday. Already up and dressed, Ferguson went to the door. Opening it, his mouth dropped open. Standing before him, Billy Johnston grinned that good ol' boy grin. Still somewhat toned because he stayed active, Johnston sported a Marine Corp baseball cap and a black tee shirt peeked out from his open jacket. The shirt, pulled tight around the midsection, hinted at a tad too much beer consumption for his five-foot ten frame. A cigarette rested behind his right ear holding his ample head of brown hair at bay and a wooden match protruded from his mouth.

Groaning, Ferguson pushed the door closed. After twenty seconds the bell rang again. Ferguson took his time and opened the door, this time unable to suppress a grin of his own.

"How ya doin' there stringbean?" Johnston said.

Ferguson shook his head; "You know something, you're a scary thing to see first thing in the mornin'."

"Yeah, well, I remember a time when you loved seein' my face in the mornin' 'cause I didn't have slanty eyes and run around in black pajamas," Johnston said.

Ferguson stepped aside to let his friend come in. "So you tie one on last night and end up on a bus comin' north or did you just miss me?" Ferguson asked.

"Naw, I missed Joanne, not your scrawny ass," Johnston said.

Looking up the stairs to the second floor, Johnston saw Joanne standing there. He took the steps two at a time and gave Joanne a bear hug when he reached her.

"Hey, sweet cheeks, how ya doin'?" Johnston bellowed.

Joanne shook her head, forcing a smile as she stared at Ferguson, "Just fine now that you're in town, honey."

"Whoee, be still ma beatin' heart," Johnston said.

"Hey, Stringbean, me an' the misses is gonna have a little talk. I'll see ya in an hour or so," Johnston said.

"If I know you, it'll only be ten minutes," Ferguson said.

Johnston came down the stairs and they retired to the kitchen. Johnston put his arm around Ferguson's shoulder.

"So why are you really here?" Ferguson asked.

"Figured you'd be hurtin', had the time off work, and got a good price on the flight," Johnston said.

"Appreciate the thought B.J." Ferguson sighed as he sat down at the kitchen table. "It's been tough but we're makin' progress on the case in spite of my boss."

"Anything I can do?" Johnston asked.

"Naw, we're okay." Ferguson tapped Johnston on the arm. "So what you been up to? You actually got a job?"

"Yep, right good job working in the cigarette industry. Kinda like you," Johnston said.

Ferguson looked blankly at him.

Johnston puffed up like a rooster, "Got me an executive position at S&S Distributing in Greensboro. We sell cigarettes to a lotta stores around Greensboro."

"Even after grabbin' that huge General Motors pension from that executive position on the assembly line in Lansing? Why, with all that money I can't imagine you'd ever need to work again!" Ferguson said.

"Well, they needed me and I couldn't leave'em in the lurch," Johnston said.

"Who's they?" Ferguson asked.

"Buncha you damn yankees own it. Couple a guys from New York and another guy who seems to show up every once in a while from up here in Michigan," Johnston said. "Strange too, 'cause they're doin' a great business even though they ain't been around for very long."

"So what do they have you doing?" Ferguson asked.

"Loadin' trucks," Johnston responded.

"Thought it was something important like that," Ferguson said.

Finishing breakfast, Johnston and Ferguson moved to the great room, admiring the view of Ferguson's property, ten acres of prime land that backed up to a state forest.

"Wanna take a walk?" Johnston asked.

"Sure, let's do it, B.J.," Ferguson said.

Stepping outside, Ferguson shivered at the cold for a moment but the bright low sun warmed him a bit. Pixley, Ferguson's golden retriever, bounded back and forth as if clearing the way for the men. Picking up a stick, Ferguson threw it for the dog. Pixley raced after it.

Ferguson and Johnston walked in silence for a minute taking in the mixed pine and maple trees scattered about the property. Ferguson remembered that Young Rascals song-It's a Beautiful Morning from the 60's and started to hum.

"You still into all that music shit, Sean," Johnston asked. "You never played Hank Williams or George Jones. Always that canned shit. What was that?"

"Canned Heat." Ferguson paused. "You shoulda stayed here instead of headin' south, B.J."

"Yeah, but Maggie's arthritis really acted up in the cold or I'd be here," Johnston said.

"So why'd you come up? It isn't close enough to just pop in anymore."

Johnston stopped and kicked at some pinecones lying on the ground. "Just knew how you were in 'Nam when guys checked out and thought you might wanna talk to someone, that's all. Specially since it was Katie."

Ferguson cleared his throat. "Not gonna tell you it doesn't hurt, Billy. Hurts worse than anything I can remember- even when my dad passed away." Ferguson swallowed hard. "I'm going to get these bastards no matter what it takes and you can take that to the bank."

Billy crouched down, grabbed a few pebbles, and shook them like a pair of dice.

"At what price, Sean?"

"Whaddya mean?" Ferguson asked.

"You prepared to sacrifice your family for that?"

"Whaddya mean?"

"I probably know you better than anyone- agreed?"

"I suppose."

"I know how you were when we lost guys you barely knew back there in 'Nam. Are you shuttin' out Joanne and the kids now 'cause you blame yourself for Kate? I'm willin' to bet you are," Johnston said.

82

Ferguson flinched at this revelation. He crouched down beside his friend. "Maybe I am. Can't help myself. I was responsible for her and I screwed up, Billy. You understand that?" Ferguson said.

"Ain't your fault, Sean. And you know what the real crime is? Not only did the asshole kill Kate but now he's killin' your family."

"I'm tryin', Billy, I really am. It's as though Joanne and I are strangers. I can't even talk to her. I used to look forward to calling her everyday from the office but now I avoid it like the plague."

The pair stood and strolled on in silence for a few minutes. Reaching the back of his property, Ferguson patted his friend on the back. "You're a good pal, B.J. Thanks for comin' up."

They spent the rest of the day comfortable in each other's presence. After a few beers that evening, or maybe it was more than a few, Ferguson's curiosity got the best of him.

"So who are these guys that own your cigarette wholesaler?" Ferguson asked.

"You just can't let anything go, can you?" Billy asked, grinning at Ferguson. "I know the guy who comes down from Michigan is named Moussa. He's got an Arab name but he never saw the old country. I'm sure of that. The two New York guys get nervous when he's around so I think he's connected to the top dog. He reminds me of a gangbanger- not smart enough to run a business, just muscle."

"So who's the real owner and why is he down in North Carolina?" Ferguson asked, more to himself than Johnston. Maybe Dempsey at ATF could help him find some answers.

Ferguson stepped onto the porch of the 1950s brick colonial near the Lodge freeway in Detroit bright and early Monday morning. He knocked on the wrought iron storm door. A boy about five pulled the heavy wood door open and peered through the decorative metal of the storm door. A woman appeared behind him—attractive even without make-up and nice clothes.

Ferguson flashed his tin. "Mrs. Lancona?"

Her eyes became slits as she eyed him warily. "Yes."

"My name is Sean Ferguson. I'm a fraud agent for the Treasury department. Could I talk to you for a few minutes?"

She unlocked the storm door and pushed it open. "Come on in, Mr. Ferguson."

The home was clean but it was obvious that they didn't have much money from the well-used furnishings. She motioned for Ferguson to sit and sat on a chair across the room, the boy never leaving her side.

"Now, what can I do for you?" she asked.

"I'm trying to find Moochy. Have you seen or heard from him in the last two weeks?"

Her eyes clouded over and her hands began to tremble. "I haven't seen him and the police haven't either. I filed a missing person report but he's gone. I-I..." She looked at her son, gave him a kiss on the forehead, and told him to go play with his trucks. As the boy disappeared from sight she continued. "I'm sure something's wrong. He would never leave us and just walk away. He always spent a lot of time with us, especially Timmy." She paused.

"Something else?" Ferguson asked quickly. He felt a pang of guilt at his situation with Joanne and the girls.

"I-I received a package yesterday. It was delivered by a courier and was wrapped in a plain brown wrapper- no markings or address anywhere." She closed her eyes and sighed to gather herself. Opening her eyes, she rose. For a moment Ferguson didn't know if their talk was over.

"Just a second, Mr. Ferguson," she said, walking to a closet near the door.

Shaking visibly, she returned with a shoebox loosely wrapped in brown paper. She put it on the coffee table and sat down.

Ferguson moved to the table and gently removed the paper as if it were a bomb. Ferguson lifted the top off. His eyebrows rose as he peered inside.

"You don't know who sent this?" Ferguson asked.

Mrs. Lancona shook her head.

"Did you count it?" he asked.

"$100,000," she said quietly.

Ferguson looked at her, knowing she had agonized over what to do with the money. He smiled warmly. "I'm sure it's not illegal, Mrs. Lancona. I would just use it for the two of you."

Ferguson knew from Lancona's phone call the day of the funeral that he would not be coming home. He also knew that the woman had never seen this much money. Mrs. Lancona slumped as if a huge weight had been lifted from her shoulders. Ferguson stood to leave, patting her on the shoulder.

"If you think of anything or if your husband contacts you I'd appreciate a call,"

Ferguson said handing her a card knowing a call would never come.

Ferguson drove to Lansing thinking about Mrs. Lancona and her son. He slid his briefcase onto his desk at the office. He sat trying to concentrate on the mundane paperwork associated with audits of people who made a living avoiding taxes. Ferguson still lived for the days the team made a difference and caught someone in a fraud scheme.

He heard the click of the security door outside his office and guessed who would step across the threshold.

"Sean?" Jessica said. "You here?"

"Yeah, Jess," Ferguson said.

She glided in and sat down. "I wanted to update you on Lancona."

Ferguson perked up.

She held up her hand. "Nothin' good, I'm afraid. Hound Dog and I have beat the bushes. We got nothin'. It's like he's gone from the face of the earth. How about his wife?"

Ferguson slumped back. "Nothin' there either, Jess?"

She just shook her head. "We'll keep trying but it doesn't look good."

"I think his wife would know if he was hiding out but she is truly devastated. I even verified she has been on the phone every day with the police. She just doesn't know," Ferguson said.

"It sounds like he may be part of the food chain somewhere to me," Jessica said.

"The way he talked to me the day of Kate's funeral I knew he was scared out of his skin. I'll tell you one thing- she just received a package by courier service with a $100,000 in it. My guess is that's a payoff for Moochy's family." Ferguson shook his head and sighed.

"A hundred grand! Wow, I wonder how he negotiated that perk," Jessica said.

Chapter 11

George Dempsey, the agent in charge of the Detroit Alcohol, Tobacco, and Firearms office, sat across from Ferguson in a surveillance van near the warehouse district in southwest Detroit. Ferguson's talk with Billy had piqued his interest and Dempsey could get information Ferguson didn't have access to.

"Sorry you had to come down here, Sean but we been sittin' on this guy for four days waiting for him to make a move with some assault rifles he's peddlin'- about a hundred of'em. Snitch also said he's got some heavy-duty explosives. This thing is supposed to go down sometime today. I just couldn't leave but I knew you'd want to know about this," Dempsey said.

Ferguson looked at the electronic eavesdropping equipment, a lot like Hamood's store, mounted on one wall of the stepvan. Wire lockers held Kevlar vests, firearms, and night vision headgear. Two men manned the van, wearing headphones and controlling recording equipment.

"I appreciate that, George. We can use all the help we can get." Ferguson felt a nervous rush course through his limbs, hoping this might be the lead they needed to take out Hamood.

"Got a call from a guy named Gary Portnoy who claimed he bought illegal cigarettes at a store on Eight Mile in Detroit. Said not only did he buy Tareytons with tax stamps from another state on them but he heard the owner and another guy behind the counter talking about the agent who was killed and how it served her right," Dempsey said. "Portnoy sounds legit, Sean. Gave me the name of a Detroit cop who referred him to me and left his cell phone number if we need it."

Sliding the notes across the table, Ferguson's eyebrows raised when he saw the address. "The Keg and I on Eight Mile in Detroit? Hamood's stores are in Livonia and Canton."

"Isn't Hamood. Some guy named Ghaleed," Dempsey said.

Ferguson stared blankly at the wall of the step van. A furrow deepened in his brow. How could this guy be involved? He knew Hamood was the bad guy or had he misread him? Maybe Hamood and Ghaleed were related. Ferguson pinched his forehead between his thumb and fingers as he closed his eyes.

"Know anything about the guy yet, George?" Ferguson asked.

"Only that he grew up about ten miles north of Detroit. Never been in trouble. Had the store for the last twenty years. Family run and owned all that time."

Something struck Ferguson as odd. Ghaleed didn't seem to fit the profile of any smuggler he had ever put away. This man has roots. Ferguson doubted the information that Ghaleed was dirty.

Stepping outside the van, Ferguson squinted in the fall sun and lit a Swisher. Ferguson looked at his friend. "George, we've been at this game a long time together, haven't we?"

"Sure have and I notice you're still smokin' those Sweets."

"We all got our vices," Ferguson said grinning at Dempsey. "By the way, could you check someone out for me, off the record?

I've gotta friend down in Greensboro who said
he's working for a cigarette wholesaler. The
name is S&S Wholesale and they are growin' big
time from nothin' two years ago to the biggest
player in the area. Maybe, there's dirty
money in there. I was just wondering if you
could check'em out. My gut says something
isn't right."

Jessica's cell phone chirped as she was
leaving her Ann Arbor condominium. She ripped
the phone from its holster like a gun fighter
in the old west to stop the annoying ringing
and knowing it was Sean Ferguson.

"Morning, Sean, what's up? Where are you
and when do you want me to meet you?" Having
returned Ferguson's calls hundreds of times
Jessica knew the regimen. She always felt
good when Ferguson got an idea and needed her
to help execute it.

"How'd you know it was me? Doesn't
anyone else ever call you? We need to find
you someone. Maybe a man would help, Jess,"
Ferguson rattled off, pretending to be
irritated.

"Well, daaad, it's like this," said
Jessica.

"Hey, hey, hey, I'm not that old, young
lady," Ferguson said. "Only a few years older
than you."

"You can't prove it by me. Fourteen
years is more than a few, I would say.
Anyway, what do you need, Sean, or has your
geriatric brain forgotten already?" Jessica
didn't really think of Ferguson as that old
and in fact had strong feelings for him. She
liked to think of it as a schoolgirl crush but
her admiration and friendship seemed to boil
over into something else when she fantasized.
Jessica would walk through fire for Ferguson

and she was sure he knew it but never was out of line like a lot of law enforcement types.

Ferguson ignored the extra curricular comments and got to the point.

"Got a call from Dempsey. Someone reported stamped packs at a store on Eight Mile. I need you to run down there and see what we've got. Take the Hound with you."

Closing her cell phone, Jessica dropped it onto the seat of the Camaro as she got in. Pulling her aviator sunglasses from the neck of her heavy T-shirt, she slid them onto her face. Feeling like Tom Cruise in Top Gun with the shades, she pushed the accelerator and the car jumped to attention.

Hound Dog met Jessica at the office and the two checked the equipment they would need. The camera with the telephoto lens and lots of film were primary.

"Where'd this tip come from, Sugar?" Hound Dog asked.

"Don't know. Sean called me and said it was a priority one. He got the information from Dempsey. Said to make the buy in Tareytons."

"Tareytons. Who smokes that shit anymore?" Hound Dog asked.

"Evidently someone does. So I'll handle the buy and you drive the wheels?" Jessica asked.

"No problem."

The two rode in silence listening to the strains of classic rockers Kansas and Bob Seger on the radio. Eight-Mile was a conglomeration of boarded up buildings, fast food restaurants, convenience stores, and topless bars.

The Keg and I was a gaudy building on the corner of Hastings. The side of the building

was painted in huge red letters announcing the
name. At first glance the wall appeared to be
a huge paisley 1970's head shop advertisement.
Hound Dog drove past the store and turned
right at the next side street. An alley ran
directly behind the storefronts. Jessica took
a look as they rolled by. Old tires and a
mattress lay on the ground like an obstacle
course on the disintegrating black top.
Broken bottles and overgrown weeds covered the
rest of the byway.

Jessica noted the back of the stores in
case they needed to execute warrants in the
future. The importance of knowing the lay of
the land could not be overstated. Hound Dog
stopped next to the huge sign at the side of
the building and Jessica got out of the car.

"I'll be back in a flash, Dog. You just
keep yourself real up close and personal,"
Jessica said.

"You just keep yo' booty warm and safe,"
Hound Dog said.

"Holy shit, Dog, you sexist buffoon. You
watch your step or I'll have to kick yo'
booty! Or maybe you'd like to walk your black
ass outta here when I take you out of that
car?" Jessica retorted, feigning irritation.

"Okay, okay, princess, sorry," Hound Dog
said. He tried not to smile though it looked
like his face might crack from the effort.

Jessica rounded the corner onto Eight
Mile and sauntered toward the door. The
windows were plastered with painted signs
advertising beer and cigarettes. Small
diameter holes perforated the windows in a few
places, sending a shiver up her back. Jessica
walked to the double doors and saw the heavy
steel gate pulled aside to allow access.
Stepping inside, she looked around the store.

One side was nothing but glass faced coolers loaded with beer and pop. In the center of the store stood a maze of metal shelving. She picked up a few cans by two fingers, blowing the layer of dust from the top of them.

The wall opposite the coolers was made of sheets of Plexiglas. The inch thick clear plastic protected the clerk from the unwanted demands of people who made a living stealing from others. It probably didn't hurt that there was also a 12-gauge shotgun sitting on a shelf behind the clerk, standard issue for stores in this area. At least the plastic walls also protected her from him should he consider doing something stupid. On a wall near the door hung a series of framed pictures of the Winston Cup stock car racers. Dale Earnhardt's number 3 car and Jeff Gordon's ride were prominent. Jessica approached the glass castle and smiled at the clerk.

"Hi, three packs of Tareyton, please," Jessica said, smiling at the clerk. After pulling a ten-dollar bill from her pocket, she nodded toward the pictures. "How much for the Earnhardt picture? My boyfriend's a big fan."

"Nineteen-ninety-nine," the clerk said. The man looked to be of Middle East descent but there was no hint of an accent. "You know, he won at Daytona a few years ago. And now that he's gone, that could become valuable."

"Maybe next time. I'm a little short right now," Jessica said. "Thanks."

In the car outside, she pulled a pack of Tareytons from the bag. Hound Dog studied the bottom of it.

"Nothin', Sugar," he said, sounding disappointed. There were no marks on the protective cellophane. The cigarettes were legal. He pulled the second pack, shaking his head no. "Not a mark."

"Shit," she said.

Pulling the last pack from the bag, Jessica scrunched up her nose as if to will a tax stamp on the bottom of it.

"Bingo!" both said simultaneously. A tax stamp was clearly visible on the third pack.

Driving away from the store, Jessica was on the cell phone to Ferguson.

As soon as Ferguson answered Jessica talked. "He's dirty, Sean. We got a stamp."

"What we got is probable cause to get a search warrant," Ferguson said. "We need more than one pack of cigarettes to make a case. Did you get any shots of our man?"

"Not yet, but we will now," Jessica said. "If this guy is our man, Sean, I don't want him to breathe without us knowing it." Her voice cracked as she finished her statement.

"After you called this morning, Jess, I started checking records in Wayne County and then up in Lansing. Seems Paul Ghaleed bought the store property last year for cash-$400,000 in cash. Does the name Ghaleed ring any bells?"

"Nope," Jessica said. "He must be low profile."

"I ran a check through Secretary of State vehicle records and came up with a truck registered to Ghaleed- an '87 Ford pick-up. Got anything to say about that?" Ferguson asked.

Jessica thought for a minute. Where was the Ford truck? Was Ghaleed driving it the night in Chamberlain? But what about Hamood? Were they partners? Every step they took just created more questions. "Chamberlain?"

"Bingo," Ferguson said.

Chapter 12

When Ferguson returned to his office in Lansing the morning after starting the investigation on Ghaleed, a manila envelope sat on his desk. The envelope had an ATF return address. Ferguson brightened, knowing this was the information on S&S he was waiting for. Turning it over Ferguson noticed it had been opened and resealed.

"Anyone see who dropped this off?" Ferguson asked of the agents in the office.

"It was on the floor just inside the door when I came in," Simmons said. "I was first in this mornin' after an all night surveillance."

"Thanks," Ferguson said. He wondered when it had been left and made a mental note to call George.

Reading the sticky note attached to the papers left by the ATF man, he noted that Dempsey had more documents coming but that he knew Ferguson wanted to see anything he got post haste. Nothing he saw glared at him right away regarding the company Billy Johnston worked for in North Carolina.

A corporation named Ventures Unlimited that had incorporated in Delaware owned S&S Wholesalers. Turns out Ventures was jointly held by companies named Specialty Risks, Farhill Farms, and six other shell corporations that hold few assets up and down the Eastern seaboard. Farhill seems to be the majority holder and is incorporated in Delaware. Specialty is a New Jersey company. Ferguson thought there was an awful lot of paper and legal maneuvering to incorporate one cigarette wholesaler. Ferguson didn't even

find a real name until annual reports for the
corporations were checked. The only name he
found made the hairs on his neck stand up.
His head started to spin as he thought of the
ramifications if this turned out to be true.
The name of M. Lancona appeared on documents
relating to Specialty Risks in New Jersey.

"Jess, I need you now," Ferguson yelled
out to his agent sitting at her desk.
Everyone looked up to see what the commotion
was as Jessica jumped up and headed for
Ferguson's office.

"What's up, Sean?" she asked as she
stepped into his office.

"You did the work up on Moochy Lancona
when we collared him three years ago, didn't
you?" Ferguson asked.

"Yeah, dug real deep on him but he
slipped out," Jessica said.

"Was he ever in New Jersey?" Ferguson
asked.

Jessica put her hand to her chin as the
furrow in her brow deepened and didn't say
anything for a few seconds. "No, he was born
and bred here and as far as I know never set
foot in New Jersey. Why?"

"His name shows up in a check on one of
the companies that owns B.J.'s cigarette
wholesaler in Greensboro. Seems odd to me and
Lancona isn't that common a name," Ferguson
said.

"I can see in your eyes you're not buyin'
it's a coincidence that they have the same
name," Jessica said.

Ferguson smiled. "I've got a post office
box number in Trenton. I'll see if I can get
an address from them. In the meantime an
address in Pittsfield, near Ann Arbor, turned
up on one of the companies. Might be a nice

day for a ride, wouldn't you say Jess?"
Ferguson said, smiling.

This was the way most days went. The
fraud agents reviewed records the majority of
the time. Following people and busts were
only a small percentage of their time. The
attorneys always wanted the paper trail and
the agents jumped through hoops most of the
time to supply the documents. It also meant
that they knew by a cursory look what stunk
and where they would find problems. Since the
majority of the convenience store owners in
Michigan these days were of Middle-eastern
descent and they failed in many cases to keep
any records.

Arriving at the address, it didn't
surprise Ferguson that it was a vacant lot.
Fake addresses were used extensively for all
kinds of fraud and this could be one of the
biggest ever. A check with the postal
authorities did turn up a post office box in
Ann Arbor. Ferguson was fairly sure it was a
scam but he needed to make sure.

As he stepped to the counter, he pulled
his identification from the breast pocket of
his shirt.

"Hello, I'm Sean Ferguson with the
Michigan Treasury. Can I speak to the
postmaster, please?"

The postal clerk eyed the identification.
When satisfied it was genuine, he motioned
Ferguson to a side door where he was buzzed
into the work area. After a few moments a
tall beefy man appeared and thrust his hand at
Ferguson.

"David Barringer, Agent Ferguson. I'm
the postmaster here. How can we help you
today?"

"I'm checking on an address and a post office box as part of an official investigation." All postmasters loved to hear there was an official investigation. It made for good dinner conversation and put a little excitement into what Ferguson thought must be a mundane existence.

"I have a box number and I need to know the address behind it," he said.

"Sure. What's the number?"

"It's box 12428."

Barringer walked to a file cabinet and pulled out the information on the boxes.

"Okay, box 12428. Let's see. Here it is," he said, raising it proudly over his head. "The address is 1246 Chamberlain in Pittsfield Township."

"Sorry, Mr. Barringer but that address is a vacant lot. Any other information? How about a signature?"

"There is a signature but I'll be damned if I can read it." He shoved the card at Ferguson. The signature looked like the scrawl of a one-year old.

"How's the box paid for?" Ferguson asked.

"From what I see here, it's paid with a money order and has been in use for three years. Money order is mailed here to pay the fee."

"That figures," Ferguson said. Another dead end did not surprise Ferguson.

The break on Ghaleed came with good old-fashioned legwork on the part of Jessica and Hound Dog. The white surveillance van with the tinted side and back windows sat a half block from the brick and aluminum ranch in Southfield that belonged to the suspect.

Inside, agents watched for the 1987 black Ford pick-up truck registered to Michael Ghaleed they had chased near Ann Arbor the week before. Jessica briefed Ferguson while Hound Dog held the binoculars on the subject's house.

"He's spent most of his life here in the states, came over from Lebanon thirty-two years ago. He's a citizen."

"Boy, you guys have been busy since I called." Ferguson was impressed. "You must have been burning up the phones."

"We on him like white on rice, man," Hound Dog said. "Gotcha." He grabbed at air as if catching a buzzing fly.

"Might be," Ferguson said, "but I'm not sure yet. Things may not be what they seem." His favorite words were "convince me and you know we'll get a conviction." It was a game the agents always played. They came to enjoy Ferguson's challenge and felt great pride when he finally said to make the call to the attorney general or prosecutor. The team had enjoyed a phenomenal run, convicting 95% of those charged with cigarette felonies.

"Find the truck and maybe we'll have something, right Sean?" Jessica said. Ferguson grinned. Ferguson felt pride well up in him because his agents had learned their lessons well.

"Do you think this is the creep who's responsible for Kate's death?" Jessica asked softly.

Ferguson sat quietly for a minute. "I'm not convinced until we have the truck and a tie to Hamood. So, have you started?" he asked as he sipped coffee.

Jessica looked at his boss.

"Started what, Sean?"

"The affidavit for the search warrant for this guy's store, of course." Ferguson shook his head. "Let's head back to the office, Dog."

The affidavit took two hours to prepare. All the facts had to be documented so a judge could follow the trail logically. There had to be probable cause to believe that there was illegal activity going on at the convenience store before any judge would issue a warrant.

"You ready to rock n' roll, mama?" Hound Dog said as he prepared to leave. He was to meet with Wayne County Sheriff deputies and State police detectives while Ferguson and Jessica got the warrant signed.

"I think we're in business. Sean and I will talk to the judge," Jessica said.

"OK, man, we'll be waiting at the staging area," Hound Dog said. The agents and police met at a staging area away from the taxpayer's business to organize when warrants were to be executed.

At precisely 2:00 p.m. the deputies, state police, and treasury agents entered the store. The uniforms were to make sure peace was maintained while the search was made. When treasury agents asked for Michael Ghaleed, the man inside the plastic room strode toward them.

"Are you Michael Ghaleed?" Jessica asked as she flipped open the case that held her credentials.

"I am, and what can I do for you?" he asked, not bothering to look at the identification.

"Sir, I would like you to step outside of the security wall so I can have a word with you," Ferguson said in his most authoritative voice.

"What do you want, ahh," he squinted to read the identification, "Mr. Ferguson, is it?"

"I need you to come out right now, Mr. Ghaleed," Ferguson repeated sharply. Redness crept into his face.

"Yes sir," Ghaleed said as he opened the door and stepped outside. "I apologize for this enclosure. We've been robbed many times; last year my brother was shot and killed over a bottle of liquor. It's been very difficult for me," his voice trailed off.

"Mr. Ghaleed, my name is Sean Ferguson and this is my assistant, Jessica Davies. We are here to execute a search warrant. Before we proceed, though, I need to know if there are any firearms on the premises." They knew full well that in this neighborhood most people had a gun for protection or to rob someone.

The search progressed from the front of the store to the rear storeroom and upstairs to a small office. Hound Dog and Jessica started at the cigarette storage first.

Almost immediately Hound Dog called to Ferguson. "Looky here, boss," he said proudly displaying contraband cigarettes. "And there's more where these came from."

"All of'em?" Ferguson asked.

"Naw, but quite a few," Hound Dog said. "They seem to be mixed in with legit stuff."

Ferguson looked at the storage area. He turned to Ghaleed.

"Mr. Ghaleed, can you tell me why you have illegal cigarettes in your store?"

"I don't buy illegal cigarettes. I never have and I never will. It's not worth the hassle," he said through clenched teeth. "If there are illegal cigarettes in there then

101

your people put them there. There are only two keys to that storage area and I control both of them."

"Mr. Ghaleed," Ferguson pressed, "you're telling me no one else has access to that storage facility, is that true?"

"That's right."

"Mr. Ghaleed, can you tell me where your 1987 black Ford pickup truck is?"

"I don't own a pick-up truck, certainly not a Ford." He hesitated. "And even if I did own it, I wouldn't let you see it," Ghaleed spit. He sounded like a mad kid who was going to take his toy and go home.

"Can you tell me why the Secretary of State- Motor Vehicles would show you own this vehicle? Can you also tell me when you sold the 1986 Oldsmobile Eighty-eight that was titled to you? Can you? Did you know we had an agent killed by a man in a 1986 Oldsmobile?" Ferguson puffed up with each comment made. "Mr. Ghaleed, can you also tell me if you like to work on cars? Do you like fast cars? Do you?"

"It's none of your business what I like," Ghaleed snapped. The police officers tensed and sidled closer as they rested their hands on their holsters. Jessica stared at Ferguson. She stepped in and changed tack trying to diffuse the situation.

"Now, just cool off, Mr. Ghaleed. We're just trying to find out the facts. If you haven't done anything wrong, you have nothing to worry about, right?" Jessica put her hand on Ferguson's shoulder and pushed him a few feet away. "What's the matter, Sean? You okay? I want the guy as bad as you, but we have to be cool. If he's guilty, we'll find the evidence."

"Sorry. You're right, Jess." Ferguson rubbed his temples between his thumb and first finger. A trickle of cold sweat ran down his back.

"You're the one who taught me that the man isn't guilty until he's convicted, remember? We can't do anything about the truck until we find it. Just chill out, please. Now, let me talk to Ghaleed."

Patting Ferguson on the back, Jessica coaxed him back to the storeowner. Ghaleed, with his jet-black hair, heavy growth of beard, and dark piercing eyes, appeared ominous. He was now mad as a hornet.

"Mr. Ghaleed, we are executing a search warrant to find the facts. Nothing more. Let us do our job," Jessica said.

"I don't smuggle cigarettes and I don't cheat," the man said quickly. He was still just under the boiling point and Jessica knew it.

The search continued for another two hours as boxes of records accumulated near the door. Jessica and Ferguson stood near the locked cigarette storage closet and looked around.

The small office upstairs was the last area of the store to get a thorough going over. Jessica sat at the desk and looked into the drawers. Papers were stacked everywhere. The center drawer held pencils, business cards, and car keys—Ford keys. Jessica took the keys from the drawer and hung them by two fingers for Ferguson to see.

"Looky here, Sean," Jessica said, "Ford keys." The two went down the stairs and walked to Ghaleed who leaned against the rear wall of the store.

"Thought you never owned a Ford, Mr. Ghaleed," Jessica asked holding the keys for the man to see.

"Those aren't mine. I only buy General Motors cars."

"Good, then can I take them?"

Ghaleed shrugged his shoulders but did not answer.

As Jessica went through the drawers of the file cabinet in the office upstairs, one thing was apparent. There was no organization to anything in the room.

"Shit, I can't make anything of this," said Jessica, "there are invoices with price lists, some from '96, some from '97."

"Take everything, then," Ferguson said. "We'll sort it out later."

Eight evidence boxes and seventy cartons of cigarettes later; the agents loaded a truck and pulled away from the store. The one item not inventoried because it had slipped in between the papers was the shiny new key in box number seven.

Ferguson lit up a ten-dollar cigar and slowly exhaled out the side window of the truck before passing it to Jessica for the victory smoke. She grabbed the Dominican and took a long drag.

"Where the hell is the truck? That's what I want to know," Jessica said.

"Same question I have," Ferguson said, "but right now I'll take any success I can get." Ferguson hummed the theme from Cops and then broke out into his own rendition "Bad boys, bad boys, what ya gonna do."

Jessica laughed as a broad grin erupted on Ferguson's face.

Chapter 13

Three days after executing the search
warrant on Ghaleed, the agents got a break.

"Agent Ferguson, this is Sergeant Joplin
with the Southfield police department. We
found your pick-up truck and wondered if you
want to take a look at it. It's hidden behind
a strip shopping center on Lahser about a half
mile from Michael Ghaleed's house."

"We can be there in thirty minutes,
Sergeant. Just keep everyone away from it,
will ya?" Ferguson said as he stood to go.

"Will do, Ferguson," Joplin said.

Walking out of his office, Ferguson
motioned for Jessica to come. "Got a break on
Ghaleed. Grab the keys we took from Ghaleeds
and meet me outside. I need to radio Dog to
meet us," Ferguson said.

When they arrived at the strip center
they found two police cruisers guarding the
truck. Ferguson flipped open his
identification as he walked to the truck,
fumbling with the keys they had found in
Ghaleed's store. Before trying the key he
turned to his agents.

"Looks like the truck, doesn't it?"
Ferguson asked.

"It's the truck, boss," Hound Dog said.

Jessica nodded after checking the license
plate. "That's the plate number."

Ferguson moved to the door and inserted
the key. It turned easily and the door
opened. Trying the key in the ignition, he
started the truck; a low rumbling that could
shake teeth loose reverberated from under the
hood.

"Pop the hood, boss," Hound Dog said.

The hood sprung loose and Hound Dog raised it to reveal a huge engine. Engine, wires and accessories took every inch of space under the hood. It was obvious this engine was not original equipment.

"Holy shit," Jessica said, shaking her head.

The three agents went through every inch of the truck, finding the registration, insurance papers, and even invoices from a North Carolina wholesaler for cigarettes made out to a name they all knew was fictitious.

"Whaddya got to say now, Sean?" Jessica asked as she gave him an impromptu hug.

"I guess I'd say we should have another cigar for a victory moment," Ferguson said. "But since we don't have one- Does anyone want a Swisher Sweet?" Ferguson plugged one into his mouth and lit a match.

They sat in the Camaro, doors open, waiting for a wrecker to take Ghaleed's 1987 Ford truck to the impound. Ferguson lit another Swisher and shoved the box toward Jessica. She pulled one from the pack, slid it under her nose as she sniffed the aroma, and licked it the entire length.

"Light me," Jessica said as she leaned over to Ferguson's side of the car.

Jessica laid her head against the back on the seat looking out at the truck as she exhaled a cloud of smoke.

"We got him, Sean," Jessica said. She looked so content as she rolled her head to look at Ferguson. Taking another drag from the cigar she took the smoke deep into her lungs.

"What's the matter, Sean?" Jessica asked as she sat up, the cigar protruding from her mouth.

He flicked an ash onto the ground and rolled the edge of the little cigar on the ashtray over the console of the car.

"Nothin' I guess. Well, maybe there is something but I can't put my finger on it," Ferguson said.

After reviewing the records from Ghaleed's store, an indictment was issued against Michael Ghaleed for smuggling cigarettes. Rarely did any case move this quickly but this was special. The agents wanted desperately to tie him to Kate's murder with a conspiracy charge but the evidence just wasn't there.

Mixed among the legitimate invoices from southeast Michigan cigarette wholesalers were bills from a North Carolina distributor, Associated Tobacco- the same Greensboro wholesaler found in the truck. While reviewing the records of the company, agents found a new brass padlock key in box seven amongst the records. Jessica checked the packing box and found that the contents had been taken from the office desk upstairs. Picking up the key from box number seven, Ferguson turned it over and over in his hand as if it would talk to him. Checking supplier records, no tax had been paid on 500 cartons listed on one North Carolina invoice. Guaranteed conviction.

"Something's wrong," Ferguson said as Jessica walked in. "Too pat, Jess. We're being set up."

"Nobody would be dumb enough to leave invoices, would they?" Jessica asked.

"I don't get it, Sean," Jessica said, "Ghaleed wouldn't cooperate. He hid the truck and..."

"We don't know he hid the truck," Ferguson broke in. "It wasn't on his property and he said he had no knowledge of it. It could be a set-up. You're the one who reminded me of the need to stay objective. Remember?"

"Yeah, right, Sean. He just happened to have the keys to that very truck in his desk at the store. And the truck just happened to be registered to the guy."

"Things are not always what they seem, Jess," Ferguson snapped.

She stared at her boss.

"Okay, okay, Sean, calm down. I'm on your side, remember?" Jessica said. "I'll make some calls and we'll see about Ghaleed, okay?"

Ferguson sighed. He knew all evidence pointed to Ghaleed and he wanted the people responsible more than anything he could remember but he wasn't sure, his gut wasn't sure.

"Sorry, Jess, I guess this is wearing on me."

"Me too, Sean," Jessica muttered.

"Now, back to Ghaleed," Ferguson said. "Let's check out the distributor in Greensboro, North Carolina. Get two tickets on Northwest for tomorrow and we'll go down there. As long as we're down there, I'd like to see Billy Johnston, if that's okay with you? I'll call Wellston and get the authorization. Shouldn't be any problem."

"Okay. You got it."

Ferguson dialed the phone to his administrator. In a minute he was talking to Steve Wellston.

"Morning, Steve?" Ferguson said.

"Sean! Anything new on Kate's case?"

It was always the first question everyone asked.

"Might have something in North Carolina on this Ghaleed character. I wanted to fly down and talk to some people in Greensboro. I asked Jessica to make flight reservations and wanted to get your approval."

There was a pause.

"Do we really need to go any further with it, Sean? When I reviewed the evidence, it struck me that the case was open and shut. This guy is toast."

"Steve, I agree that this case is solid but I wanted to check the cigarette distributor to see if they recognize Ghaleed or any of his relatives who work the store."

"I'm sorry, Sean, I can't authorize the flight or the time. We're so far behind now and the case is so strong, I don't see any reason. I think we've got our man."

Now it was time for Ferguson to pause.

"Why not?" he blurted. "This may not be our man. I just want to cover all the bases."

"First, Sean, I don't have to give you an answer but I know the stress you've been under. I've already given you my reasons. We've got too much to do and no time to do it. So, let's just drop it."

"But we need to..."

"I said no, Sean. Isn't that clear enough for you?"

"Yes sir, that's very clear," Ferguson said.

"Now, Sean, just cool off. This case is finished. You've done a good job. Now let's drop it, okay?"

"Yes sir." Even as he hung up the receiver Ferguson was making arrangements to go to Greensboro. It troubled him that

Wellston had been so adamant. It was worth the ticket price to seal the case against Ghaleed.

"What was that all about?" Jessica asked. "You breathin' fire again?"

"Just a little disagreement with our boss, that's all."

Jessica knew better than to pursue it with Ferguson.

"Okay, no problem. What do you need me to do, Sean?"

"I still need a ticket, but just one. I'm going down to see Billy Johnston. It's about time I took a little vacation, don't you think? He's wanted me to come down. Course, if I just happened to have a few pictures in my bag and if I just happened to have some free time..."

"When do you want to go, Sean?" Jessica interrupted.

"As soon as possible. And I need you to keep your eyes and ears open around here and let me know what's happening. Can you do that for me, Jess?"

"Sure, Sean."

As Jessica moved to the door of the office, Ferguson was already making mental notes of things he needed for his trip. Within an hour the flight was booked on Northwest Airlines for the following day. He picked up the briefcase his wife had given him as a gift when he started with the department. The initials stamped and dyed into the case twenty-five years ago were now faded almost to a memory in both Ferguson's mind and on the luggage. He could not bring himself to call his wife right then. He was too drained for another argument.

After making his travel arrangements
Ferguson drove to the state police training
facility to meet Jessica and talk to the
commander of the Lansing post. He parked in
the lot; gazing at the security- ten foot high
fences lined with gleaming razor wire, guard
shack and security cameras everywhere.

After concluding their business Ferguson
and Jessica walked to their cars.

"Little chilly today, Jess. Edith like
that new starter?" Ferguson asked, referring
to her Corvette.

"I don't know if she does but I sure do,"
Jessica said as she pulled the key from the
back pocket of her jeans.

"How far away will that thing work?"
Ferguson asked.

"Not sure but I did it from my bathroom
the other day," Jessica said.

When they were no more than twenty-five
or thirty feet away Jessica pointed the remote
at the Corvette and pushed it. They heard the
engine crank.

The initial blast took both T-tops a
hundred feet in the air and then back to earth
but they didn't see that. Ferguson remembered
the searing heat that he thought would ignite
his clothing and skin in flame. The force of
the blast threw them like kites in a
hurricane. While in the air Ferguson knew he
would land and that it would hurt but he could
do nothing. Where was Jessica? Oh my God!

When Ferguson woke he lay on the parking
lot as two state troopers hovered over him.
Raising his head, all he saw was thick black
smoke where Edith had been. Terror griped him
as he frantically tried to scoot away- hands
and feet clawing at the cement.

"Whoa, take it easy, Ferguson. It's all right, settle down," one trooper said. There was nothing left to see but twisted, charred metal and melted rubber from the tires.

Ferguson sat up with the help of the troopers. "I-I'm fine, I think. Just scrambled up a bit," Ferguson said in a hoarse voice as he shook the cobwebs from his head. "Where's Jessica? Where is she?" Ferguson tried to clamber up as his head darted from side to side looking for his agent.

He ran to where she was being helped by other troopers. Blood trickled from her nose and she looked dazed.

"Jess! You alright?"

"No, Sean. I'm not alright," she whispered in a raspy voice. "Those assholes killed Edith. I will see their balls on a skewer." A tear escaped from the corner of her eye.

Ferguson knelt down and hugged her. "At least you can still skewer their balls, Jess. If you hadn't used that remote when you did we'd both be dog food right now."

Looking at the car, a chill ran up Ferguson's back causing him to flinch. The bomb must have been in Edith when Jessica drove in. Who and why was all Ferguson wanted to know. He thought of Hamood and a burning hatred bubbled to the surface. But even Hamood wouldn't be stupid enough to do this. Or was he?

Chapter 14

The morning after the bomb blast, after a few Valium, Dramamine and Tylenol, Sean Ferguson slid onto a plane to Greensboro. He moved like an old man, shuffling along, but was determined to continue his investigation. When he deplaned, a full set of grinning teeth met him.

"Well, well, I don't believe it. I heard it but I sure didn't think you'd really do it," Billy Johnston said as he shook his head. "You always hated flying when we did 'Nam."

"The power of Valium and Dramamine," Ferguson said calmly. The two men embraced, Ferguson wincing.

"I always found that beer does the same thing," the grinning Johnston said. "Course it's a lot more expensive than those little pills." He thought for a few seconds. "But those pills ain't near as much fun."

"Okay, okay, Billy, I get the drift," Ferguson said, waving him off.

"So, why you look so sore there partner? You look like you're on the losing end of battle with a freight train."

"A freight train would have been easier. Someone almost made me fertilizer with a bomb yesterday," Ferguson said, trying to loosen up a bit.

"No shit. You okay?" Johnston asked.

"Just a touch sore. I'll be fine in a year or so," Ferguson said.

"We'll just have to get some anesthetic for those tired old bones o' yours. You want eighty or a hundred proof," Johnston asked as they pulled out of the airport parking lot.

After an obligatory look at the homestead, Ferguson and Johnston sat, reminisced, and exchanged barbs. A fifth of Jim Beam and a six-pack of Coke sat near Ferguson while Johnston pulled one of his eighteen Budweisers from the refrigerator. Twenty years ago, Ferguson and Johnston had done this on dozens of occasions but Ferguson was now out of shape for the activity. He lit a Swisher and extended his hand with the box to Johnston. Johnston waved him off. Had Billy's wife, Margaret, been home for the last seven hours, the evening undoubtedly would have turned out differently. She had gone to Mobile to visit family and would be back in a few days.

"Hey, Sean. Remember that song we used to sing in 'Nam when we wanted a big laugh. I thought about that song the other day," Johnston said.

"Oh, yeah." Ferguson cleared his throat. "Barry Sadler's Green Berets. Biggest propaganda song they ever recorded. I remember listening to that song in '66 just itchin' to get my chance to join up. Boy, was that stupid or what?" Ferguson said, slurring his words. He was ready to pack it in. "If you're not busy tomorrow, maybe you'd like to be my chauffeur. Specially after what you did to me tonight." Ferguson blew out a huge plume of smoke.

"Nothin' I'd rather do, string bean," a mellow Johnston said.

The next morning Ferguson awoke to the eerie buzzing of an insect outside the house. The loud shrill noise was heard over the drone of the central air conditioning unit. He rolled over and tried to focus on the small clock radio. The red digital numbers appeared

a blur until he squinted three or four times
in between shakes of the head. Ten-o'clock.
That couldn't be right! He hadn't slept that
late in twenty years. He also hadn't drunk
like that in twenty years. He jumped up and
nearly toppled over from the pounding in his
head. Holding onto the wall like a lifeline
every inch of the way, Ferguson walked
tentatively to the bathroom.

"Hey, Sleepin' Beauty," Billy chortled,
"thought ya died in there. You always been a
early riser."

"You did this to me, you stupid
hillbilly," Ferguson countered.

"Well, come on in the kitchen and get you
some coffee and grits. We got to get you in
shape for another go round tonight. The
problem with you is you drink that liquor.
You stick to beer like me and you never wake
up late and in pain. Got it?"

"Bullshit." It was all Ferguson could
spit out. He picked up a Swisher Sweet but
immediately thought better of it and threw
them back onto the counter.

A few coffees and three pieces of toast
later, Ferguson was beginning to think he
might survive after all.

"So, Sean, want to go to the zoo while
you're here? We got us a dandy zoo and it's
only an hour away in Ashboro. Me an' Margaret
go down there all the time."

Ferguson could see his friend was serious
for a change. "I've got some work to do first
and then I'm yours."

"Who you on the trail of anyway?"
Johnston asked.

Ferguson rubbed his face as if to clear
the cobwebs. "You know how tough it is for me
losing Katie."

"Yeah," Johnston said somberly.

"Well, the suspect bought cigarettes down here at a supplier by the name of Associated Tobacco. I just had to poke around because the case at home is a pat hand, a royal flush. The evidence couldn't have been more condemning if it were planted. I'm just not buying it. Everyone else, including my boss, is ready to put the guy away, but I'm not bitin' yet."

Johnston shook his head. "Associated is old family around here. Been around for years and years, they say. There's some bad blood now, because my company moved in three years ago and seems to be doing everything right. We're growing and Associated is goin' down the chute. Go figure."

"I just want to flash some pictures around and see if our suspect or any of his people made buys down here," Ferguson said. He was gaining steam for the afternoon shift.

"Well let's get goin' then," Johnston said.

Associated Tobacco was definitely old time. The loading docks located at the back of the building appeared to have been made for horse and wagon, not for the big rigs used today. The loading docks were stacked with a few bales of cardboard compacted by machine, acknowledging the company's entry into the late twentieth century.

The front of the building housed the administrative offices of Associated. Stepping through the door was like stepping into the past. The oiled oak counter and wooden desks and chairs had a thirties look to them.

A woman in the later stages of middle age peered at them over her reading glasses. The

116

bows of the spectacles were attached to a
fancy chain that draped around her neck.
There was no emotion on the face. She was all
business. The small nameplate, which sat in
front of her, announced the name as Gertrude
Masters.

"May I help you gentlemen?" she queried.

"Yes, ma'am," Ferguson said. Johnston
stood in the background glancing around with
his head bowed. "My name is Sean Ferguson and
I'm an agent for the Michigan Treasury
Department. We're currently working on a case
in Michigan and found a few invoices from
Associated Tobacco. I just wanted to see if
any of your people might recognize these men."

"Don't know if I can help you or not,"
she said. It was obvious Ferguson's
credentials did not impress her. "I know
everyone who buys from us. We're like family
around here. Let me see what you got." Her
eyebrows rose when she looked at the invoice.

"Something wrong, ma'am?" Ferguson said.

"The invoice. Whoever fills an order,
initials the order form down here. Harley
James was an employee here. Bad as they come.
He worked for us for four months. Never
trusted the ape as far as I could throw him.
Trouble, just plain trouble. We let him go
'bout a month ago."

Now it was Ferguson's eyebrow that rose.

Master's eyes moved to the photographs.
"Never saw any of these characters. They've
never bought from us, at least not in the
forty-two years I been here."

"Are you absolutely positive, Ms.
Masters?"

"Young man, I haven't taken a day off in
the last three years and I know these mugs

have never been in here. Do I make myself clear?"

"Yes, ma'am. I don't doubt a word you say. Thank you for your time, ma'am. Have a great day." Ferguson was back-pedaling and Johnston could only stand by the door and grin. He scratched his beard to cover his mouth so that he would not draw the wrath of the diminutive woman himself.

As the two men left the building Johnston snorted, "I think that went well, don't you, Mr. Treasury man?"

The battered metallic gray Lincoln swung onto the street where S&S Wholesale's new warehouse was located outside Greensboro. The loading dock, with bays for four trucks, stood on the west side. Semi-trailers with no markings occupied two. Markings of manufacturers would only tip thieves of the $1,000,000 payday that lay inside a forty-foot semi-trailer loaded with cigarettes; a risk the manufacturers did not wish to take.

To the casual observer, this business was the classic success story, an instantly profitable newcomer. In this case, the owner, never seen by the employees, seemed to make all the right moves.

Moussa stopped the Lincoln at the rear of the building away from the activity of the business and reached for the electronic door opener locked in the glove box. When he was satisfied no one was watching, he pushed a button on the opener and heard the quiet whirl of a motor as the overhead door rose. Open sesame, he thought, as he drove in. The property backed up to woods and afforded privacy. Surveillance cameras hidden at

Farhill Farm

various locations in the woods guaranteed no
one could approach undetected. Even if a
burglar should disable the cameras, there were
still motion detectors to circumvent.

When inside he stepped from the vehicle
and threw the switch for the overhead lights.
As his eyes became accustomed to the dim
lighting, the man looked around the twenty-
foot by eighty-foot area.

Against one wall was a desk, much like
the farm, with a row of video monitors. The
three monitors blinked to different cameras
located on the property. Moussa recognized
the image on the screen as the door he had
just entered. As quickly as it flicked to
another camera, an image of the inside of the
warehouse appeared.

This room had two doors, one overhead to
access the building and one sixty-inch double
door leading to the main section of the
warehouse. This door, however, was never seen
from the other side. Two palates of
cigarettes obscured the view on the other side
of the door at all times. Only two employees
knew of the door, Gene Sawyer and Vincent
Scarponi.

Four palates of stacked, shrink-wrapped
cigarettes were in the room. He scanned the
names on them until he found the one he was
looking for, the one marked Babcock. Moussa
would be happy when Bat recruited a new man so
he could stop making the cigarette runs. He
felt it beneath him to smuggle the contraband.

Apprenticing on the streets of Chicago,
Moussa had learned his craft well. As a gang
member, his first run in with the police was
at age ten for stealing cars. He didn't
witness a murder until near his thirteenth
birthday and it had a profound effect on his

life. Even though he had not been the
triggerman, he was totally immersed in the
feeling of power the gun seemed to grant. It
was intoxicating to him and he immediately
started to carry a small 22-caliber handgun
with him everywhere.

He pulled a miniature cellular phone from
the breast pocket of his shirt. With fingers
that looked like the appendages on a daddy
long legs spider, the phone fit comfortably in
the palm of his slender hand. He punched in
the area code and number as the roam button
blinked on and off at him.

"It's me," he said when the other end of
the line answered after four rings.
"Everything looks good here. We've got three
runs plus mine ready to go. I'll talk to
Scarponi when I go up front."

"Everything may be fine there, Mr. Moussa
but here they are not. Ferguson is down in
North Carolina and I want to know what he
knows. I also want to know how the hell he
knew to go down there. Have Scarponi make
your run. You find Ferguson and find out what
he is doing down there," Bat said. "And make
sure everything and everybody are up to snuff.
You know how I despise mistakes."

Moussa's skin crawled as the connection
was broken but he shook it off. After
scanning the security monitors, Moussa stepped
into the bright sunlight and looked around,
checking for unwanted eyes. His eyes watered
as he squinted in the light. After closing
the overhead door, he strolled to the corner
of the building, quickly walked toward the
front, and up the steps leading to the loading
dock.

He noticed three men sitting on the
corner of the dock smoking. They made no

attempt to jump up or even to appear busy. They looked at Moussa, surprise on their faces, as he sauntered through the overhead doors into the warehouse.

"Have you seen Scarponi?" he asked of no one in particular.

"Thought I saw him ten minutes ago headin' for the office," one of the men said with obvious effort. It was hard to hear the man over the roar of the huge industrial fans that blew volumes of air around the warehouse.

Moussa continued into the warehouse and looked at the cases and cases of cigarettes, tobacco, and cigars stacked in neat piles on palates. Eight men and women scurried about to prepare store orders for shipment. More cigarettes would be going out tonight but these people would not be filling those orders.

Moussa sensed he was being watched as he stepped through the door into the administrative section of the building. A small camera had followed him as he crossed the warehouse floor, his movement recorded for posterity on tape. Eight other state of the art miniature cameras prowled the warehouse like junkyard dogs, daring anyone to invade their turf.

Entering the offices, Moussa looked around the modern office with two fax machines and a state of the art phone system. Scarponi, the manager of the warehouse, stood at the far end of the room mulling over what appeared to be spread sheets.

"Hey, Scarponi, how's it hangin'?" Moussa asked. Moussa was not normally congenial, especially when business was to be discussed.

"Moussa! What's up?" Scarponi asked. "I didn't expect ya 'til tomorrow." Two of the office girls looked up from their work, but just briefly. Moussa's looks didn't impress many people.

"We need to talk, now," Moussa said.

Scarponi walked to his spacious secure office. The walls insured no listening by unwanted ears and electronics in the room took care of any bugs.

Moussa locked the door after they entered and went to a walnut paneled wall. Reaching up, he pushed the moulding at the top of the wall. Two four foot sections of the wall silently slid back and to the side to reveal a small hidden room. One wall inside the room held six locking file cabinets. Moussa knew the contents; legal papers, including articles of incorporation for the forty odd companies Bat had started to hide his identity. On the floor were two brand new tax-stamping machines, used by various states to identify cigarettes already taxed. The small half-inch detailed stamps usually were brightly colored so they could instantly be recognized.

"We got new stamping machines?" Moussa asked.

"Bat just made a call," Scarponi said. "Next thing I know, here they are. Ain't supply and demand great?"

Moussa, who was never very impressed by anything, was obviously taken by how fast Scarponi had gotten the machines. Of course, he had his doubts that Scarponi knew what supply and demand was, but that didn't matter.

"We're just waitin' for the stamps now, but our supplier has assured us we will be able to obtain the stamps a week after they are approved by Michigan. Pretty slick, huh?"

"Not bad," Moussa said, shaking his head. Bat never failed to amaze him. He was always one step ahead of everyone.

"You makin' a run today, Moussa?" Scarponi asked.

"Nope. You are. Just talked to Bat. He wants me on something else. Looks like others are coming in today too," Moussa said.

"Shit. Why me?" Scarponi shook his head. "Never mind, I'll be outta here in a few hours. Just gotta put some clothes together," Scarponi said.

Scarponi picked up a phone and dialed a number.

"So tell me, Moussa, what happened to Lancona. All we know is..." Scarponi held up a finger.

"Yeah, we need a load in two hours." As he hung up the phone he returned to Moussa.

"All we know is Lancona ain't coming no more."

"Just leave it that he fucked up, and his contract was cancelled. That's all you want to know. Believe me," Moussa said.

The two men walked into the warehouse and wilted when they hit the heat. As they headed toward the loading dock, Scarponi saw one of his men near the door.

"Johnston," Scarponi said, "have you pulled the order for Safeway yet? They called a few minutes ago."

"You betcha, boss, pulled and loaded," Johnston replied. Johnston eyed the stranger, the same man he had seen come from the rear of the building. The tall thin man returned the gaze.

"What you lookin' at, boy?" Moussa said.

"Nothin', man, you just looked familiar to me, that's all. Sorry."

Johnston looked down at the floor and turned to leave.

Moussa, who had never liked anyone looking at him, once had decked a guy just for straying eyes. He was in a good mood today, lucky for Johnston. Scarponi distracted Moussa just in time.

"Hey, come on Moussa, relax. Let's go get some coffee," Scarponi interjected. He patted Moussa on the back. Moussa whipped around and glared at him.

"Don't ever touch me! You got that?" Moussa said through clenched teeth.

"No problem, man, no problem," Scarponi said as he held up his hands to ward off Moussa.

The two men returned to the offices in the stares of the four employees who had heard the exchange. Johnston just shook his head as the men disappeared through the door.

"I can't believe that guy. Something fishy goin' on there, I swear," Johnston muttered. He decided he would make a point to keep tabs on the man called Moussa.

An hour later Moussa came out of the office and walked to the loading dock, his eyes constantly shifting to the left and right. He quickly bounded down the stairs and hurried to the rear of the building, checking behind him for unwanted attention.

The door to the storage area was already opening when Moussa turned the corner. He ducked in as the door was returning to the closed position and savored the air-conditioned coolness inside. Quickly moving to the bank of monitors on a desk, he looked at them. Everything was normal until he saw a man coming down the stairs from the loading dock and slink down the side of the warehouse to the corner.   Moussa pushed a few buttons on a console and one of the cameras zoomed in on the lone man.

"Johnston," Moussa whispered.   "Shit."

What had he seen?   Anything?   He couldn't have, reasoned Moussa.

Moussa watched as Johnston turned the corner and looked back in confusion.   It was clear from his demeanor that he had expected to see something.   Moussa picked up an intercom phone that was linked to the hidden room in Scarponi's office.

"Moussa?" Scarponi asked when he picked up the phone.

"Yeah, listen, you know that asshole that was eyeballing me in the warehouse?   I just saw him on the monitor following me out.   You need to watch him.   Understand?"

"Did he see anything?   He didn't see anything, did he? Aw dammit," Scarponi asked. He fiddled with the machine on the security system to retrieve the tape of Johnston. "Shit," he spat when the machine wouldn't cooperate.

"Just keep an eye on him, dammit," Moussa said.

Chapter 15

Bat picked up the phone and dialed the number. "What did he do in North Carolina, Moussa?"

"He visited Associated but we got it covered. There's nothing to find there. That old bag couldn't spot one of our guys if her life depended on it. We're back on the ground at Metro. Ferguson's on his way home," Moussa said.

"I'm not sure he's going to lay down even after our little show of force. Ferguson has no fear of dying. What he does have is loyalty to his friends and that will drive him farther than anything else. I believe we should slow the runs down for a few weeks, Moussa, and make sure we're out of sight. Is that clear?" Bat said.

"How long do we follow him?" Moussa asked.

"Until we know what he's going to do. This man is not stupid, Moussa. Never, never underestimate Ferguson. He will burn us. Now, call whoever you need but I want to know where he goes and who he talks to," Bat said. "And make sure no one does anything to Ferguson. Just follow him and, for God sake, don't let him know. Since Hamood is so into that spy stuff and gave Ferguson a sniff of our operation, see if he can help," Bat said.

Bat could not let Moussa know but he was nervous about Ferguson. He tugged at the collar of his shirt and noticed the dampness in it. How could someone like Ferguson hope to compete with him? Bat took a deep breath and exhaled slowly to calm himself. The wholesale operation in North Carolina was

Bat's trump card. He couldn't let it fall under any circumstances and that buffoon Moussa led Ferguson to North Carolina with those invoices. He never should have trusted Moussa to fabricate evidence against Ghaleed.

"Make sure you have muscle people available to do what's necessary should we need them, Mr. Moussa. And watch Ferguson like a hawk," Bat said.

"Don't worry, boss, I'll take care of it," Moussa said.

Bat hadn't worried before but with an agent as good as Ferguson on your trail anything could happen. He would not lose what he had built. In his mind everyone was expendable. He just had to know what Ferguson would do and how far he would take this investigation. He knew people like Ferguson and in his experience the only way to stop them was to kill them. Perhaps that would be Ferguson's destiny but for now he had to be patient. The heat was on and to throw more fuel on the fire would not be very bright, especially if that fuel was a dead agent named Ferguson.

Ferguson was working at his desk in Lansing trying to put the pieces of the puzzle together when the phone rang.

"Hello."

"Whaddya say, partner? I got a message from Gerty for ya."

"Who?" Ferguson asked when he realized it was Johnston.

"Gerty. Don't tell me you've forgot her already. You heartbreaker. And you made such a great impression on her."

"Oh, yeah, her," Ferguson said. "And why this call. I just left you a week ago. Miss me, already?"

"Naw, I had to call 'cause I was at work the other day and this dude comes in like he owned the joint. I don't know who he was. His car had Michigan plates and he met with the manager for about two hours. He's definitely one of you yankees." Johnston waited for Ferguson to retaliate, but it never came. He continued. "I heard him talkin' in the warehouse. As a matter of fact, he threatened to take my head off just for lookin' at him. I seen his car before, an old Lincoln Towncar, sort of a silvery gray color. I thought you might want to check him out."

Ferguson made a mental note to call George Dempsey.

"Give me the tag and I'll see who it belongs to."

"Let's see here, it's GGGJ42," Johnston read.

"What does this guy look like?"

"He's about six foot, real skinny, blond hair and his face looks like someone tapped danced on it with golf spikes, you know, not an ad for that skin stuff that stops zits."

"Nice description. I'll check him out, buddy," Ferguson said.

"I'll see what else I can find out when I go in tomorrow," Johnston continued. He was eager to please and liked the cops and robbers stuff.

"You'd better watch your step there, partner, or you may be looking for another job," Ferguson said chuckling. "Some bosses don't appreciate their employees investigating them."

"I always tell them, I was lookin' for a job when I come through the door," Johnston said.

"Okay, Billy, but don't blame me if you get canned. I'll check out the car and let you know if I find anything."

"You do that and I'll keep a low profile while I'm playin' secret agent man," Johnston whispered.

Ferguson did the one finger punch on the terminal connected to the mainframe computer at the Secretary of State license plate section a second and third time but the result was the same each time, no record. The plate number Billy had given him did not exist. He then called directly and had them manually check the number. Still the same results, no record. Johnston would not have made a mistake on the number. Ferguson asked them to check again while he waited.

Billy Johnston answered the phone on the third ring.

Speaking in an atrocious British imitation, the man said, "This is Bond, James Bond."

"Well, this is Ferguson, Sean Ferguson." There was a pause.

"How did you know it was me, B.J.?"

"We secret agents got all kinds of spyin' gizmos," Johnston said. "The hi-tech ultra expensive gizmo I used this time was caller ID. Pretty slick, huh."

"Yeah, real hi-tech, hot shot," Ferguson said.

"Well, Gerty would be impressed I bet," Johnston said.

"Okay, okay, I give up. Billy, I ran the plate you gave me and there's no record. You sure the number was right?"

"Hell yeah, I'm sure...I think."

To Ferguson, he didn't sound that sure.

"Okay, okay, Billy. If you see the car again, check the plate. Capeesh?"

"Yeah, yeah. So anyway, Sean, how you doing? Things settlin' down for ya?"

Whenever Johnston asked how he was doing Ferguson knew he wanted to talk. The two had been close since they were cast together in a war that only the politicians wanted. Talks about their innermost values and concerns had taken up many boring days. They had shared the horrors of war, the inhumanity of it all. The two were closer than most brothers were because their survival had depended on each knowing the other.

"I don't know, Billy. I can't get Kate out of my head." Ferguson's heart started to race when he remembered the day she was shot. "There isn't an hour that goes by that I don't see something at the office or at home that reminds me of her. I can't sleep. Her death and the hunt obsess me. If my work doesn't contribute to the hunt, I can't focus."

"Sean, Joanne is worried," Billy said quietly. "She called me the other night. She doesn't know what to do to help you. She said you're shuttin' her out. Man, ya gotta work through this."

The phone was silent except for an occasional breath. Ferguson knew Billy was right. He knew Joanne wanted to help. He knew he had to let her in. But he couldn't.

"I'll try." That is all he could squeeze out. More silence on the line.

"I know ya will, partner," Johnston murmured. "You also know I'd go to the line for ya. Don't you dare cut me outta this if ya need help. You got that, Ferguson?"

"Yeah, I got that, Johnston," Ferguson whispered. He sat in silence before putting the receiver back on its cradle.

Ferguson strolled to his car after walking for an hour. Driving to Jessica's apartment on the off chance she was home, he parked in a space marked Guest and got out of the car. Because of the shadows reflected off the living room window from the television, he knew she was home.

He knocked. Jessica opened the door, a glass of wine firmly clutched in her right hand.

"Don't mind if I do," Ferguson said as he grabbed for the wine.

"Sean." She laughed. "Come on in. I'll get you a fresh one."

"You sure I'm not interrupting anything, Jess?"

"No, no, I'm just watchin' some sappy chick flick. That's what I do when I'm alone and don't have to prove I'm as tough as the guys. Just started fifteen minutes ago."

The two sat in silence for a few minutes watching the television and sipping wine. Ferguson felt at ease. He was surprised how feminine Jessica looked, the baggy sweatshirt and boots gone, replaced by a silk nightgown and robe. The house smelled of potpourri and cinnamon.

"What's goin' on, Sean? You never come here and to be honest you look like you're one step away from a homeless shelter."

He reached up to feel his weekend growth of beard and admitted that he probably looked pretty used up.

"Jess, I just needed to be somewhere other than home right now."

"You don't have to explain to me. You know you're welcome anytime, Sean." There was a pause. "Well, almost any time."

"Jess, you think I've been out of whack lately, since Kate's death, I mean?"

"Yeah, some, but knowing you, it's not surprising. You've always felt responsible for everyone on the team, even Hound Dog."

He sipped his wine absently. Staring at the television screen, he did not see the movie. When it ended, Ferguson did not even know what it had been about.

"I need to get home, Jess. See you tomorrow at the office."

Ferguson walked into the crisp night air and drove home, thinking about what to say to his wife. He now had a new problem to work out, one which was more disturbing to him than Kate's death. He was losing his wife and kids to these people and he couldn't do a thing.

Chapter 16

Ferguson started his new Ford Mustang, requisitioned after the loss of his Taurus and Edith a week ago, and started his drive home. His heart hurt as he chewed on Billy's words. He knew he had avoided his family because of his obsessive behavior and he was determined to patch things up.

Dialing his home, the answering machine picked up after five rings. Hearing his wife's voice gave him some comfort. "This is the Ferguson residence. We're at the game. Leave a message and we'll call you back."

The message jogged his memory and he remembered tonight was a home basketball game. He had not seen Emily play this year and guilt flooded in as he drove toward the high school. Arriving just before half time, Ferguson stood in the doorway of the gym looking for his wife and daughters.

He spotted his wife and youngest daughter, Annie, and strolled toward the bleachers. He thought about his youth and remembered the Sly Stone song- We Are Family but for some reason couldn't recall the year. Good thing Hound Dog didn't ask this one. Joanne clapped and yelled encouragement to Emily on the court. Ferguson stepped onto the bleachers as his wife looked at him. A metamorphosis took place and the woman he had just seen smiling and enjoying herself scowled at him. Sitting next to his wife, Ferguson fumbled with how to begin a dialogue with her. His mouth felt as if it were stuffed with cotton.

"Annie," Ferguson said.

Annie turned and a wide smile creased her face. "Dad! You came," she said. "Great." Being a girl of few words with her parents Ferguson was gratified by her comment.

As the first half of the game ended Emily grabbed a towel and looked up at Ferguson. Grinning from ear to ear, she waved vigorously to acknowledge his presence. Two out of three isn't so bad, Ferguson thought.

"Hello, Joanne," Ferguson said tentatively.

"Sean," she said. Her response was ice. So much for we are family.

"Can we talk?" Ferguson whispered.

"Talk about what, Sean?" Joanne whispered, but barely contained. She quickly looked around self-consciously. "Talk about the fact that you are never home? Talk about the fact that every waking moment is spent investigating who caused our niece's death? Talk about the fact that last week you were almost killed by a bomb but you didn't bother to even tell me before you traipse off to North Carolina? That I had to find out from your best friend? Gee, Sean, I don't know what we could possibly talk about."

Ferguson didn't have a response. His mouth hung half open as he tried to collect his thoughts. He looked down at his feet as he sat there with his elbows on his knees.

"I-I'm sorry, Joanne," he whispered. "I just didn't want you to worry, that's all."

"Didn't want me to worry? I think the fact that I could have been sitting here mourning today gives me the right to know when something like that happens, don't you?"

Ferguson felt spent. His hand shook imperceptibly as he rubbed his eyes. He

sighed loudly. "I know I haven't been there
for you. I'll try harder," Ferguson said.

"And that's supposed to fix it, Sean?"
Joanne said. She sat silent for a moment.
"This isn't the time or the place." Those
were the last words directed at Ferguson. She
returned her attention to the game as the
teams started to warm up for the second half.

Ferguson sat in silence for the rest of
the game, trying to put everything in
perspective but the numbness never left him.
How much longer could this go on? Should he
accept things as they appeared? Was his
common sense warped from the events of the
last month?

Back in North Carolina three days after
shadowing Ferguson, Moussa parked the Lincoln
in the small area at the front of S&S. He had
returned on a flight to pick up the Lincoln
left unexpectedly in North Carolina when
Ferguson had been spotted. He now could
resume watching that Johnston character who
had caused his worry.

He knew Johnston was scheduled to work
and had intentionally put the car in a spot
not seen from inside the building. A hidden
camera would, however, watch for anything out
of the ordinary.

The Lincoln now had a North Carolina
license plate mounted over the Michigan plate.
Moussa walked past the elaborate landscaping
with colorful rhododendrons and white pines.
Red pine bark filled the beds that were
bordered by cement edging. The door had a
horsehair mat proclaiming a welcome to all who
crossed the threshold and gold three-inch
letters on the glass door announcing S&S
Wholesale. No mention of cigarettes or
tobacco products was made. The only sign of

security was a small camera lens conspicuously mounted overhead in the soffit and protruding an inch from the overhang.

Moussa walked through the door, past the receptionist, and to Scarponi's office.

"Scarponi, I want you to watch all the cameras until I leave. I think we got a rat and I set a trap."

"Naw, Moussa, I can't believe it. We got a good crew here."

"Just humor me, then. I tell you we got us a problem. I know it."

Moussa made a swing around the warehouse and spotted Billy Johnston near the loading dock. Johnston saw him at the same time but averted his gaze.

For three hours Scarponi watched the monitors as they constantly roamed the building and grounds. He kept a particular eye on the back of the building and the front near the Lincoln. Moussa relaxed nearby in an executive chair while he played solitaire.

"Moussa, come here," Scarponi whispered. Billy Johnston's image flickered on the screen as he slowly walked toward the Lincoln. He looked left and right and turned around completely to verify he had not been seen. When he reached the rear of the Lincoln he glanced down. He couldn't hear the whirl of the zoom lens on the camera hidden less than thirty feet away. He did a double take as he noticed the North Carolina plate on the car. He looked away and scratched his head before returning his gaze to the license plate.

"He must not believe his eyes," Moussa said as he leaned over Scarponi's shoulder. Johnston knelt down and took the three-inch folding knife from its scabbard on his belt. For a moment, he stopped and looked around.

"Yoohoo, Johnston," Moussa said. "Don't forget to look up here." Johnston could not have heard him, of course, and didn't realize he was on candid camera.

Johnston turned one of the screws until the right side of the North Carolina plate fell, revealing the fake Michigan plate that Johnston had reported to Ferguson. He quickly replaced the screw, stood and nervously walked toward the side of the warehouse.

"Oh, oh," Moussa said shaking his head, "he shouldn't a done that."

Moussa punched two buttons on the security console and a new camera jumped to life. These cameras showed the loading dockside of the building; one strategically hidden camera with a wide-angle lens showed the corner and much of both adjoining sides.

Johnston walked into the picture and strolled down the side of the building. He stopped near the loading dock and looked inside the warehouse before continuing down the side of the building. As Johnston rounded the corner, he turned back to review his steps, not once but three times. He continued until he reached the overhead door on the rear wall of the building. It stood as the solitary break in the eighty-foot wall. Johnston stood looking at the door. He looked perplexed. Stepping back from the wall, he quickly moved back to the corner of the building and up the loading dock stairs. A second later he was out of sight of the west side cameras and inside the warehouse. Minutes later Johnston emerged and took unnatural long steps back to the corner, appearing to talk to himself.

"What the hell is he doing?" Scarponi asked.

"Damned if I kn.," Moussa said. "Shit, the lousy bastard knows. He's counting the steps to see how long the building is."

The two men sat stunned as Johnston completed his awkward walk to the corner of the warehouse. They watched as a grin spread across his face.

"Damn it," Scarponi said, "I don't believe that dumb hillbilly bastard figured it out."

"Well, he did," Moussa said quietly. "Too bad for him. We need to keep Johnston in our sights from now on 'til we figure out what to do with him. Call in some help to baby-sit. I want to see the personnel file on him. I just don't believe it."

Chapter 17

Moussa and Scarponi scrambled to call in
help and figure what they needed to do with
Johnston. They could not afford to let him
out of their sight. If anyone found out about
the secret room at the rear of the building
the operation would be toast.

"I want to see the personnel file on him.
What do we know about this guy? I just don't
believe this," Moussa said. "Don't let him
talk to anyone in the back Scarponi."

Scarponi jumped up and scurried out to
the loading dock before Moussa could say
another word. Johnston was coming up the
steps onto the dock when the two ran into each
other.

Moussa watched on the security monitor as
Scarponi talked. Johnston looked startled.
Moussa thought he saw a bead of sweat on
Johnston's upper lip. "You better sweat,
Johnston," Moussa murmured to himself.

Scarponi walked back to the office.

"What'd you say to him?" Moussa asked.

"Asked him to stick around for an hour or
two," Scarponi said. "Said he would."

Moussa wandered around the warehouse,
keeping an eye on Johnston. Moussa then made
his phone call, paging Bat. The 911 after the
number alerted Bat there was a problem.

"Mr. Moussa," Bat said quietly, "I trust
this is very, very important. I'm in a very
sensitive meeting."

"Yes sir, it is," Moussa gulped. Moussa,
who thought his place with Bat secure, now
knew how Babcock must have felt before the
beating. His palms were sweaty and his mouth

dry. "Some one knows about the building down here."

"What? Give me sixty seconds. I'll call you back," Bat said. The call disconnected before Moussa could acknowledge Bat.

Moussa jumped when the phone rang a minute later.

"How'd Ferguson find you?" Bat asked without waiting for a greeting.

"Huh?" Moussa asked. "Oh, it's not Ferguson. One of the employees down here found out about the private room, boss."

"Moussa, how the hell did he do that?" Bat asked. Formality gone, Bat wanted answers.

Moussa had never heard Bat rattled before.

"I don't know but I took the liberty of calling a plumber."

"Do whatever it takes but we cannot lose S&S. Stop the leak, wherever it is? Understood?"

"Yessir."

"Call me when it's done. Leaks can cause a lot of damage if unchecked, and you know how I feel about mistakes."

"Yes, sir, I know." Moussa said but Bat was already gone.

"We've got to make sure that sonofabitch doesn't talk to anyone. Is Sawyer here yet?"

"Yeah, just got here." Scarponi called Sawyer into the office.

"Okay, this is what we got," Moussa said. "We can't let Johnston talk to anyone, and he has to have an accident. Those are the only rules. I can't drive the Lincoln so I need a car. Sawyer and me will tail the guy and look for an opportunity to bag him. Scarponi, you stay here and keep a lid on this. After we've grabbed him, we'll figure out what to do."

Sawyer and Moussa set up on either side of the cigarette wholesaler on English Road about a block away. They were in contact with each other by cell phones that were not secure—but they would have to do.

On cue, Scarponi walked slowly into the warehouse and told Johnston to go home.

Johnston appeared deep in thought and scratched his head. Carrying his brushed metal thermos, he jumped into his red 1995 Chevy pick-up truck and drove away.

Moussa punched in a cell phone number. It barely rang and Sawyer answered.

"Yeah," he said tensely.

"Time to roll," Moussa said calmly.

The outskirts of Greensboro were not busy. Johnston pulled onto English Avenue and rolled past Sawyer's vehicle. Sawyer was bent low across the front seat of his white Dodge Intrepid. After Johnston passed he sat up, his hand already shifting the car into gear. Moussa drove past him at a slow pace.

Johnston drove east and turned north onto Summit. The area was more rural, and the road looked as if it was about to be swallowed by the vines and trees growing over the road. A clearing on the left side of the road came up quickly as he cruised at sixty miles per hour. Johnston pulled his truck into a parking lot at a bar called C.B. Good Buddies.

Johnston opened the massive pine door, looked around, stepped in, and closed the door. Moussa waited a few minutes before following. Having found a hat in the borrowed car, he slid it onto his head, pulling it low to cover his eyes. After removing his shirt to reveal a black t-shirt, Moussa followed

Johnston inside. Four men sat at the bar,
chains attached to belts from wallets
protruding from their rear pockets. Johnston
had stepped up to the 1930's vintage wood bar.

Moussa saw that cigarette burns had
scarred the surface; beer stained paper
coasters advertising Goebels beer laid at
various points along the twenty feet of
polished mahogany. In addition to the money
pouches, the men wore John Deere or
Caterpillar sweat encrusted baseball style
hats. He did not wish to tangle with any of
them. When no one noticed him, Moussa moved
quickly back to the door and slipped outside.

"He's in there sitting alone at the bar.
I don't think he's talking to anyone, but
we've got to grab him as soon as he comes
out," Moussa said.

"What are we gonna do with him?" Sawyer
asked.

"Hell, we'll just have to take him when
he leaves," Moussa said.

"Where do you want me, Moussa?" Sawyer
asked.

"Stay on the north side. When he comes
out, he'll go to his truck. Get behind and
knock him out and we'll put him in my trunk."

Thirty minutes later, the overhead
mercury light started to buzz, signaling
night, as Johnston emerged from the bar. But
instead of turning left to go to his truck, he
turned right. Damn, thought Moussa. Where
the hell is he going now? Moussa was able to
make out the panicked face of Sawyer sitting
in his car as Johnston passed within ten feet
of him.

Johnston continued his quick step across
the parking lot to a pay phone hanging from a
pole near the road. The light on the phone

box flickered; graffiti was etched everywhere. He picked up the receiver and punched in an eleven-digit long distance number.

Moussa moved closer. He heard Johnston speak.

"Hey, Sean, me boy," Johnston said, "how ya doin'?"

"This here's James Bond, again. I got some secret agent info for ya. The building..." Those were the only words Johnston got out.

The phone rang at 5:30 a.m. Ferguson answered quickly. He had been up for an hour already even though he hadn't gone to bed until 1:00 a.m.

"S-Sean." He barely recognized the voice.

"Margaret?" he asked hopefully.

"Bad news." Her voice choked. "They found Billy's truck upside down in a culvert a few hours ago. Billy was still strapped into the driver's seat. He's gone, Sean."

Ferguson gulped hard. "I'll get a flight down, Margaret," he assured her. That was all he could say. He hung up the phone in a fog. He made a phone call to book a flight, not recalling much of the conversation when he finished. He was working on reflex now. None of this was really happening. He would wake shortly and everything would be fine.

Billy Johnston was just conducting another one of his practical jokes. Practical jokes. Now what was that one he pulled a few months ago? Calling up and getting the girls worked up about something. Ferguson was out of touch for the moment. He lay his head down, but rest eluded him.

"What's wrong, Sean," Joanne asked. "Was that Margaret?" The sound of her voice jolted him fully awake.

"Oh my God," Ferguson whispered. "He's dead. Billy's dead. Traffic accident. She said he's gone." Ferguson began to sob. He floated back to a time when his friends were dying all around him. What would he do now without his other half?

Joanne clutched him. They wept, clinging to each other. Ferguson finally stood and wandered out of the bedroom to nowhere in particular. He was unable to play comforter, even for his wife. He stared blankly through the window in the living room that overlooked his land. Joanne lay on their bed, not making a sound. After regaining some control Ferguson went to his wife in the bedroom, but the moment she needed him was past. They embraced but it was empty. He told her of the flight.

"Have to get ready. Do you want to come? Margaret will need some support," Ferguson asked. It was an obligatory request and they both knew it.

"No, I'll stay home and hold down the fort. The girls will need support, too." That jab found its mark so Ferguson slipped to a neutral corner of the house.

He showered and dressed. Joanne made coffee and prepared hot cereal for him. They ate in silence except for the whirl of the blower fan on the furnace and the clink, clink of the icemaker in the refrigerator. Ferguson marveled that the benign house sounds would come as a relief from the deafening silence.

"Better get to the airport. Don't want to miss my flight," he exclaimed.

"Wouldn't want you to do that," she said.

Ferguson hugged his wife tightly and plodded out the door with his suitcase in tow. He arrived at Metropolitan Airport two hours earlier than he needed to.

Waiting for his flight, Ferguson felt tortured. He had not felt so numb since his father had died of cancer when he was only sixteen. Memories haunted Ferguson- memories of Billy Johnston and the love he had for the man. Their wives had been allowed to share them but there was a bond between both men no one could penetrate. He stared into space as he sat at the gate for his flight, no one within earshot.

Ferguson found himself questioning his relationship with God again, just as he had when his father had died. Ferguson had given up on God when his prayers to save a father ravaged by cancer had gone unanswered. The events of the last two months only seemed to confirm what he had felt for the last thirty years. No God would take away the only people in the world Ferguson loved more than life itself. Why was this happening to him?

Chapter 18

Ferguson puffed on a Swisher cigar as he drove to Johnston's home from the Piedmont airport outside of Greensboro. Pulling up in front of the house, he glanced at the covered front porch where he and Billy had shared a few drinks and conversation just days ago. Those precious memories flooded back to him.

Margaret stood in the door as he stepped onto the porch. With hair askew and face red and wet from crying, she looked totally spent.

"Oh, Sean," she whispered.

"I'm so sorry. Margaret, are you okay?" he asked, removing his hat and giving her a hug.

"I'm all right. I just can't believe he's gone."

"Me neither." He led her to the old metal glider at the end of the porch. They sat.

"Have the police told you anything, Maggie?"

"Only that he drowned in that culvert and that they suspected alcohol was a factor."

"I guess we both know Billy liked to drink a bit so that's not surprising," he muttered.

"Sean, the only problem I have is where they found him. The culvert where it happened is on Deer Track. That road is five miles south of Good Buddies where he always goes to have a beer. He would not have turned out of the bar and gone south. He drank in that bar dozens of times since we moved down here."

"Billy called me last night but I thought he was joking like he did about the secret agent stuff. The conversation was cut off, as

he was about to say something. But if he did
have too many, he could have become
disoriented."

"Sean, I'm telling you something's wrong.
I don't know what it is, but I intend to find
out."

"Let me poke around. It's obvious I was
the last one to talk to him," Ferguson
responded, now upset by this news. "Do you
need any other help—you know with the
arrangements or anything?"

"The boys are here. Thanks, Sean."

"As long as I'm here maybe I can help
with the investigation. Who's the officer in
charge?"

"I think his name is Conway," she said.
"He gave me his card and said to call if I had
any questions." She went to the kitchen
counter and picked up a business card. She
handed it to Ferguson with a shaking hand.

"Thanks, Margaret." He gave her a hug.
"Can you tell me how to get there? I'd like
to see where they found Billy."

A few minutes later Ferguson was on his
way. Deer Track was twenty minutes southwest
of the Johnston house. Ferguson turned onto
the road and realized it was isolated.
Ferguson didn't know the exact location of the
"accident" but found it easily by the trampled
grass and bright yellow crime scene tape
remnants scattered around. Ferguson stopped
and got out. He strolled over to the edge of
the road, eyes scanning every inch.

He needed to see where Billy Johnston had
taken his last breath. Looking down, he could
see the tire tracks from the tow truck that
had labored to free the pickup. Ferguson
squatted and picked up some pebbles while he
pondered his friend's fate. He shook them for

Rick J. Barrett

a moment and then casually tossed them into the culvert, watching the ripples extend out from the source.

"Well, Billy, old friend, what happened here?" Ferguson muttered as if speaking to some presence. "We've known each other a long time and, quite frankly, I don't know what I'm gonna do without your ugly butt around." Ferguson stared into the rippling culvert as tears overflowed his eyes. Standing up, he cleared his throat while shuffling back toward the main road. Lifting the MSU hat from his head, he brushed the tears away with the sleeve of his shirt.

Five hundred feet down the road; he looked down at the long lush grass on the side of the road and noticed it had been trampled. A wide tire track suggested a vehicle had spun out as it left, mangling the grass and throwing up loose dirt. Looking closely at the marks on the road, he searched the area and found nothing until the glint from an object that lay in the middle of the road caught his eye. Ferguson bent down and picked up a bottle opener attached to a small chain. He turned the metal over and over in his hand, hoping it would give him insight. When it did not, he put the opener in his pocket and headed back to the car.

He drove in silence back to the Johnston house.

"Sean, why in tarnation are you knocking?" Margaret asked. She sounded stronger than she had earlier. No doubt the boys, in from Chicago and Colorado, had calmed her.

"Margaret, I need to ask you something. I'm sure you're as whacked out as I am, but I found something at the site of the accident

148

that seems important." Ferguson dug deep into his pocket and pulled out the bottle opener and chain.

"W-where did you find that, Sean? It's Billy's. I know because I got it as a promotion at some bar more than ten years ago. Billy always said it was the best gift anyone had ever given him." She clutched it and Ferguson knew she would never let it go. "He said it meant more to him than anything in the world. You know, I believed him. To this very day, I believe him."

"Get some rest, Margaret. I'm checked in at the Shady Grove down the road. I'll see you in the morning." Ferguson hugged her and walked away.

The day following Billy's funeral, Ferguson put his wife and daughters on a plane home.

"Sean, why don't you come home with us? You can always fly back to Greensboro in a few days," Joanne asked.

"I just have to tie up some loose ends and help Margaret."

"But the boys are here. They can help her," she said tartly.

"I just want to talk to the police and look at a few things. I'll be home soon, I promise." Ferguson said.

Joanne shook her head. "You know, Sean, some day you're goin' to realize what you lost by ignoring the girls and me all these years. Are you so far gone you don't even see that we hurt too?" She turned and walked to the boarding gate.

Too stunned to say anything Ferguson put out a hand in a feeble attempt to explain only to let it collapse to his side as Joanne walked briskly away. His daughters gave

Ferguson a peck on the cheek and trotted off
after their mother to the plane.

He ached to talk to his wife but repeated
phone calls to their home went unanswered.
They should have been home from the airport
hours ago, he thought. He grabbed his cell
phone and took his time driving into
Greensboro to the county jail. As he walked
to the building he read a sign posted on the
door that said, "No firearms allowed past this
point. Check them at the desk." He buzzed
and a deputy opened the door.

"Looking for Sergeant Conway," Ferguson
said as the deputy eyed him.

"Go through the door at the end of this
hall and turn right. That's the detective's
room," he said pointing down another hall in
the maze.

Ferguson had seen many county jails while
working with various sheriffs, state police
and local departments. This one was no
different than most except that it desperately
needed a coat of paint. The walls of the
detective's room proved no different. The
yellow residue of tape long ago removed and
holes left from hundreds of punctures from
pins were all that remained of memos, wanted
posters, and reports. Ferguson's gaze
gravitated to the only occupied desk.

"Sergeant Conway?" Ferguson said as he
extended his hand. "I'm Sean Ferguson. We
spoke on the phone yesterday."

"Oh yeah, how are you doing Ferguson?"
Conway said. He half rose from his chair and
slumped back while shaking Ferguson's hand.

Gerald Conway was a mountain of a man,
but the mountain seemed to have settled around
his copious middle. The buttons on his shirt

strained to contain the ever expanding flesh.
His balding red head hinted at hypertension.

"So how can I be of help?" Conway
mumbled. "This inquiry have anything to do
with the Michigan Treasury?" His attention
returned to a file on his desk.

"No, no, nothing like that. Johnston was
a friend of mine, that's all. I just wanted
to touch base with you. I know you've
probably been busy with the investigation of
Johnston's death. Is there any new
information about the murder?"

"Who said anything about a murder?"
Conway asked.

Ferguson sat upright. "It had to be
murder."

"The results of our investigation aren't
complete but we're inclined to say the truck
crash was accidental. After all, the man was
dead drunk. We found the empty whiskey bottle
in the truck. Course the water took care of
some of the evidence."

Ferguson's heart beat faster. "So you've
decided that this was an accident. Would it
help you to know that it could not have been
an accident?"

"Oh yeah, and why is that?" Conway asked.

"Because the man never drinks hard
liquor, that's why not. He was talking to me
last night when he was abducted. I was
listening to him when the line went dead,"
Ferguson said.

"Well, maybe he decided to take liquor up
and maybe he forgot to put enough money in the
payphone. The coroner thinks it was
accidental."

"Who the hell is your coroner, Dr.
Seuss?" The veins in Ferguson's neck bulged.

"Now look here boy. You better watch your step. We don't need no Yankee smart ass coming down here to tell us how to run an investigation," roared Conway. The balding man began to sweat.

"I'm not your boy," Ferguson said.

Oh shit, Ferguson thought. It had taken him only thirty seconds to awaken the sleeping bear. Ferguson gritted his teeth. "My point is that I've known this man for twenty-five years. It seems unlikely to me that he would take up drinking liquor now. He hated the stuff. Another thing, I was at the crash site and found this lying on the road about five hundred feet before the accident site." Ferguson tossed the bottle opener on the desk.

"So, what's this?" Conway asked as his interest rose for a moment. "Looks like a church key."

"I spoke to Johnston's wife and she said it was his. She gave it to him as a joke years ago."

"Guess she shoulda given him something else, huh, so he wouldn't become a drunk. What's your point Ferguson?" Conway was now on the defensive and Ferguson knew he had to be calm. He took three deep breaths and sighed deeply.

"My point, Sergeant Conway, is, why was his opener lying in the middle of the road 500 feet from the crash site?" Ferguson said.

"Don't know, but I'll go back and take a look," he said matter of factly.

"Can you tell me what the autopsy said? Can I see the report?"

"You're not going to see jack shit Ferguson," Conway said. "In fact I think visitin' hours is over. We'll let you know the results of the investigation."

"Now you listen, Sergeant," Ferguson snarled, "that man was my best friend and only a blind baboon couldn't figure out there's something suspicious about this accident. So why don't you get off your dead ass and find out what happened?"

Conway struggled to his feet and lumbered around the desk. Three uniformed deputies had heard the commotion and rushed into the room to stop a major brawl, one that Ferguson could not possibly have won.

When Ferguson realized whom he had almost started a fight with, the deputy holding him back did not have to work so hard to contain him.

"Get him the hell outta here before I take him," Conway spat.

"You haven't heard the last of this, Conway," Ferguson said. He pulled away from the deputy, grabbed the bottle opener from the desk, and headed out the door and back through the halls.

Ferguson drove, stopping at S&S Wholesale on his way back to the Shady Grove. Ferguson parked across the street from the cigarette wholesaler in a lot surrounded by a stand of tall pines.

"Well, B.J., what's going on in there that you were so interested in? Am I too close to this? What about the building? Is this the building you meant? Is this a murder or just an accident?" he whispered.

Chapter 19

Jessica sauntered into Ferguson's office before he was even settled. He had been away from the office for five days and the paperwork had accumulated like rabbits multiply. It was only three days after Billy's funeral but Ferguson felt more comfortable being back to work than at home. His doubts about Ghaleed had been nagging at him and he needed to find out the truth.

"Glad to see you, Sean," Jessica said. "Sorry to hear about Billy." She gave him a peck on the cheek and a hug.

Ferguson sighed. "Thanks. Been a tough week, Jess."

"You still look like shit," she said, giving him an impish grin.

"That makes me feel better," Ferguson said, his face breaking into a smirk as he shook his head. He slid his cap from his head and tossed it toward the coat rack in the corner. It bounced off the top and fell to the floor. "How do they do that every time? Yeah, I'm all right. I still can't believe he's gone. We lived through 'Nam and he gets taken out by someone here five miles from home. Anything new on Hamood or Ghaleed?"

"Wellston got involved in Ghaleed and has been pushing for an indictment. He says we've got him cold and it's time to move on to greener pastures."

"I think Steve's getting heat from upstairs, and he folds when that happens," Ferguson said as he tapped his pencil on the desk pad. Jessica knew Ferguson had something in mind when she saw the pencil and the incessant tapping, as if some pent up energy

threatened to blow him sky high if not
released.

"I'll tell you one thing, Jess. I think
we need to put more time into Hamood and
Simmons. One of them is the key. But this
has got to be kept quiet; the rest of the team
doesn't need to know."

"No problem. So what's the deal on
Billy?" Jessica asked.

"They've pegged B.J. as a drunk who
rolled his truck into a culvert but I'm not
buying it." He thought a few seconds. "Maybe
I'm too close."

"No way," Jessica said. "Anything I can
do?"

"Appreciate that but I need to think this
one out. I'll let you know."

"Anytime, anywhere, Sean, you know that."

As Ferguson punched in a number on his
phone, he was already thinking about Hamood.
He had one connection to the Greensboro area
and decided it was time to ask for a favor.
He dialed the ATF office.

"Dempsey," the man answered.

"George!" Ferguson asked.

"Hi, Sean. What's up?"

"Remember that outfit I asked you to
check on, S&S Wholesalers?"

"Yeah, got some info on them, and I asked
someone down there to keep an eye on'em."

"I don't know the connection, George, but
a good friend of mine worked there and was
murdered last week. The locals are saying it
was an accident but for my money, it was
murder."

"That's too bad, Sean. Anything I can do?
What do you need to know?"

"Mostly I need background. I'm workin' on
the case as much as I can."

"I'll give you Fred Moffat's number. When you get down there, give him a call. If there's something to find, he'll find it. I've got some more info for you. Another corporation showed up in the search." Ferguson heard the rattle of paper over the silent phone. "It was SW Jackson Inc. That one showed up as part owner in Farhill. Traced it back through four companies to a P.O. Box in Grand Rapids. It was incorporated in Delaware again."

"Appreciate it, George. Got one more for you. Remember that day when Jess and I were in your office and you put us onto Ghaleed at the Keg and I?"

"Yeah. In fact, I saw the notes I took the other day. Let's see. Where'd I put those? I keep everything, unfortunately," Dempsey said. "Here they are. What do you need, Sean?"

"We did a work-up on the guy and everything fell into place, like a puzzle—but I don't buy it. If Ghaleed were the smuggler we're looking for, he never would have been caught so easily. The people we're after are sharp. They don't make stupid mistakes. I wanted to look closer at him, but I need more information. Who called the complaint in that day?"

"The informant was Gary Portnoy. His number is 200-9677, a pager as I recall. He said he had phoned the Detroit Police, downtown, a Sargeant Hoover."

"Thanks George, that'll get me started. I just don't feel comfortable with this one. I'm going to have to buck Wellston so I'd appreciate if you'd keep this quiet."

"I won't say a word, Sean. And if you need anything, anything at all, you call me."

"Don't worry, I'll be in touch."

Ferguson hung up the phone and pondered his next move. A few phone calls would either confirm or deny the allegations against Ghaleed. Ferguson decided to go to the source first, dialing Portnoy's number.

After listening to the pager message, Ferguson punched in his cell phone number at the signal and hung up to wait for the return call. It came three minutes later.

"Hello, this is Karen Jenkins. I received a page."

"I'd like to talk to Gary Portnoy. This is Sean Ferguson from the Michigan Treasury Fraud Unit."

"Who?" she asked. Ferguson could almost see her nose scrunching up. "I'm sorry but you have the wrong number. What number were you trying to reach?"

"The number is 200-9766," Ferguson replied, but he already knew that was not Gary Portnoy's number. Dempsey had not written it wrong, either.

Driving up to the barn at the farm, Bat saw Moussa's Lincoln parked near the house. Grabbing his Al Kaline Louisville Slugger, Bat stepped into the barn to find Moussa and Abdul pulling cigarettes for delivery to a store in Flint. Abdul dropped an order and nervously bent down to pick the cartons up. Abdul had never met Bat but he knew it was him. Was it the Al Kaline Louisville Slugger he was carrying? Or did someone describe Bat to him? Stacks of cases of cigarettes stood in rows six feet high and twenty feet long.

Bat picked a carton of cigarettes, turning it in different directions as if looking for something. "Mr. Moussa, what do you figure we have in inventory here, a million, maybe million and a half? We have made millions of dollars by selling these and now I find someone is plotting to take it from me."

Moussa nodded as a look of surprise spread across his face. "Plotting? Against you?"

"Yes. Isn't that right, Abdul?"

Abdul was sweating, now. "What? I don't understand."

"Oh, I think you do," Bat said.

"You know, Abdul, just because you talk in your native language doesn't mean people don't know what you're saying. Now, take your conversation the morning Faisal died. I record everything and have someone who will translate for me. Imagine my surprise when I'm told what you said."

Abdul fumbled in his coat to pull something out of his shirt but Bat was too quick. A flick of his wrist and Abdul's right wrist was broken cleanly and he was doubled over screaming in pain. The next blow took out the vertebrae in his neck and Abdul crumpled to the ground as the bone severed his spinal cord.

"You sonofabitch. How dare you send money to those people so they can kill innocent people here in America. I can assure you that Hezbollah will receive nothing more from you."

In a frenzy now, Bat beat Abdul ruthlessly until the man was nothing more than a mass of broken bones and bleeding tissue. In less than ten minutes it was over but Bat continued to swing for some time longer.

Bat picked up a towel from the communication desk and slid it down the Al Kaline Louisville Slugger to clean it up. Bat

felt terrible. He had lost control. How dare
a terrorist try to blow up his country and
kill Americans. His regret was that he had
not found out the entire chain back to the
Middle East. Inspecting the bat he noted the
need for refinishing because the bone
fragments had scratched the surface.

"Clean up this mess as soon as you can.
Also, I believe Ferguson realizes that there
is no Gary Portnoy, or at the very least
suspects it. He knows Ghaleed was set up.
We've got to stop him and do it now," Bat
said.

Moussa patted the holster under his arm.
"Not a problem. Just give me the word and
Ferguson will be gone."

Bat sighed. "We are only inviting
trouble if we kill another agent, Moussa. You
can't bully the whole damn state into
submission like some street punk but we've got
to do something. Ferguson may not respond to
the fear of his own death but maybe threats
against his family may be productive. I leave
it to you but under no circumstances are you
to take out Ferguson unless I tell you to. Is
that understood?" Bat asked.

"Yeah, I understand," Moussa said.

"Very well, Mr. Moussa, handle it," Bat
said. "But do it quietly. Also, did Mrs.
Lancona get her husband's severance pay?"

"Delivered the hundred grand myself,
small bills and no way to trace where it came
from, just like you wanted," Moussa replied.

Bat nodded while scanning the warehouse.
"Stock looks a little low and there will be
thirty or forty orders in the next few days.
Call Greensboro and tell them we're going to
step up the runs to catch up." Bat always
wanted to see the warehouse full just in case

something unforeseen happened, like the wrath of the government.

"Scarponi will handle it," Moussa said.

"Oh, and tell Hamood we need a few more people here. I'm sure he can find someone in the family. There's so many of them I can't keep track."

Bat rubbed his eyes and drew in a long breath before exhaling quickly as Moussa went to the cell phones at the desk.

Bat was concerned about the investigation- not worried but just concerned. He cursed the shooter again knowing the situation was completely preventable. A few calls would step up his involvement but could stop a total shutdown of the operation. The risk of exposure was worth it if he could salvage control.

"Wellston," the administrator of the fraud division answered. He sat in his office in the Treasury Building in downtown Lansing.

"Steve, it's Sean."

"Yeah, Sean, what's new? Got something on Kate's case for me?"

"Sort of, Steve. I've got something on the Ghaleed case."

Ferguson was like a kid in a candy store. He had made progress on one case, even if it was not the direction he had anticipated.

"I've got information that our informant on the Ghaleed case supplied us with bad information. The phone number he left was wrong, and the man he identified at Detroit PD and talked to, a cop named Hoover, doesn't exist."

Wellston didn't answer. Ferguson continued, "Ghaleed only buys GM- never owned a Ford in his life."

"Sean, I understand what you're saying, but there was contraband at the store and records supporting the illegal purchases. That is conclusive evidence of fraud."

"Yeah, Steve, but there's also information to support his claim that he's innocent and that stuff could have been planted."

"Oh, come on Sean. There's no conspiracy here. I think the evidence points to Ghaleed being dirty, but I'll give you forty-eight hours to prove he's not. Then you've got to drop it. Agreed?"

Ferguson hesitated.

"Agreed?" Wellston said emphatically.

"Agreed," Ferguson said, knowing he wasn't going to get anything more from his boss.

"And then we get back to the caseload we've got, right?"

Ferguson did not answer. His plate was too full already. He'd been able to put Billy's death aside for a few hours out of each day and work.

After returning to his office, he sat in silence wrestling with the order from Wellston. Jessica popped into his office. "Takin' a little nap there, Dad?" she said with a smirk.

"Come on in, Jess. Just tryin' to figure out what else we can do to clear Ghaleed so Wellston will go for it."

Ferguson opened his desk drawer and stopped short. His shoulders sagged as he picked up a picture with shaking hands.

"Sean, what's the matter?" Jessica asked.

With a melancholy look, Ferguson handed the photograph to Jessica.

"Oh, shit. I'm sorry Sean," Jessica said. She laid the picture on the desk- a nine-year old photo of Kate with Emily and Annie the summer Kate had been a babysitter for Ferguson. She had just graduated from high school and looked forward to adult life. At the time Michigan State had been the farthest thing from her mind. She had wanted to find herself and enjoy life. The photograph had made it clear what he had to do regardless what Wellston and the others wanted. Ferguson would find the truth whether authorized by the department or not.

Chapter 20

The meeting took place at Steve Wellston's office in the Treasury Building. Ferguson and Jessica sat across from the administrator, who had a copy of the findings on Ghaleed in a file folder on his desk. He opened the folder while asking questions.

"So, what have we got?" Wellston asked. Wellston doodled on his deskpad, drawing precise tiny cubes and pyramids with his left hand. Ferguson watched him intently.

"I think- no, I know Ghaleed was set up, Steve," Ferguson said. "Every bit of our evidence is contrived. He never owned a Ford pickup. He's strictly a GM man. The truck was transferred into his name after our little chase, and the informant who called this in to ATF is non-existent. Ghaleed claims to be a straight arrow and I'm inclined to believe him. I'm not so sure about Simmons."

"Simmons! What the hell does Simmons have to do with this?"

"Nothing, I hope," Ferguson said. "But he showed up in a security tape at Hamood's. ATF also found his name on a document"

"C'mon Sean, we cleared Hamood. It must have been coincidence Simmons was there. You're talking about another agent, Sean. Do you understand that? And proof. What've you got for proof- a security tape of the guy buyin' something in a store? If there isn't anything else, you got squat. Unless you've got hard evidence just leave Simmons and Hamood alone," Wellston said impatiently. Wellston looked at Jessica for input.

"I admit, Steve, I think Ghaleed's innocent. I agree with Sean," Jessica said.

"Don't ask me who and don't ask me how, but I agree with Sean."

"Let me look at your report," Wellston said. "I'll talk to Shapiro and the Attorney General." Wellston looked pensive. "But what about the contraband at the store? Where did it come from if Ghaleed is innocent?"

It was evident Wellston wanted Ghaleed prosecuted for the cigarette felony at all costs. Kate's murder was another story. Ferguson rose silently and turned to leave. Jessica scrambled up to follow.

"Thanks for your time, Steve," she said back peddling out of his office.

When the agents were outside the Treasury Building, Jessica glanced at Ferguson. "What the hell was that all about?"

"I don't know. Wouldn't you think if there was evidence to prove someone innocent, it would be considered?" Ferguson asked.

"Yeah, of course," Jessica said.

"So why is Wellston so hot to prosecute this guy? And why did he blow off Simmons as a possible?"

"There's a lot of pressure to close the case on Kate's murder. If he can tie the smuggling to Ghaleed with the fast cars and other circumstantial evidence, I think he'll try to make the murder charge stick," Jessica said.

"Maybe, Jess, maybe. Or is it something else we can't see?"

"Are you going where I think you're going?" she asked.

"You know me better than that. I never make accusations until I can prove them. I'm just asking, that's all."

A note was on the well-used message board, the primary source of communication for a family with teenagers.

This particular message said, "Went to basketball game with girls. J." He thought about going but his last visit had not gone well.

Ferguson's pager bleated at him. Pulling the tiny box from his belt, he looked at the number. It was not familiar to him, but then many were not. He dialed the Lansing area code and punched the number. The person on the other end of the line surprised him.

"Hello, Sean?" That voice. He knew it.

"Yes sir. I was surprised by your page, it seems late for it."

"Oh, I'm sorry. Is this a bad time?" Treasurer Shapiro asked.

"No, no sir, not at all. I was just surprised, that's all."

"Okay. Sean, I just wanted to touch base with you. I only get Steve's perspective and I need to get another opinion. Steve is a little worried about you. He says he feels comfortable with where we're at with Ghaleed but says you've got a problem. Is that correct?"

"I don't think he's guilty. He was set up, and I want to pursue that direction. Steve didn't agree," Ferguson said.

"Steve will be in Detroit tomorrow. Maybe, I can smooth it out for you after I get all the facts. He's usually willing to work with me at the drop of a hat. I don't feel it's productive to interfere with his authority, if I can avoid it. You can reach me with a page or at my private number."

"Yes, sir, I'll be in touch." Ferguson pushed the end button.

At eleven o'clock Ferguson let Pixley out for his final business of the evening. Joanne and the girls had come in and immediately retired for the evening, never saying a word. The dog always stayed within the boundaries of their property and always came when called, usually after a fifteen minute run. That way the dog would be in before the weather and sports.

Precisely at 11:15 p.m. Ferguson called to Pixley and whistled. No answer. A whistle always brought a bark in return. Ferguson whistled again. No answer. Ferguson wondered what the dog had gotten into. He retreated to the television to hear the weather. At 11:30 p.m. Ferguson called again. Still, no answer. Ferguson pulled on his coat and grabbed a flashlight. The clear sky and bright moon made the flashlight unnecessary but Ferguson carried it with him anyway. He breathed deeply in the crisp night air. His shoes slipped on the frosty ground as he traversed the boundary line of the property.

"Pixley, here boy, come on Pixley," he shouted, but only silence and an occasional rustling of branches from a stray breeze found its way through the trees. Ferguson reached the edge of the state land that bordered his property. A branch snapped somewhere beyond his vision.

"There you are," he said to the dog. He shined the light, but saw nothing but pines and naked trees. He froze. No further sound escaped from the woods. No running animals, no birds, nothing.

"Pixley, here boy," he repeated slowly and not as loudly.

He resumed his journey along the rear of his property. A few hundred feet farther, a small clearing appeared. The family had shared a campfire here on many occasions. The beam from the flashlight played across the land until it came upon brown fur. Ferguson walked toward the mass of fur.

"Pixley, what are you doing?" But the fur never moved except for the hair that blew in the wind. Ferguson walked up to the mass and found it was indeed his dog. He bent down over the animal and carefully turned him. There was no panting. There was no grinning. He lifted the head. The dog's tongue slipped out the side of his mouth. He was no longer breathing. Pixley was dead.

Ferguson looked around. The beam of the flashlight skipped across the ground with a new urgency. What had happened to his pet? There were no marks on him. The dog was not that old. And then he saw it. Lying on the ground near the dog was a piece of meat. Not very large- only the size of a small apple. It was a piece of fresh meat; probably beef if he were to guess. He wrapped the meat in a few large oak leaves and put it in the pocket of his coat.

Picking up his friend, he carried him back to the house. He carefully wrapped the dog in a blanket and gently laid Pixley down in the storage shed near his house.

The phone began to ring just as Ferguson opened the door into the house. Answering it on the third ring, he heard nothing but the wind and breathing for a moment.

"How ya doin' tonight, Ferguson?" the man asked.

"Who is this?" Ferguson countered.

"Oh, just a friend. A friend who wants to make sure nothin' happens to your family, that's all since you don't listen so good."

Rick J. Barrett

"Who the hell are you, you asshole?" Ferguson screamed.

"Oh, my, my Ferguson. You need to settle down and just listen."

"I saw you pick up your dog and carry him back to the house. Something wrong with him?"

Ferguson whirled and looked through a window that gave him a view of his property. His head spinning, Ferguson thought he would vomit as he struggled to get outside.

"What did you do to my dog, you sonofabitch?" he said through clenched teeth.

Standing in the door, Ferguson scanned his property. The wind blew across the land moving the pines and tree limbs but he could see no one.

"Did I say I did something to your dog? I don't recall saying I did something to your dog." There was a pause. "Lookin' for me Ferguson. You can't see me without night vision glasses."

With only a sliver of moon Ferguson knew the man was right. Without lights from a city it was almost pitch black outside. Tiring of the game the man spoke up. "Look here Ferguson. We know your wife Joanne and your daughters Emily and Annie. We know where they go and when. We know what cars they drive. Do I make myself very, very clear? You either back off this investigation or something is going to happen to your family. And don't bother tellin' anyone about this because no matter what you do we can get to them."

There was again silence until Ferguson heard himself swallow hard through his constricted throat.

Ferguson started out slowly. "I promise you this. You harm one hair on any of my family and I will hunt you until the day I

168

die. There will be nowhere on this earth you will be able to hide from me. My life will be dedicated to finding and killing you."

"Yeah, sure Ferguson but just remember this. They'll all be dead, hotshot," the caller said. The line went dead and Ferguson stood there frozen, his head reeling from the words.

Ferguson walked to the living room and slumped into an overstuffed chair that faced the rear of his property. He tried to clear his head- to replay the phone call in his head. They had found his home- the only sanctuary he had from the drug dealers, cigarette smugglers, and other crooks he lived with every day he worked. He felt violated, sapped of all his strength. He replayed the words. Oh, my God, he thought, they know my children's names and my wife. They know everything about me. How? How do they know?

Chapter 21

The smugglers now had upped the stakes. By killing his dog and threatening his family they now had 24-hour babysitters.

"How dare you bring this on us, Sean?" Joanne said. The girls and me will be out of here tomorrow. Is this a big enough price for you now? Your daughters are living in fear, your dog is dead and what have you accomplished? Nothing." Joanne turned and stormed off before Ferguson could even say a word.

These people will pay for this, Ferguson thought. There would be no place they could hide when he found out who they were. His stomach in knots and ragged breathing, he needed to find something to do before he worked himself into an uncontrollable frenzy. He decided the office was the only place for him at that moment.

The fax from Ron Moffat in North Carolina arrived at Ferguson's office in Lansing at 8:30 a.m. Ferguson was wrapping up an affidavit of search warrant for a case they had been working for the last eight months. After his conversation with Wellston the previous day he had decided to try and clear his desk before pursuing the Simmons angle. Jessica pulled the 15 pages from the machine and looked at the ATF transmittal sheet. As soon as she saw who had sent the documents she walked them into Ferguson's office and dropped them on his desk.

"Important?" Ferguson asked looking up.

"From a guy named Moffat with ATF," Jessica said.

Ferguson grabbed the fax and rifled through the papers. After the initial once through Ferguson started over, much slower this time, finally settling on two sheets. The furrows on his brow deepened as he read further. He stared at the last page as if he couldn't believe his eyes and his jaw dropped like rock. He looked blankly up at Jessica.

"I don't believe it," Ferguson said quietly.

"Don't believe what, Sean?"

He turned the papers around and slid them at Jessica who stood in front of the desk. Looking at the papers Jessica collapsed into a chair, staring at the document. She threw it back onto the desk as if it were poison.

"This is the famous smoking gun thing, isn't it," Jessica said, grinning at her boss.

Clearly on the line marked resident agent for a corporation registered in North Carolina to operate in Michigan under the name of Specialty Risks was the signature of T. Simmons. One of the officers listed was a Paul Hamood.

"You bet your butt it is, my dear," Ferguson said. He pulled a Swisher Sweet from his pocket and slid it into his mouth to gnaw on for a while before stepping outside for a mini-victory smoke.

"You know Wellston isn't gonna buy it, right?" Jessica said.

"Let's just keep this kinda quiet for a few days," Ferguson said as he slid the papers into a desk drawer.

Walking outside, Ferguson stepped into his Jeep and opened a folder. He had Simmon's address, the vehicles he owned, his neighbors names, and other informal information he had gleaned from various conversations with the

171

man's teammates and a look at his personnel
file. Driving as he looked at the map,
Ferguson reached Simmons' home in Canton forty
minutes after leaving his office.

Simmons was a fraud agent who had been
with the department nearly as long as
Ferguson. With a brush cut, it was sometimes
hard to tell his hair color, especially when
it was buzzed. At five-foot, eleven inches
and 175 pounds, most of which was muscle, he
was a formidable adversary. He completed
cases faster than any other agent in the
department did but had problems with many of
them. Simmons philosophy was complete the
case as soon as possible and to hell with the
consequences. To do this, he routinely cut
corners.

Ferguson drove into the subdivision where
Simmons lived and found Chippewa street
easily. All the streets had Indian names-
Cheyenne, Ojibwa and many others Ferguson had
never heard of. Parking across the street and
down three houses from the Simmons home,
Ferguson settled in to watch for him. The
home, a brown brick ranch on a hundred foot
wide lot, was the nicest on the street. After
watching the house for an hour, Ferguson
cracked the window of the Jeep for some fresh
air. At that moment he heard the tap of metal
against glass. Ferguson froze as his breath
caught in his throat. He swallowed hard
knowing the sound could not be good news. The
cold metal of the gun barrel touched the back
of his head. Sweat immediately formed on
Ferguson's neck. He closed his eyes and
exhaled.

"Get outta the car now and I better see
those hands at all times or you're gonna make
a big mess in your car when the bullet goes

through your head." Ferguson recognized Simmons voice.

"O-okay, just be cool Simmons, it's me, Ferguson," he said, placing both hands on top of the steering wheel.

"Shut up and get out, now," Simmons repeated.

"C'mon Simmons, don't be stupid," Ferguson said.

Simmons pushed the barrel of the gun harder into Ferguson's neck grinding it into the flesh as if trying to draw blood. "Do I have to coldcock you with this gun or are you going to shut up." Simmons said, snarling like an animal.

How could he have let Simmons pick him up? Would he survive this night? Glancing around he hoped someone was watching but saw no one peeking through curtains. Nuts! Ferguson thought there had to be a neighborhood busybody. He could hardly make his legs work. He was always careful. Ferguson remembered the open flap on the envelope in the office and Simmon's remark about knowing something was up.

"Walk to my garage, and keep those hands where I can see'em. I don't want my family subjected to this."

"What're you going to..."

"I said shut up Ferguson." Simmons pulled the gun from Ferguson's back, moved as if he were going to use the butt of it on Ferguson's skull but stopped in midswing.

"Jessica knows where I am." Ferguson said as his only defense.

"So what. What are you doin' watchin' me?" Simmons pulled the hammer of the gun back until a click split the air.

"Hey, Hey! You know what I'm working on and your name turned up."

"It's not my name, Ferguson."

"That's funny. I was sure the name was T. Simmons on the papers I saw from ATF."

"That's right, T as in Timothy, not T as in Thomas."

Ferguson stopped in his tracks causing Simmons to run into him. "Who's Timothy?"

"My brother. Keep walking." He pushed Ferguson in the back with the barrel of the gun. Stepping into the garage, Ferguson saw the small wood burning stove that heated the room.

Trying to sound nonchalant, Ferguson said, "Your brother?"

"Know what your problem is, Ferguson?" He didn't wait for an answer. "When I worked for you, you were always objective and patient. Hell, how many times did you jump my ass because I didn't let every step play out to its conclusion? Now you missed the boat and even though we aren't on the best of terms, you slam dunk me without looking for any other answer or even talkin' to me."

Ferguson slowly nodded his acknowledgement. "So, what the hell is your brother's name doing on the documents."

"I can only guess. But it's probably because he's just a screw-up, just that simple."

Ferguson didn't know if Simmons would elaborate but couldn't think of anything to say.

"You know anything about me, Ferguson?" Simmons asked.

Silence. Ferguson didn't answer.

"I grew up in southwest Detroit. Can you possibly understand what it was like for an

Anglo kid in that neighborhood with the Mexicans? Can you?" More silence. "Let me enlighten you. We were one of two things down there. Dead or tough. We chose to be tough but we always watched our backside. That's how I picked you up tonight. My dad was never around and when he did show up, he was usually drunk. I met a Mexican man who helped me out- kinda like a mentor. My brother wasn't so lucky. He died about a year ago; knife slit his throat when he crossed the wrong people."

Ferguson didn't know what to say. "What was your brother into?"

"Anything that would make him a buck. He found out about cigarettes when I shot my mouth off about how easy it was to run them a few years ago. My mistake. Before that he just hung with the gang and caused grief for a lotta people. They'd boost cars or run scams to make a few bucks but he liked the big bucks the cigarette smuggling pulled in."

"What were you doing at Hamood's?"

"Just buying a candy bar. It was just a random stop. I could've stopped anywhere. I just chose that store."

"I guess that answers the questions, Simmons. Sorry."

"If you would've asked me I'd have told you. It's just something I'm not too proud of," Simmons said as he put the gun in its holster in the small of his back and pulled the baggy sweatshirt over it.

"Understood." Ferguson walked back to his car as Simmons watched.

"Well, Mr. Moussa do you feel better now that there is one less dog to watch us? What

in the hell were you thinking? I ask you to
handle one small job and this is what you do?"

Moussa was on a speakerphone in the
communications center at the farm.

"Who thought of that one? Both you and
Scarponi, I suppose?" Bat was in no mood for
excuses and Moussa knew it. "You know, Mr.
Moussa, that is why I am the employer and you
take orders from me. Do you honestly think
that Mr. Ferguson will cower in a corner
because of your feeble attempt to dissuade him
from an investigation? If that's the case,
sir, you are sadly mistaken, I promise you.
Mr. Ferguson will not back down from this."

Bat let these statements sink in for a
few seconds before continuing.

"I would suggest you do nothing else
unless it is cleared by me. Do you
understand, Mr. Moussa? It is obvious we need
to bring in some help because of your inept
bungling. The only thing we agree upon is
that Ferguson is getting to be a major problem
and at the point he causes us to alter our
business schedule is the day he will die."

Moussa looked at the cases of cigarettes
ready for delivery to various stores in the
metro Detroit area trying to ignore Bat's
constant bantering. He marveled at how
profitable the business had become. They had
the legislature and the moral majority to
thank for that.

"Yes, sir, it's real clear. It won't
happen again." Moussa had always known when
to fight and when to bide his time. He had
learned that lesson the hard way. As a boy he
had been chastised and humiliated by his
drunken mother and beaten by a father who
barely knew him.

"Mr. Moussa, I want you to find some trustworthy people and I want Mr. Ferguson put on a leash, a long leash. Understood? Do nothing else unless I tell you to unless it's an emergency."

Moussa did not understand why Bat was so protective of this agent. He could never prove anything, but if he stumbled onto something it could be very damaging. Moussa would wait. He would bide his time. He would keep one eye on Ferguson and the other on everything else. And if necessary he would deal with the agent regardless what the little man wanted.

Moussa made the call to the phone number Bat had given him. After two rings a man with a deep raspy voice answered the phone, wherever it was.

"Yeah."

Moussa waited but nothing more was forthcoming from the mysterious voice.

"I've got a job for you," Moussa said. It was all he could think to say.

"Meet me at the train station off Plymouth in Ann Arbor at 1:00 a.m. tonight. Don't be late." Click. The mysterious voice was gone.

Chapter 22

At 1:00 a.m. Moussa parked his car outside the small train terminal in Ann Arbor and waited. The station was located within a few blocks of the University of Michigan campus and a few students rode bikes down Depot Street even at this late hour. A smoker, no doubt banished from the inside of the building, leaned against a post on the platform near the tracks. No one looked as though they were waiting for anyone. When no one approached him after twenty minutes of sitting, Moussa started his car to leave when he saw headlights switch on in the shadows of the residential street across from the station. A dark green late model Mustang slowly pulled out and entered the station parking lot. As it approached the smoked glass side window on the passenger slid down revealing a beefy blond man behind the wheel.

"Get in Moussa."

"Where are we going?" Moussa asked.

"Just get in, dammit."

Moussa stepped out of his Lincoln and got into the sleek Mustang, instinctively patting the gun in the holster under his arm.

"We're going to Ferguson's house," the man announced. "I'll do the work and you'll take the trigger."

"Do what work?" Moussa asked. "We can't go there. The place is hot with cops after the other night."

"There are only two. We can get by them. You'll see," he said. "I'll make it easy to keep tabs on Ferguson, that's all. And if Ferguson gets stupid I'm puttin' a little surprise under his personal car. I may not be

able to get to his State car but this one is
open game."

Moussa looked around nervously. He
stared at a screen that illuminated the
interior of the Mustang an odd green hue. The
electronics were mounted on some sort of
platform in between the two men. A grid on
the computer screen made it look like an
expensive game.

Arriving at Ferguson's home after the
fifty-minute drive, the man opened the door of
the Mustang allowing a rush of frosty night
air into the vehicle.

"Let's do it," the man said. Standing
outside, he tossed a backpack at Moussa.

"What's this?" Moussa asked.

"The dynamite, of course," he said.

A look of horror spread across Moussa's
face. Grasping the bag with both hands, he
held it away from his body as if that would
protect him in the event it exploded.

"You're fuckin' psycho, you know that,"
Moussa said, gulping for air.

"Why? It ain't gonna do nothin' until I
arm it," the man said, looking puzzled.
"Uncle Sam trained me. Best training money
can buy."

Moussa sagged momentarily as the man set
off for Ferguson's house a few hundred feet
down the road.

Arriving at the house, they were
surprised to see the Jeep Cherokee parked
outside and only one guard sitting on a wood
pile toward the rear of the property.

"Well, whaddya know, the Jeep's outside,
one guard is outta the play, and there's no
moon," the man said. "Piece a cake."

Sticking a small flashlight in his mouth
as he lay down, the man wiggled underneath the

Jeep from the rear. A slight glow emanated from the undercarriage of the car as the man moved to a spot directly under the driver's seat. About ten minutes into the project Moussa froze.

"Shh, something's happening up here," Moussa whispered. He crouched and pulled his thirty-eight from its holster under his coat. A porch light popped on, illuminating the drive. Moussa flinched at the light as both men scrambled to avoid its glow.

"Shit, why didn't we take care of that," the man under the vehicle said trying to scoot away from the light as if it were poison.

Moussa stepped around the corner of the garage to remain in the shadows as the door to the house opened.

"Dammit, I hope you gotta a gun, Moussa, cause my ass is hangin' out here," the man whispered in a panic.

As if to answer him Moussa cocked the hammer of the gun. He hoped the sound calmed the bomber.

Ferguson stepped out of the door and down the steps from his house. He turned toward the Jeep, lighting a cigarette or cigar of some type.

Moussa's forehead broke into a cold sweat even though the temperature hovered around freezing. He took a deep breath and blew out making sure to exhale away from the light. Ferguson couldn't have been more than twenty feet from him and substantially closer to "BoomBoom" under the car. Closing his eyes, Moussa felt fortunate that Ferguson's dog was gone. His mouth felt dry and his knees knocked a bit. Moussa hated being in this jam. Anyone else and the guy would already be dead, a bullet through his head. But if

Moussa killed Ferguson, Bat would have his head on a pole for sure. Shit, why hadn't Ferguson just stayed inside? Now Moussa was going to have to kill him and ruin everything. And to make matters worse the thirty-eight wasn't the most accurate gun ever made at a distance.

Moussa looked down at the man under Ferguson's Jeep. He was mouthing something but Moussa couldn't figure out what he was saying. The man looked terrified, the whites of his eyes huge. Squinting to make out what he was saying, Moussa finally understood. The man mouthed "Blow his ass away now, you sonofabitch."

Hearing the chirp of the keyless entry system to the Jeep, Moussa returned his attention to Ferguson, nearly firing as he twitched at the sudden noise. Muscles in his hand strained as he held them in check waiting for the last possible moment to fire, hopefully into Ferguson's head.

Taking his time, Moussa followed Ferguson with the gun praying he wouldn't have to take him out but knowing he had to protect himself and "Boom Boom" underneath. Ferguson came around the Jeep as Moussa bit his lip. He didn't want to run from Bat but knew he would have to if his finger twitched enough to release the hammer and fire the gun. He moved the fingers around the handle of the gun trying to dry the sweat that had made it slippery.

Moussa decided he had no choice but to take Ferguson out. He would just explain to Bat that Ferguson had seen the bomber under his car and was going to shoot him when Moussa nailed him. Bat would believe that. Maybe. Shit! Why didn't he just go back in?

Moussa composed himself after a few deep breaths, closing his eyes and slowing his breathing. He trained the gun on Ferguson, now only eight feet away and facing the door he had come from. Moussa slowly began to squeeze the trigger. Say goodnight Ferguson, he thought.

Jessica parked the Taurus next to Ghaleed's store on Eight Mile and walked in. Since it was on her way home she had decided to stop and see if Ghaleed was in even though it was ten o'clock at night. As she strolled into the store, Jessica scanned the interior of the building. Ghaleed was not behind the counter- another man of middle-east origin was. Jessica glanced at him first.

"Mr. Ghaleed in? My name is Jessica Cooper," She said speaking through the Plexiglas wall.

"He's in the back. I'll call him," was the reply.

The man turned and pushed a button on a beat-up intercom conveniently mounted to a shelf. Jessica stared at him. She recognized the man from somewhere but couldn't place where. Was it at work? No. Was it at a bust? She was not sure. Was it just the dark scar on the man's cheek? As Jessica focused at the man behind the glass wall, Ghaleed approached from the rear of the store.

"May I help you?" Ghaleed asked. Jessica turned to face him.

"Mr. Ghaleed, Jessica Cooper with the Treasury Department, remember me?" Jessica held out her identification and badge.

Ghaleed's jaw dropped noticeably and his demeanor was immediately hostile. He stared at Jessica; his thin black hair and bushy eyebrows the first thing she saw. Even though he was clean-shaven, the outline of his black beard was clearly visible. His deep-set eyes sunk into his head, the color of the iris barely discernable.

"Yes, I remember," he said. His voice was cold. "You're the ones who are trying to put me in jail and take my store. How could I forget since I haven't slept in two weeks?" Ghaleed opened the door to the counter and liquor area and stepped in. There was no hint of an accent as the man ended his tirade on Jessica. He must have been second generation here. Yet, from his appearance he could have been new to this country.

"Wait a minute, Mr. Ghaleed," Jessica said defensively. "I'm here to talk to you off the record. Sean Ferguson believes you're innocent and I'm pretty convinced too."

"Ferguson. He's the jerk who was ready to put me away that day. It's very comforting to know he now knows I'm innocent. And now, after you arrest and charge me on the record, you want to come here off the record." Ghaleed reached under the counter and Jessica took a step backward, never taking her eyes off him. She released the air from her lungs when Ghaleed came out with a coffee mug and took a swig.

"Look, Ghaleed, what have you got to lose by talkin' to me, then?" Jessica said.

Jessica saw the fire in the man's eyes extinguish as he contemplated the words. The seconds ticked by as an uncomfortable silence persisted.

"You have five minutes," Ghaleed finally said.

"Okay, okay, here's what we know," Jessica said. "The Ford pick-up is registered to you, right?"

"That truck isn't mine. I told you I only buy GM, but you chose not to believe me."

"I know, I know, but I did check with the Secretary of State and the records bear you out, at least for the last four vehicles you've owned. That black Ford pick-up was originally titled in North Carolina. You are the first owner in this state." Jessica paused as if this would mean something to Ghaleed.

"Stay with me on this Mr. Ghaleed." Jessica pulled the shiny brass key attached to a ring tag from an accordion file folder.

"So what's this?" Ghaleed asked.

"We found this key in between the invoices on your desk upstairs. Do you know what it fits? It's definitely a padlock key."

"I've never seen this key before."

"Let's try it on the cigarette storage padlock."

"It can't be to the cage because I have the only key. We had a problem with people stealing cigarettes a few years ago so I changed the locks. No one gets cigarettes unless I'm in the store."

"Humor me and go try this key, will you?" Jessica asked.

The two walked into the storeroom and strolled to the wire cage. Jessica handed the key to him.

"It won't fit, I have the only key," he said confidently. The key slid into the tumbler easily. Ghaleed turned the key and a loud click signaled the lock opening. He stared at Jessica, a puzzled look on his face.

"Discrepancy number two," Jessica muttered.

"But, how?" Ghaleed asked. He was clearly confused. He took his tangle of keys from the ring attached to his belt and stared at the key to the lock on the cage. He held the two keys up to compare the cuts as if he thought the shiny brass one had some magic.

"Is this some sort of trick? How did you get the key to make the copy?"

"We had to establish that someone else had access to the storage. Now we have," Jessica said.

"So now what?" Ghaleed said. "You still continue to harass me even though you know I've done nothing wrong? That's just great. Get outta my store now before I do something we'll both regret Ms. Cooper." Redness had crept into Ghaleed's face.

She shoved a business card at Ghaleed as she retreated.

"My cell phone number is on the back. Just call us."

Jessica backed through the front door of the liquor store and around the corner to her car. She had been so intent on watching the door of the store she did not see the man parked near the alley behind the store. Cigarette smoke swirled out the partially open side window of the gold Lincoln Towncar. As Jessica pulled away from the curb and turned the corner, the driver of the Lincoln put the car in gear and spoke into a cell phone.

Chapter 23

A cell phone chirped as Ferguson walked to the Jeep outside his home. Moussa closed his eyes and took a deep convulsive breath- surprised he hadn't shot Ferguson reflexively when the phone rang. Ferguson retreated to the house, taking a drag from his cigar as he listened to whoever was on the phone. Moussa was able to make out some of the conversation.

"Good job, Jess," Ferguson said. "The key fit, too? Great!" A pause. Ferguson moved to the porch and put a foot up on the first step. "At least Ghaleed should be off the hook."

Moussa watched the blue plume of smoke rise from Ferguson's lips through the light cast by porch lamp. He sat tensed but now lowered the gun thinking Ferguson had bought himself a few more days of life. Even though the ordeal only took a few moments, Moussa felt the muscles in his arm and hand shutter from the tension. As the door closed and the lights extinguished, he collapsed against the side of the garage.

"Moussa, why didn't you blow his ass away," BoomBoom asked scrambling up from under the Jeep. "He almost made me. Shit, he damn near stepped on my fingers."

Moussa never answered as they made their way back to the car. They rode back to Ann Arbor in silence. Arriving at the train station, Moussa got out and turned to the man before closing the door.

"You know what to do, right?" Moussa asked. Moussa had never felt comfortable working with strangers, especially when it involved bombs. He guessed it was because he had seen a guy in Chicago lose his head when a stick of dynamite went off prematurely during one of the many gang wars fought on the south side when he was a kid.

"Yeah, just follow the guy and report. I'll call Bat. He told me I was to keep him informed of anything that happened. Don't punch the button to make him dog food unless ordered by your boss. Right?" he said in a raspy voice.

Moussa nodded. Bat had not even told him anything about Boom Boom and Moussa was getting a lump in his throat. BoomBoom was told specifically to call Bat, not Moussa. It sounded to Moussa like his boss was making some kind of plans and they evidently didn't include him.

"You got it." Moussa wanted to appear in charge but they both knew who was calling the shots. "I gotta catch a flight to Greensboro in two hours but here's my pager and the cell phone numbers if something comes up. Don't do anything. Call me if you have any problems," Moussa said.

He stepped into the night and the Mustang roared away. Moussa wondered if BoomBoom would ever call even if, or maybe when was a better word, Ferguson blew the whole operation sky high.

Standing next to his car, Moussa bit his lip. He regretted not killing Ferguson when he had the chance and felt that the decision not to shoot would come back to haunt them. It was time for a backup plan in case he had to get out of town. The first twinges of doubt about Bat tickled his brain. Caught between a boss who he now knew was crazy and a Treasury agent who would dog them until his dying breath didn't give him any comfort. He was certain Ferguson would have to go soon.

Almost as if he knew Moussa's thoughts Bat's number popped onto his cell phone as it started to ring. He sighed long and deep before answering.

"Mr. Moussa?" Bat said.

"Yeah, boss," Moussa said.

"Did our man do his job?"

"Yeah, Boom Boom put the bug and the bomb on the Jeep."

"Who?" Bat asked.

"Yeah, we got Ferguson wired up and if we need to we can push the button to take him out," Moussa said. He paused. "Ferguson's getting' too close. I almost had to do him tonight," Moussa said, instantly regretting his words.

"You don't do anything unless I tell you, Moussa. Is that clear?" Bat said. "I told you before we're not killing any more agents and especially Ferguson."

"Would you rather he find us out?" Moussa asked, getting bolder.

"Listen you street punk. I picked your ass up from a Chicago gang and I own you. You'd have been dead long ago if I hadn't been there for you. I expect you to listen very carefully to me and I'm saying we kill no one unless I order it. You got that? To put it in your vernacular," Bat said, almost growling, "You fuck with me and I may have- what did you call him? Boom Boom- pay you a visit one night."

Moussa heard the call disconnect and knew he had made a mistake. Would Bat really take him out? Was he really that dispensable? Moussa had no doubt Bat would kill him unless he moved first to kill the madman. Moussa

turned and looked at his surroundings. He
would make sure he wasn't sucker punched by
another of Bat's people- including the new
guy- Boom Boom.

The cell phone on the desk in the office
at S&S in Greensboro rang, startling Moussa
from his daydream.

"Moussa?" he said.

"The man drove to the airport tonight and
parked the car in the long term lot at Metro."
Moussa did not have to ask who the caller was.
The raspy growl was all he needed. "Guess
where he went?"

Moussa was in no mood for twenty
questions. It had been a long day and his
back had tightened to the point of pain.

"Disney World?" he asked.

"Cute. How does Greensboro strike ya?"
Boom Boom said.

Moussa sat up instantly. The pain in his
lower back seemed to have subsided.

"You sure?" Moussa asked.

"Saw him get on the plane myself. Flight
coming in to you." There was a pause. "Right
about now I'd say."

"Thanks," Moussa said as he switched off
the cell phone. A thousand questions passed
through his mind. He rubbed his forehead as
if to think more clearly and was surprised to
feel wetness on his fingers.

Shit. Why was Ferguson coming to
Greensboro? Did he know someone here? Moussa
remembered Bat's words. Did he know
something? Did Ferguson have a lead on them?
It was weird. Ferguson could not possibly
know anything. Moussa exhaled. He chuckled
to himself at his initial reaction. Ferguson

was not clairvoyant. He had no crystal ball. Greensboro is a big area.

"The guys still talk about Johnston. They really miss the ornery bastard. Other than that, everything is goin' smooth. You coming in today?" Scarponi asked.

Arriving at S&S, Moussa stepped from his car and looked around. Across the street he looked at the parking lot for the plant. Movement from inside one of the cars drew his eyes to the blue Chrysler Intrepid. But there was nothing to see. Moussa casually walked into the building and immediately went to a blinded window in the office overlooking the front of the building.

For five minutes Moussa watched from the darkened office. He focused on the car. And then he saw the person sit up. He squinted to see the driver. He rubbed his eyes.

"No fuckin' way," he murmured. "That's impossible."

Sean Ferguson sat watching the tobacco distributor from a parking lot across the street. Moussa was instantly on the cell phone. He called the number reserved for emergencies. It was the equivalent to the president's red phone. The phone rang but once.

"Yes, Mr. Moussa?"

"Major problem. I'm down at the warehouse and someone's sittin' on the building. It's Ferguson. We gotta kill the bastard. He's on to us."

"I'll call you back in five minutes." The line went dead. Moussa rubbed his forehead as if he could erase the vision of Ferguson.

When the phone rang, Moussa pounced on it.

"Mr. Moussa?"

"Yes sir," Moussa said.

"You're absolutely sure it's Ferguson watching the building, correct?"

"Positive. We gotta take him now before he tells someone."

"Settle down, dammit. If he knew something we'd already be in jail. Okay, I need to get some information. Don't do anything until I call you. And I mean nothing, Moussa, you bungling fool."

"Yessir." Moussa felt the anger begin to grow inside him. How dare the little jerk talk to him like that! Moussa would remember the comment for a long, long time.

Moussa called in Scarponi and told him of Ferguson. Scarponi went to the window and carefully pulled the blind back an inch. He lifted a pair of binoculars to view the man close up, committing the face to memory.

"No problem. Let's put him outta commission," Scarponi said.

"Our orders are to do nothing. The boss will handle everything. This guy was pretty hot on us in Michigan and he's well known and liked. That's why I'm worried. He's an agent for the Treasury."

"Oh fuck," Scarponi said, shaking his head.

For most of the next day Moussa and Scarponi watched Ferguson watching them. All runners had been contacted and told to scatter into Tennessee, and other parts of North Carolina. Moussa had moved his Lincoln to the rear of the building and had put legitimate plates on the car. He hoped Ferguson had not recorded the bogus plate. If checked, the new tags came back to a Lincoln from Greensboro. Moussa stood in front of the window he had occupied for the last two days drinking coffee. Scarponi walked into the office laughing at something said in the reception area of S&S. Moussa whirled toward him, spilling coffee on the carpet.

"Can it, you asshole," Moussa said. "We're sittin' here waiting for the Feds and maybe Michigan agents to come and take us and you're yuckin' it up. We got a nut case for a boss and he ain't the one goin' down if he guesses wrong about what Ferguson knows."

Chapter 24

Ferguson met Jessica at a McDonalds restaurant at the Fowlerville exit off I-96 midway between Ann Arbor and Lansing at 9:00 a.m. after arriving home late the night before.

"What's been happening up here, Jess," Ferguson said. "You been takin' care of business the last few days?"

"Oh, yeah, big time, Sean. I seem to be on everyone's shit list."

"Well cheer up, cause I'm back in town. No farther ahead than when I left, mind you, but I can just feel good things getting ready to happen." Ferguson took a big hit from his coffee.

"Well, don't be surprised if Wellston takes a big chunk out of your ass. He's really pissed off."

"Just look at the bright side, Jess. At least he's decisive about something. Right?" Ferguson had always been able to reason with Steve Wellston. He had, in fact, been his right hand man when Wellston had been a supervisor in the field, much like Jessica was to him.

"I suppose. So what did you come up with down there?" Jessica said.

"Not much. That ATF agent George called for me was a big help though, and he's got guys keeping an eye on S&S. Got some stuff to check records on here and some more in Delaware."

"So what's the problem with Ghaleed? I thought he'd like to have us in his corner," Ferguson said.

"He won't even talk to us. Your hunches were right on the money but when I went to talk to him he ran me out of Dodge. Of course, he had nothing but praise and admiration for you."

"Oh yeah, I bet he did," Ferguson said, shaking his head and pursing his lips. "I really blew it, Jess."

Jessica continued. "He wasn't too happy when I told him our conversation was off the record. What was I going to tell the guy? Sure, I believe you buddy, but my boss wants your nuts hanging from a pole." She tossed her empty cup onto the tray and closed the Styrofoam container that had held her cinnamon roll. "And now we have to go talk to a shit for brains boss who I'm beginning to think is stonewalling us. Ain't life great?"

As Ferguson and Jessica prepared to drive to their office in Lansing, the man in the gold Lincoln parked in the Big Boy restaurant lot forty feet away, saw them through the window and prepared to leave as well. He spoke to someone on a cell phone and slid the Al Kaline Louisville Slugger under the front seat.

Approaching downtown Lansing, the dome of the State Capitol was clearly visible over the other buildings in the area. Directly west of the capitol was the nondescript concrete and glass four story building that was home to the Treasury Department. Administration was on the second floor; access cards gave people the ability to enter the floor through security.

Ferguson and Jessica walked to fraud administrator Steve Wellston's office and spoke to the secretary. Steve Wellston stuck his head out of his office as if he were waiting to pounce. "Come in."

Silently, they stepped into the office and sat across from Wellston. The desk was immaculate with awards prominently displayed for everyone to see, the ten-year service certificate, the certificate for ATF training from the academy in Maryland, and hats. Wellston had fifteen or twenty baseball style hats for every agency he had ever had contact with: State Police, Wayne County Sheriff, Oakland County Sheriff, ATF. Jessica thought Wellston probably bought them because he certainly would never have received them as gifts of appreciation.

"Sean, I wanted to talk to you about a problem," Wellston said. He obviously enjoyed the feeling of power. "I've talked to Jessica about the Ghaleed case and I have the feeling you two are working against me on this. I want to clear the air and state the position of the department on it." Wellston paused to let this sink in. "I understand you were out of state and that's fine but I have to be able to contact you at all times. Is that clear?"

"Yessir, clear," Ferguson muttered.

"I thought it was clear that the Attorney General and the rest of the administration are comfortable that we do have the right man."

"I'm sorry, Steve, but just give me a few minutes to review what we have. I know Jessica found some evidence that bears out what Ghaleed said. No one in North Carolina-"

"What the hell are you doing in North Carolina representing this department? How dare you!" Wellston spit. He looked like a geyser about to blow. "You were not authorized, no, you were told not to go down there to pursue this case. Do you remember that, Ferguson?"

"Now wait a minute Wellston," Ferguson said through clenched teeth. "I went to bury my friend and if you want to check on that, you chicken shit jerk, make a phone call. Anything else I did was my business and in the best interest of something you wouldn't understand, the truth."

"Okay, that's it," Wellston hissed. "I can see we're not going to agree on this."

"Agree! Agree! Shit, this isn't about agreeing. It's about prosecuting an innocent man, period. You pompous ass! So what's going on? You've never made a decision in your life and now, all of a sudden, you've passed judgment on this guy. Who's behind this decision?"

"The Attorney General passed on it based on the evidence, so it's a go. And as for you, Ferguson, you're suspended. Give me your ID now."

That was it. Ferguson felt numbness as he tossed his credentials on the desk. His knees knocked as he silently turned and walked out of the office. He questioned his motives. Was it him? Or was it an administration that would not admit a mistake no matter the consequences? Ferguson only knew that he was no longer a part of it- the one thing he had once loved to do. His whole life seemed to be folding up before him. How long had it been since he just talked to Joanne? Days to be sure. She still hadn't forgiven his absence from Katie's funeral even after his explanation. Hell, he hadn't forgiven himself. The chasm between them widened with each day and now he had lost the only other stabilizing factor in his life- his job.

"Sean! Ghaleed called me about ten minutes ago. He wants to meet with us in two hours," Jessica said to Ferguson over the phone the day after his suspension. Even though Ferguson was off work status Jessica tied her allegiance to Ferguson.

Ghaleed was the only avenue they had left to travel. Ferguson needed his help to find the perpetrators, knowing Hamood was involved somehow. It would only take one small lead to start anew and he desperately wanted that chance but he was apprehensive about meeting Ghaleed. How ironic that Ghaleed might be the link to the Arab connection needed to crack the case.

"You sure it's us or doesn't he know I'm coming?" Ferguson said. "After all, there is this little thing called a suspension I'm on."

"Naw, he knows you're involved, honest. He decided to help us when he thought about the murder of your best friend," Jessica said.

"How'd he know about that?"

"I told him that was the reason you weren't with me when I talked to him the other day. He told me how hard it was after his brother was killed."

"Okay, okay, where does he want to meet?" Ferguson said.

"Dunkin' Donuts on Telegraph in Southfield," Jessica said.

"I'll be there. Got some free time on my hands," Ferguson said.

Ferguson arrived at the donut shop twenty minutes early scoping out the place in case there was a problem. Arriving at the shop, Ferguson was relieved to see Jessica's shiny Corvette parked off to the side of the building, away from all the other cars. As he got out of his Jeep Cherokee, he saw Jessica step out of her sports car and push the keyless alarm button.

"Evenin', Sean." Jessica said. Ghaleed's inside at the far end of the counter."

Ghaleed tried to blend into the building, sitting at the farthest seat from the door with his back against the wall. The aroma of fresh brewed coffee permeated the air as the sweet smell of donuts backed it up. Ferguson and Jessica strolled over and sat down next to Ghaleed.

"What can I get for you boys?" the waitress asked as she cracked her gum that smelled like Juicy Fruit. All he could think of was the Waffle Houses down south, where Ferguson had eaten many breakfasts during the time on the road years ago.

"Medium coffee- black, and a glazed, please," Ferguson said as Jessica nodded for the same to the waitress.

Scribbling on a pad, the tired-looking woman turned and walked back towards the donut displays to get the orders.

Ghaleed turned on the stool toward the wall and sipped on a coffee, appearing to ignore them.

"Mr. Ghaleed." Jessica was the first to break the ice. "How are you?"

"I'd be better if these charges against me were dropped." There was bitterness in his voice but it was evident he had softened.

"I think you remember Sean Ferguson," Jessica said diplomatically trying to avoid any confrontational statements.

"How could I forget this man?"

"Mr. Ghaleed, I'm sorry we got off on the wrong foot when we first met, but I want to assure you this isn't a scam." Ferguson paused. "We really want to help," he said in

an attempt to calm the man's fear and
bitterness.

"Oh, now you want to help me, Mr.
Ferguson," Ghaleed said. The words were meant
to sting and they found their mark.

"Okay, I understand you're angry and I
don't blame you, but I wouldn't be here if I
wasn't sincere about helping you. I'm a fair
man."

"I know you are Mr. Ferguson. I made
some calls of my own," Ghaleed said. "But it
still hurts that I'm the one who stands to
lose everything here."

"Mr. Ghaleed," Jessica interjected.
"Sean was suspended for trying to clear you.
You need to know that."

Ghaleed's face did not betray his
thoughts but he seemed to relax.

"What do you want me to do?" he said.

"I don't know if you saw the news article
or story about one of our agents being shot
and killed by a smuggler a few months ago but
we're trying to catch the people responsible."
Ferguson paused for a few seconds.

"I saw it. It was on the news a few
times, wasn't it?"

"Yeah, there are still a dozen detectives
assigned to the case, but the trail is going
cold. Whoever is responsible is organized and
well connected. Their tracks are covered."

"So what can I add? If there's anything
to find, the detectives are gonna find it,"
Ghaleed said.

The returning waitress put the coffee and
donuts in front of Ferguson and Jessica.
Ferguson nodded his thanks to her and she
walked away.

"I know this is a lot to ask but this is
very important to us. The Arab community is

very tight and from our experience, certain factions will smuggle cigarettes to supplement income. We all know it's done." Ferguson cleared his throat. It was suddenly very dry. Jessica took up the story.

"Mr. Ghaleed, we need to know who's behind the operation that caused the agent's death. We have reason to believe they're of Arab descent. Coincidentally, we also believe they're the people who framed you."

"How do you know they are Lebanese? What proof do you have? These people would not do this to one of their own, I can assure you of that."

Ferguson looked down at a scratch on the counter top and ran his finger over it. He sighed.

"I know it's hard to believe, but the man who shot the agent had just come over from Lebanon seven months before he was killed. We have confiscated illegal cigarettes from people he associates with. It's virtually impossible for anyone not of Arab descent to penetrate the organization."

"Do you realize what you are asking of me, Mr. Ferguson? Do you?"

"Yes, but I've got to find the truth and unless I miss my guess I'll bet you want it too."

There was silence again as Ghaleed pondered the request.

"People in this community look up to me because I grew up here. For those who need help, they trust me." He paused and shook his head slightly. "I'll think about it, Mr. Ferguson. Not because I feel I owe you anything, just because I want to find the truth also. I'll be in touch." Ghaleed stepped off the round stool and walked quickly

from the counter. Ferguson and Jessica
watched as the man left the building and got
into his 1995 Pontiac Transport. In a few
seconds he was gone.

"He won't do it," Jessica said. "He's got
too much to lose. We don't have a prayer of
gettin' him."

"Then we might as well call it a day,
Jess, because we're all done without him,"
Ferguson said. There was dead air for a few
seconds.

"I will not accept that," Ferguson said
clenching his hands into fists. He had never
been stonewalled like this in his life and did
not know how to act.

"We'll get'em, Sean. I know we will,"
Jessica said with so much conviction Ferguson
almost believed her.

Moussa decided the time was right to
confront Bat. Stepping into the empty
warehouse at the farm, Moussa nervously looked
around. When he did not see Bat he exhaled
deeply and slumped. After what seemed an
eternity Moussa felt something poke him in the
back. Twisting to see, panic overtook him
when he saw what had poked him- a Louisville
Slugger. His breath caught in his throat and
before he could pull his gun Bat pushed the
Slugger into Moussa's ribs. Where the hell
did the man come from? It was spooky.

"Why Mr. Moussa, you look as though
you've seen a ghost. Anything wrong?" Bat
asked, wickedness in his voice.

Moussa backed out of Bat's swing plane,
never taking his eyes from the man.

"Yeah, look around boss. No cigarettes
mean no money and all we're doin' is sitting
here hoping that Ferguson will go away. You
really think these fifty cases are going to

Rick J. Barrett

hold us. Well, for my money, I don't think
Ferguson is going to stop and he's close."

Moussa knew Bat was good with the
Louisville Slugger but he underestimated the
speed and control Bat mustered with the
weapon. Before he could even blink the wood
bat was at his throat quivering as if Bat was
trying to prevent it from crushing Moussa's
Adam's apple.

"What is it about my orders you don't
understand Mr. Moussa?" Bat said through
clenched teeth.

At that moment Moussa didn't know if he
was about to die or not. When he attempted to
slide his hand down to his side to retrieve
his gun Bat gently tapped on his wrist with
the Slugger.

"Not a good idea Mr. Moussa," Bat said
with contempt.

Moussa backed up to a wall, pinned by the
wood cylinder.

"I'm tired of seein' Ferguson every time
I turn around. He needs to die," Moussa said,
almost in a whisper.

"You are not the one calling the shots
here, though, are you?" Bat said calmly. When
Moussa said nothing, Bat slammed the
Louisville Slugger down against the wall just
inches from his skull. Wood splintered from
the force of the blow. Moussa looked
surprised that the splintering wasn't from the
bat itself but the wall.

"There is one boss and I am that boss.
Do you think me a fool? Do you think I
haven't seen Ferguson getting ever closer to
my operation? Do you think I'm someone to
trifle with after all these years?"

Bat slammed the bat against the wall
again. Pulling it away from the wall he swung

the bat viciously, turning a nearby chair into kindling. Sweat rolled down Bat's face and his wild eyes were nothing more than slits from the deepening furrow in his brow.

"I will take care of it," Bat said, now puffing from exertion.

Chapter 25

Moussa sat in his car at Briarwood Mall off I-94 in Ann Arbor talking to Bat on one of the three cell phones he regularly monitored. Even though it was 11:30 at night, he wasn't tired even though he had been busy.

"Mr. Moussa. It's time we met regarding our little problem. Meet me at the warehouse in an hour."

"Yes, sir," Moussa said. He wanted to say to Bat, wake up, you dumb ass, this is a helluva lot worse than a little problem. Moussa knew not to tell Bat his business or that he'd taken to carrying his Smith and Wesson all the time. He pulled the gun from its shoulder holster under his armpit and looked down at it. If Bat went bonkers on him, he certainly knew how to use it and would not hesitate. He had vowed to shoot the little bastard if Bat even looked cross-eyed at him. Moussa opened the cylinder of the gun. All six chambers were loaded and ready for bear. The forty-five could blow the head off anyone who crossed him. As he replaced the gun in its holster it snuggled up to him, giving him confidence. It also didn't hurt that he carried a gun in his coat pocket just for insurance.

Moussa sat in the Lincoln for twenty minutes chain-smoking Pall Malls before driving east onto Interstate 94.

The heat was on and he was beginning to sweat, even as good as he was. Bat had always squeaked through any problems, but this time was different somehow. Moussa felt it. It seemed everywhere they went the asshole agents showed up.

Moussa reminded himself of the promise of
weeks ago. Bat would never get the chance to
screw him. The little shit would end up with
the barrel of his gun down his throat before
that happened. He thought about calling
Scarponi. Maybe it's time to jump ship and
let the little jerk drift but thought better
of this. What if Bat survived? They would be
toast. And knowing Bat, the man would not
deal death out easily.

Pulling into Farhill Farm, Moussa looked
around. At least there was little chance of
surveillance. The fields were barren and
desolate and afforded ample notice should
someone snoop around. In a few seconds Moussa
was at the barn. He looked toward the
farmhouse and saw a security man glaring at
him.

Driving to Detroit, the only sound was
the whup, whup of the wiper blades to clear
the windshield of the Jeep. Ferguson and
Jessica turned east onto Eight Mile and drove
toward the store. They had no problems
finding it because of the aura cast by the
fire in the dark fall sky. It was like a
lighthouse beacon to a ship's captain. As
they neared the fire area, lines of yellow
caution tape stretched across the eastbound
lanes of Eight Mile. Two Detroit cops stood
behind cruisers parked across three of the
lanes. The roof mounted flashers rotated red
and blue to warn away the traffic. Ferguson
slowed and Jessica stuck out her
identification for the first cop to see. He
waved them through, much to the chagrin of
other travelers routed from Eight Mile.
Ferguson pulled the car to the side of the
road a short block from the yellow fire

equipment that was being used to fight the vicious fire.

"Shit," Ferguson said. "Not gonna be much left." Jessica did not hear him because she was engrossed in the billowing smoke and flames leaping from the store. A low rumble erupted from the building. The ground shook.

"What the hell..." Jessica said.

A huge fireball leaped from the building as the roof fell into the middle of the store. They stood silently watching as the flames shot 100 feet into the air. When Jessica finally talked, it was nearly impossible to hear her because a firefighter monitoring the gauges on the pumper truck cranked up the engine to 4,000 r.p.m. Hundreds of gallons of water were charged and sent out to the hoses. One of the battalion captains stood away from the truck and called the third alarm in. Just as he finished his call, the speaker from the radio blared.

"Got a body," a firefighter yelled over the radio. "Smoke too thick to see if there's anyone else."

Ferguson and Jessica looked at each other. "Those assholes," Ferguson squeezed out. "Those rotten bastards." The people responsible didn't have names yet, at least to Ferguson and Jessica, but Hamood was part of it.

As the fire was extinguished, the true extent of the devastation came into view. The shell stood, but nothing else was left. The darkness hid much of the destruction but the smell and flickering embers told the story. Portable construction lights used for night work arrived and the fire truck engines were finally allowed a rest. The generators attached to the lights were fired up and the building was instantly bathed in bright light. The charred remains, previously illuminated only by the red lights of the fire trucks and the fire itself, now revealed total and absolute destruction.

"Damn it," Jessica said.

"What's up, Jess?" Ferguson said.

"That guy I saw in the store when I came back to talk to Ghaleed. I didn't know where I had seen him before. It just hit me. I saw him at Hamood's store when we did the search warrant."

"You sure?" Ferguson said.

"Yeah, I'm sure," Jessica said as they walked toward the building.

Ferguson looked through the hole in the wall that had been the double glass doors only a few hours ago. The glass had been blown out from the heat and lay in thousands of tiny pieces around the entrance. The glass crunched under their feet. Beautiful colors refracted from the glass as the bright lights hit them. Ferguson looked at the door. The frame remained intact, and locked.

Firefighters had entered the building through the locked doors- doors that no longer served a purpose. They continued to pour water on the rubble to prevent hot spots from flaring. As the water hit these spots, billowing smoke rose and disappeared into the night sky. Ferguson could see a yellow tarp over a mass near where the wall of liquor and cash registers had been. A firefighter stood poised with a hose to protect the corpse from further damage should the need arise.

Hound Dog approached from the east corner of the building, stopping to talk to a firefighter and a Detroit cop. No expression crossed his face.

"Hey, boss man, you been reinstated?"
Hound Dog said in a long deep drawl.

"Just an interested bystander, Dog.
Haven't been reinstated."

"Too bad."

"Yeah, I guess," said Ferguson.

"So, what happened," Jessica asked.
"This thing must have been hotter than hell
from the looks of it."

"They got the call about 8:00 p.m. that
the building was on fire. Front door was
locked according to a customer."

"Liquor store closed at eight o'clock?
Yeah, right," Jessica said.

"Lights on inside, too," Hound Dog said.
"Whoever did it used something flammable to
ignite it. Probably gas, according to the
captain."

"There's no doubt in my mind who did it,"
Jessica said. "We just don't have a name,
yet."

The agents walked around the building a
few times, not knowing what they were looking
for. Detectives looked at the rear door with
the wrought iron gate. The gate was swung
open against the wall and the heavy steel door
was open.

Ferguson looked at the door. "That door
wouldn't be open in this neighborhood," he
said.

"So, who went out the door?" Jessica
said.

"Some bad sonobitches, I'd say," Pena
said.

Investigators found the rear door of the
business open and in this neighborhood that
never happened unless there had been foul
play.

A fire investigator took Polaroid pictures, close-ups of anything that might help in the investigation. Little was left, though. The electric power line coming into the building had been subjected to so much heat, the insulation had bubbled and disintegrated. All that remained was the dull silver.

Fire officials allowed the agents inside the building but there was nothing of any importance. Ferguson found it impossible to concentrate on anything but the tarp.

"I can't stay here, Sean," Jessica said. "That poor bastard...I can't take it in here."

"Let's go. We can't do any good in here," Ferguson said.

The coroner arrived and took control of the blackened corpse. The smell is what Ferguson would remember. A cold breeze had lifted it from underneath the yellow tarp.

"Jess, I think we've attracted a lot of attention and that scares me. They knew we met with Ghaleed this morning and they're willing to do anything it takes to protect themselves." Ferguson rubbed his forehead.

"We have to watch our backs from now on and keep in touch at all times. I think you should talk to Wellston tomorrow as soon as we know the identity of the corpse."

"We need to check our cars every time we get in them. Can you call Fred Linden at Special Ops and see if he can help us?" Ferguson forgot himself for a minute. "Sorry. Forgot."

Jessica never gave it a second thought. "I'll call first thing in the morning. He's out at the crime lab at the Northville post, isn't he?" she asked.

"Last time I talked to him, he was," Ferguson said. "If there's anyone who can go over the cars and find if they've been tampered with, it's Fred. Tell him I think we have a bigger problem in our own backyard, and we need to keep this thing quiet."

Doubt crept into Ferguson's mind again. Had he gone too far? Was the price now high enough to drop the case? He remembered his teens when he wanted to quit football because he was afraid of getting hurt and how his dad never allowed even a word of quitting. His father had never quit a thing in his life and put an arm around his son when he heard of the fear, talking to him like he was a man and not a little boy. The lesson stuck and Ferguson became All-State in football as a wide receiver a month before his father died of cancer. Ferguson remembered how his dad had sat up so straight, even in a weakened condition, and how a single tear had welled up in his eyes. He had told the boy how proud he was. There was no way Ferguson would quit this investigation.

Chapter 26

As Moussa entered the code for the security system at the warehouse southwest of Detroit, Bat pulled up. Stepping from his Mercedez he strolled to Moussa as if there wasn't a care in the world.

"Mr. Moussa. How are you this beautiful night?" Bat asked.

What was so fine about this night, Moussa thought. We're lookin at fuckin' jail and he's happy about the weather.

"Okay," Moussa replied. "What did you want to talk about?" The two men stepped into the heated barn. Moussa did not remove his hand from his coat pocket.

"I heard you handled our problem. It appears some further action may be necessary to detour these agents from looking into our little enterprise," Bat said, matter of factly. "No rough stuff until I give you approval. We don't need anyone else investigating us. If another agent goes down, we're liable to have every State Police Trooper in Michigan down here looking for us. And we can't have that, now can we?"

Moussa just blinked at Bat. What the hell is he talkin' about? That agent gets close enough and we'll all be pushin' up daisies. Moussa couldn't remember where he had heard that phrase but he liked it. Bat would probably think it crude.

"No, can't have that," Moussa muttered.

"Mr. Moussa, I'm going to suspend operations for a few weeks. Have the stores put in orders from different wholesalers here. Spread them out. They need to be careful that the orders are spaced so no one gets suspicious. They also need to pay for these cigarettes with money orders so there is a trail." Bat stopped when he saw he was losing Moussa.

"Look, we got to do something with the agents that are doggin' us," Moussa said. "These people are gettin' too close for comfort."

Bat stared at Moussa as his demeanor changed instantaneously. "You, Mr. Moussa, are not to do a damn thing until I say so. I am not a fool. I realize they need to be addressed but I make the decisions. When we move, when we stop, when we pull out. Do I make myself clear, Mr. Moussa?"

Moussa's hand closed around cold hard metal in his coat pocket. His smile almost turned into a snarl as he turned away. His hand shook as he worked to pry his fingers from the gun in his pocket.

"Mr. Moussa?"

"Clear," Moussa spit.

"And I want all vehicles in the warehouse now. Deliver the product we have here and call Scarponi. Scarponi needs to know. He also needs to know there might be ATF agents watching his location. Do it now, Mr. Moussa. We will take all three agents out together if possible and hope no one else is involved in the investigation."

Bat moved toward the door. Ready to leave the barn, he returned his gaze to Moussa. "I also want you to increase security here. They'll never find this place but move out the cigarettes anyway. Understand? Just the cars stay here."

"Yes, sir," Moussa said. He didn't know what Bat had said but he always replied the

same way—yes sir. And then Bat was gone.
Moussa made a phone call.

"Woodchuck, I got a job for you and the
Tinman. How soon can we meet?"

Ferguson pulled into the parking lot
across from Hamood's liquor and convenience
store in Livonia at 6 a.m., two hours before
it opened for business. He had prepared for a
long surveillance, bringing a thermos of
coffee, fruit and sandwiches, cameras and a
will to remain until Hamood did something he
could turn into an indictment. His greatest
fear was that he would see the man and go
after him. Quite frankly, he wasn't sure what
he would do when the man made an appearance.
He only had an hour to wait to answer this
question.

The BMW pulled up at 7:20 a.m. and
Ferguson sat bolt upright. He didn't need the
binoculars to know it was Hamood. The fitted
leather jacket and sun glasses along with the
silk shirt open to the guys navel left no
doubt it was the pompous sonofabitch who
Ferguson would live with until he made a
mistake that would bring him down.

Ferguson raised the binoculars to his
eyes but his hands shook so uncontrollably
that he could barely see. He pulled them down
and took a deep breath. Closing his eyes,
Ferguson reached for the handle of the door.
He hesitated for a moment clenching his fists.

No one would know, he thought. He could
sneak across the street and surprise Hamood
before anyone came. The bastard would talk-
one way or another. Ferguson was no longer
bound to uphold the law. Hamood had taken

that from him, too. The rotten bastard had
taken everything from him.

Ferguson glanced down at the glove
compartment. Reaching down, he pushed the
button to open the door. The chrome on the
barrel of the handgun glinted. He picked up
the weapon, holding it in the open palm of his
hand. He stared at the instrument of
destruction contemplating his next move. An
odd calm struck him as he realized whatever
the decision it would impact him for the rest
of his life.

Ferguson pulled the door handle slowly.
He heard the click and pushed the car door
open. His hands were sweating and his mouth
was dry as if full of cotton. Standing
outside his car, Ferguson's legs felt leaden.
He couldn't walk let alone hurt Hamood. The
gun slipped into his pocket. He slid one leg
ahead of the other scraping the sole of his
shoe on the concrete.

He thought about Katie- so young and full
of life and now gone forever. She would never
approve of Ferguson being a vigilante. Sorry,
Katie, Ferguson said to himself. I can't stop
the bastard legally and people are dying at
the hands of this butcher. I can't take it
anymore, honey.

Ferguson turned back to his Jeep and
suddenly brought his fist down on the roof of
the vehicle.

Had he gone too far? Of course he had.
Was the price now high enough to drop the
case? Quit? Never!

After what seemed hours, Ferguson
gathered himself. He continued to watch the
store, periodically scanning the store through
the binoculars.

At 11:30 a.m. a nondescript white van pulled up to the store and two men got out. Ferguson grabbed the 35 mm camera. The telephoto lens weighed more than the camera and Ferguson had to use both hands to steady it. "Bingo!" he said to himself. "You are mine now, Hamood."

As the men emptied the truck, Ferguson watched intently. Open cases of cookies, canned goods and paper products left the truck as did Ferguson's hope of illegal cigarettes. Hamood would never be stupid enough to have the contraband in his store now. What was he thinking? He would follow his prey for the real answers.

Moussa strolled into a bar called the Jupiter Club on Nine Mile road in Warren. The block building had been put there for the auto plants. A painted sign advertised cocktails and "burgers that are out of this world." Moussa was sure the only cocktails mixed in the joint were boilermakers the autoworkers swilled in drinking contests. Moussa could tell it was close to lunch break in the plant because the well worn woman behind the bar started to set up shot glasses and ten ounce beer glasses.

The dark, dingy room had not seen the light of day in many years and reeked of cigarette smell and sweat. The twenty-watt bulbs illuminated the restroom doors and emphasized the signs, does and bucks. The tables and chairs were sixties vintage, metal and plastic laminate. The tables had been used so long that the gray top layer of the laminate was worn through to the white underneath. The corner afforded a dark

private area and Moussa, Woodchuck and Tinman
walked to it. Other patrons understood not to
go near if they saw people at a table.
Someone might be conducting business.

Woodchuck was the first to sit. "Shell
of Bud," he said, "and a burger with the
works." It was assumed the order was the same
for the table unless someone had the guts to
say something else. If he did, a glare would
put him in his place or if the barmaid was in
a particularly bad mood, a beer or burger
might just end up in his lap.

The three sat as Moussa looked at the
ever-present toothpick bobbing up and down in
Woodchuck's mouth. He'd picked up his
nickname years ago when, as a child, he ate
toothpicks. He still loved to chew on them
but at least he no longer ate them.

The Tinman had been honored with his
nickname when he was a deputy sheriff wearing
a tin badge. That profession was short-lived
when he became involved in a protection scam
and was busted in a sting. A year in jail had
mellowed him but did not rehabilitate.

"So here's the deal, boys," Moussa said.
"I got this person I want to take a ride.
Five K sound about right? And I would like to
see the ride as soon as possible. No
evidence. No trace. Gone. Can you deliver?"

"Shouldn't be any problem far as I can
see," Woodchuck said. He was obviously in
charge.

"Here's the particulars and some
traveling cash," Moussa said. "Balance on
completion. Understood?" Moussa slid a
manila envelope across the table. Inside were
the addresses of Ferguson's home, Jessica's
condo, and the office, along with Ferguson's
license plate and a description of his car.

There were addresses for a few other places where Ferguson might show up. A picture taken from a distance was on top of the documents.

"Kinda skinny, ain't he?" Tinman said.

"He might be skinny but I'll tell you one thing, I wouldn't fuck with him," Moussa said.

"We'll be careful with him," Woodchuck said. Tinman nodded in agreement.

"Any idea where he might be now?" Tinman asked.

"There's a liquor store in Livonia. The address is in the list. My bet is he's there. He won't be easy to pick out though, so watch yourselves."

The beer and burgers arrived. The barmaid smiled, proud that she was able to keep everything on the table. Moussa took a sip of the beer and dropped a twenty on the table.

The bill was snatched almost before it hit the table.

"Keep the change, sweetheart," Moussa said. The barmaid raised an eyebrow. Rarely did any of the shop rats leave much of a tip, let alone one this big.

"Thanks," she said. And as quickly as she had appeared, she was gone.

The three men finished the food in silence and stood to leave. When they stepped from the bar, they squinted in the bright sunlight, struggling to adjust their watering eyes.

"Do it neat and clean and call me," Moussa said. "When I confirm it's done, I'll call you for the balance."

Moussa climbed into his Lincoln and drove away from the Jupiter Club. Another bar to forget, he thought. He would remember to call Scarponi later when he had something concrete to tell him. Moussa wondered how big a mistake it was to go behind Bat's back. He knew it would not be long before Bat would find out. He felt for the gun again.

Chapter 27

After watching Hamood's liquor store in
Livonia until 7:00 p.m., Ferguson got out of
the Jeep and stretched. Hamood had not left.
He raised his arms to pull the kinks out of a
body not nearly as limber as it had once been.
Since he no longer was on a fishing
expedition, Ferguson could sit on the store
'til hell froze over. His job was in the
dumper and he had no home at the moment.
Sooner or later Hamood would make a mistake.
Ferguson started the Jeep and pulled away
from the shopping center parking lot across
from the liquor store. He switched on his
lights and headed for the freeway toward Ann
Arbor. Before he reached the expressway, he
glanced in his rear view mirror to see a black
Cadillac following. Ferguson picked up his
cell phone from the passenger seat and punched
in a number.
"Hi Sean," was the first word Ferguson
heard.
"Caller ID huh, Jess," Ferguson said.
"Having fun sitting on the man, yet?"
"Just left. What'd you find out?"
Ferguson asked.
"Hamood came over nine and a half years
ago. He's been operating a store for the last
five. Can't seem to figure where he came up
with the money to buy a store, either. Heard
the family in Lebanon pooled all their money
to buy one. Anyway, he opens this store and
all of a sudden, shazam, he's got money to
burn." Jess paused to let the words sink in.
"He's also got a reputation for violence,
Sean."

"What a surprise. Anything else?" Ferguson asked.

"Did you know that Wellston knows Hamood? Well, maybe he doesn't know him personally but knows the name?"

"What? You sure, Jess?"

"Yeah. I was over at the Trantor Building lookin' up records and came across a file that was five years old. Remember the Hassan bust in Detroit? It was Wellston's, and everyone said he built a career on the basis of that one case."

"Yeah, I remember. Seems to me I was on the grand jury and didn't work it."

"Guess who was interviewed because he was working there when the search warrants were executed?"

"No clue," Ferguson said.

"Hamood," Jessica said.

"You mean..." Ferguson stopped in mid-sentence. "Holy shit. No way. Are you sure?"

"Got the interview sheet. No kiddin', Sean. Wellston interviewed Hamood five years ago. He was only working for Hassan but the interview was put in the file. Can you believe it?"

"You've got the file, right?"

"Yeah, it's put away."

"I need to call Shapiro, Jess. Meet me at your condo in an hour."

As Jessica hung up, Ferguson was already fumbling with his address book for the private number Shapiro had given him.

The phone was answered on the third ring. "Ken Shapiro."

"Yes sir. This is Sean Ferguson."

"Ferguson? Aren't you on suspension?" Shapiro asked.

"Yes sir, but I've got some information about Wellston that could explain why I've been suspended."

"Okay. What've you got?" Ferguson explained the story to Shapiro. When he had finished, Shapiro sighed.

"Damn, Sean," Shapiro said quietly.

"Yes, sir."

"You've got to bring me everything you've got. I'll talk to the Attorney General and get his spin on all of this. Call me back in two hours."

"Yes sir."

Ferguson closed the flip phone and put it on the seat next to him. As he turned onto the service westbound ramp to M-14 toward Ann Arbor, he didn't see the car in his mirror until it rear-ended the Jeep, almost causing him to lose control. He pulled over, and without thinking Ferguson stepped from his car. Smoke glass prevented him from seeing into the car that had hit his. He stared at the older black Cadillac. Two men stepped out and walked to the front of the car to look at the damage to the cars.

"Jeez, I'm really sorry, buddy," shouted the driver of the Lincoln. "I guess I was following to close, huh?" Ferguson saw him take his hand from his coat pocket. A 38 caliber Smith and Wesson looked back at Ferguson. He froze but just for a second. Diving into his still running vehicle, he threw the gearshift into drive without looking over the steering wheel. The Jeep lurched forward. When he didn't hear any shots, he glanced into the mirrors to see the Cadillac pull away from the side of the ramp and roar towards him.

"Oh, shit," Ferguson muttered.

Bat dialed the number in Greensboro. Waiting for Scarponi to answer, he wiped his brow and was surprised to see the sweat. Bat knew he was close to losing the war. He could stand to lose a few battles but somehow Ferguson had come a lot farther than Bat ever would have guessed.

"Hello," Scarponi answered the phone.

"Scarponi, I want to shut down the operation right now. Don't ask any questions. Call all the runners and tell them to scatter until we can come up with a plan. I want the back sealed up and no one, and I mean no one, is to go near there."

"What about the loads we got pulled, boss."

Leave'em. This isn't going to last forever. I'll see to that," Bat said.

"I'll call Moussa when I'm sure we're clear," Scarponi said.

"No! You are to call only me," Bat said. "Is that clear?"

"O-okay, sure, Boss."

Bat hung up the phone and went to the vault in the library. Opening the safe, he stood mesmerized by the cash, over $2,000,000 now, before loading it in a duffel bag. If absolutely necessary, he was prepared to give up every one of his lieutenants to preserve what he could of the operation. Only weeks ago everything was running so smooth and now every facet of the operation was in jeopardy. Ferguson had proven to be an adversary he underestimated. Was Bat losing it? A few years ago he never would have blown off an opponent like that. What a shame. Especially, when Moussa wanted to kill him a week or so ago. That may have been a mistake.

Hopefully, one that was being corrected at this very moment.

Ferguson pushed the accelerator to the floor. He tried to put it through the floorboard. While watching the road and driving with one hand, he reached over to the passenger seat, fumbling for the cell phone, his lifeline to help. It was not there.

His throat tightened. Where did it go? He glanced over. Not on the seat. Not on the floor. It's somewhere, he thought. Just be calm. It has to be close. Ferguson bent and felt around on the floor. A chuckhole wrenched the wheel from his hand. He skidded left, overcorrected, and almost flew off the road on the right. "No, no," he shouted to no one. He straightened up and somehow regained control of the Jeep, for the moment.

The Caddy was on his tail. A jolt. The Jeep lunged forward. "Shit," Ferguson said. He grabbed the wheel with both hands. Got control. Glancing quickly to the floor in front of the passenger seat, he saw the phone. It might as well have been a mile away. "Oh, God," he said. Another jolt, the shattering of plastic. Tail lights smashed. The Jeep surged forward toward a viaduct. Pull left! Pull left! At ninety miles per hour he would not survive a tangle with a bridge support. The tires screamed like a tortured animal. He looked down again. It began to ring. The phone began to ring.

"Help," Ferguson yelled. He knew the caller could not hear him but he yelled anyway. It rang again. He yelled again. The tires screeched. The Lincoln accelerated to ram him again as the Jeep rushed forward. The Cadillac seemed to go that much faster. Ferguson looked down at the speedometer, 110 miles per hour. His head snapped up. He looked in the rear view mirror. The Lincoln grinned back. "Oh my God," Ferguson whispered. He was going to die. The realization—he simply was about to die. The grinning Cadillac would get him. Bullshit, thought Ferguson. He took a deep breath and tried to relax. He had to think. He had to be smart- smarter than the clown who was driving the car. He changed lanes, back and forth. He had to keep the Caddy off guard. By swaying, he was able to slow to 90 miles per hour.

"Just go away, you bastard," Ferguson screamed. The Lincoln was lining him up for one last ram. The car slowed and fell behind Ferguson's Jeep. Ferguson breathed a sigh of relief and took his eyes from the rearview mirror for a second. When his eyes returned to the mirror, the Lincoln was closer again, very close and closing. Just as the Cadillac was about to hit the Jeep, Ferguson yanked the wheel to the right and hit the brakes. The car flew past. Smoke from the tires obscured his vision but Ferguson saw the bulky Cadillac try to brake and skid into the median, spinning and throwing up mud and grass everywhere. Ferguson sat for a few seconds, still trembling from the adrenaline rush.

"Take that, asshole," Ferguson said as he punched the accelerator.

The Jeep screamed as Ferguson bent over to grab the precious cell phone that had been useless to him only minutes before. He flipped open the phone and quickly hit the redial function.

"Jess, just listen. I just got a visit from our friends. They were driving a gold

Cadillac and tried to take me. I left them in the median on M-14, stuck in the mud I think."

"You what?" Jessica said.

"I almost bought the farm. I don't know if they've got your address but you need to get out of there, now. Do you understand?"

"Now?" she said.

"Meet me at the Mickey D's on 23 near Pinckney. You got it?"

"See you in thirty." And Jessica was gone.

Ferguson pushed end and frantically entered another number.

"State Police, Brighton Post, Corporal Gordon," the trooper on the desk said.

"Corporal, this is Sean Ferguson. I'm a fraud investigator with Treasury. There was an attempt on my life about thirty minutes ago. The perps are sitting in a gold Cadillac stuck in the mud on M-14 near the thirty-seven mile marker. You can talk to Sergeant Cook at headquarters to verify who I am."

"I'll send a car, Mr. Ferguson but I need you to come into the post."

"I'll be there in about an hour. Thanks for the help."

Ferguson arrived at the fast food restaurant in fifteen minutes. It had ample parking off to the side for the big rigs that rolled up and down the interstate. He parked as far away from the building as he could, next to an eighteen-wheeler that sat idling while the driver was inside eating the greasy fare. Ferguson was exhausted. He closed his eyes, breathing convulsively while he waited for Jessica, knowing for the moment, he had beaten the bad guys.

After breathing deeply for a few minutes his heart slowed to its normal rhythm and he

melted into the seat of his Jeep. His hands
that had strangled the steering wheel,
relaxed. Shaking without control, he removed
them from the steering wheel and stared at
them, before they dropped to his side aching
and sore. He had almost died at the same age
as his father, leaving a sixteen-year old
daughter. The coincidence was overpowering.

After what seemed like only seconds there
was a tap on the driver's window. A tap made
with something metal. A sharp crisp noise.
Ferguson opened his eyes thinking Jessica had
arrived, and looked into the barrel of a 38
caliber Smith and Wesson.

Impossible. They couldn't have gotten
out of the median that fast. But there it
was. The gold Cadillac had enough mud and
dirt clinging to it to grow a garden. Another
tap from the gun brought Ferguson back.

He looked up at the burly hulk of a man
holding the gun at his window. All he could
see was the sheen of skin where the man's hair
used to be, two close set brown eyes, and one
gold tooth where his eyetooth should have
been. He looked like Curly of the Three
Stooges. The grinning mass waved the gun in a
circle to have Ferguson roll down the window.
Ferguson heard the man chuckling as the window
of the Jeep moved steadily down as he pushed
the button.

"Get out of the car, smart ass," he said.
When Ferguson opened the door and stepped out,
Curly man put his hand in a pocket to obscure
the handgun. "Ain't technology great?" he
said while Ferguson leaned against his Jeep.
The other man sat in the still running
Cadillac as Curly motioned Ferguson to get
into the car.

"Where we goin', to the car wash?" Ferguson asked.

"Just get in my car, Ferguson. And no funny stuff or you'll leak like a sieve from all the holes I'll put in ya," Curly said.

Chapter 28

The first man drove off in Ferguson's Jeep while Curly, the driver, and Ferguson piled into the mud-caked Cadillac. The car accelerated onto southbound US-23 and east on M-14, the way they had come. Slowing to exit at Gotfredson Road, Ferguson tensed. The road, lightly traveled until recently, had started to attract the attention of developers who wanted to cash in on the ever-expanding suburban sprawl around Detroit.

They slowed and pulled to the side of the road. A pair of headlights grew closer from a trailing car. The lights looked like a hound on the scent, nose to the ground, winding along the twisting road. Please let it be a cop, Ferguson prayed. No such luck. The car slowed and passed on the left, then rounded a curve. The two men watched in the darkness for a few minutes for any other unwanted guests. When Curly was sure they were alone, he ordered Ferguson from the Cadillac. Ferguson's knees felt like rubber as he was forced from the car.

"What are you going to do?" Ferguson asked through the cotton in his mouth.

"Nothin' right now," the man said as he motioned Ferguson to the rear of the car with the gun. He opened the trunk. "Get in."

Ferguson stepped on wobbly legs before he pitched into The trunk and the lid slammed shut. Even with the big car suspension Ferguson was jostled about as they traveled the winding dirt road toward a place he knew he did not want to go.

How would he escape? What should he do? Would there only be two when they released him

from his coffin-like cell? Would they simply
shoot him through the trunk? An offense is
always the best defense. Should he burst from
the trunk when it was unlocked? No. He
needed to know what they had and what they
intended to do. And then, the Caddy stopped.
Oh, shit. How far could they have driven in
what seemed to be only minutes? Damn. What
should he do? How could he survive this?
Ferguson heard a sound. Oh, shit. Was that a
thirty-eight cocking or did they have more
firepower?

They were going to shoot him through the
trunk. That's what they were going to do.
Why had he been so damn stubborn? A bead of
sweat formed on his upper lip and spread to
the back of his neck and face. He wiped his
forehead with the back of his jacket. Sweet
Joanne. Joanne didn't deserve this. The
girls would help her. Oh shit, the girls. He
hadn't seen the girls in a week. How could
this happen?

He prayed. He remembered praying for his
father's life long ago and it had not helped.
He would die just like his father but prayers
were the only thing he had left. He mouthed,
Our Father who art.

Several minutes passed. His palms were
sweating. His hands shook. The deafening
silence ended when the driver's door slowly
opened. The car rocked slightly as feet hit
gravel and the man stood. The passenger door
opened. Must be Curly, thought Ferguson. He
heard a metallic sliding sound, like the sound
of a round being racked into the chamber of a
gun. Oh, shit. His time was up. There was
nothing more to say. No more thoughts of the
future. No more time. The men were standing
at the trunk.

Ferguson heard the jingle of the keys as the trunk key slid into the tumbler of the lock. He wondered who would find his body. Where would they dump him? Maybe the Caddy would just be parked somewhere and no one would find his body for weeks. Who were these men?

The first sound startled him. Something falling onto the trunk, something heavy, and then sliding down the deck lid and off the car. A muffled noise. Something hit the ground. And then another sound, like a bowl of Jell-O landing on the ground. Silence.

The key turned and the lock was released. Ferguson flinched. The trunk lid opened enough to let shards of light from a full moon into the black dungeon. The deck lid rose slowly. Ferguson could see a belt, then a torso, then a neck, and finally teeth. Bright white teeth. Very white teeth. White teeth against black skin. Black skin stretched into a smile exposing white teeth. A broad smile. Ferguson squinted, even in the darkness.

"I guess you're happy, huh?" Ferguson said.

"Guess I am."

"Bet you're not as happy as I am," Ferguson said.

"Maybe not."

"Any particular reason why I shouldn't get outta this trunk?" Ferguson asked.

"Can't think of any," Hound Dog said. He put out his hand to help Ferguson.

As the two men waited for the sheriff's deputies to arrive, Ferguson surveyed the area. To the west he could make out a huge hill from the light of the moon. Out of place for this area. If he had his bearings correct, they were in Washtenaw or western

Oakland County. And the hill was a landfill.
Was the landfill to have been his final
resting-place? A chill ran through him. Not
because he had almost died but because the
landfill had rats. Ferguson hated rats.

"So how'd you find me?"

"Just out for a ride, man," came the low
rumble.

"Nice ride I'd say. How'd you know I was
in trouble?"

"Just did, that's all. Drove past you on
Gotfredson."

"You're kidding, that was you?" Ferguson
asked.

"No. I weren't goin' to no picnic.
Thought I'd stick around a bit. That's all."

"How long you just been ridin' round
behind me, Dog?"

"Few days."

"Thanks."

"No problem.

"You don't happen to know who these boys
you just cold-cocked are by any chance, do
you?" Ferguson asked.

"Nope."

"Any idea at all?"

"The bad guys?"

"Big help, Dog."

"I aim to please, boss."

"Sean, how long have I been thinkin' of
songs to stump your ass?"

"Long time and you still can't do it."

"Since we're sittin' here doin' nothin'
name this. Little Girl."

Ferguson gave a weak smile. "Okay, Dog,
you asked for it. Hey, little girl, you don't
want me around...," Ferguson sang. "Syndicate
of Sound on Bell Records in 1966. One of my
personal favorites."

"You and your white people music. Hell I never heard of this shit. How 'bout..." Hound Dog pulled a sheet of paper from his back pocket and opened it. "Pictures of Matchstick Men."

"Status Quo on Cadet Concept label in 1968."

"We Gotta Go," Dog said.

"The Shy Guys on Palmer label in 1966. A regional band."

"Damn, Morning Girl."

Ferguson thought for a moment. Hound Dog grinned.

"Neon Philharmonic in 1969. Not sure of the label."

Hound Dog grinned some more.

"Warner Brothers label," Ferguson finally said.

"Shit," Hound Dog said as he crushed the paper and shoved it in his pocket.

The two men sat in silence until the first deputy arrived. As Ferguson told about his abduction and car chase, Hound Dog launched a call to Jessica. Over the course of the next ten minutes, two more county cruisers and a state police car arrived. The perpetrators woke and sat handcuffed in the back of the first police car. A wrecker had arrived to tow the dirty Cadillac to a county impound.

"Jess wants to meet us at that Mickey D's on 23 now," Hound Dog said.

"A hot coffee sounds pretty good right now, Dog," Ferguson said as the two jumped into Pena's Cadillac Deville.

The agent looked for Jessica's Corvette, finding it parked an acre away from anyone else at the McDonald's.

"Shit, why she park way out alla time?" Pena said as he shook his head.

"Couldn't tell ya, Dog," Ferguson said.

"Holy shit, Sean, pretty lucky the Dog was there, huh," Jessica said.

"Guess so, Jess."

"So what's our next move," drawled Hound Dog.

"Where the hell are my wheels, that's our next move," Ferguson said.

"I don't know how they found you, Sean, but it's obvious they weren't takin' you to a picnic," Jessica said.

Hound Dog, as usual, sat looking bored by the proceedings. It had been two hours since the abduction, but it seemed like days to him.

"What triggered it?" Ferguson asked. "Something I did struck a nerve?"

"Wellston?" Hound Dog droned.

"Got to be," Jessica said. She turned to look at Hound Dog.

"I talked to Shapiro earlier tonight," Ferguson said. "He's got the Attorney General involved."

A pager chirped and all three looked to their belts. Jessica pulled hers from her waist and looked at the number.

"Office."

A few seconds later and another pager went off. The ritual was repeated. This time it was Hound Dog's turn.

He dialed the office and waited. "Yep." He listened. "Are you sure?" Hanging up, Hound Dog turned to his comrades. Wellston wants us in Lansing right now and said bring Sean. He said Sean was right all along."

Even as tired as Ferguson was, he smiled, "Let's go then."

"At ten o'clock at night?" Jessica said.

Very good, Steve," Bat said. "When the agents get to the Treasury Building, bring them to your office and Mr. Moussa will help you take care of them. We're just going to take them out the fire escape door. Mr. Moussa can disable it so you can get them out without any interference."

"You're sure this will work. Ferguson will never let go. I can't take this much longer," Wellston said.

"Steve, take a deep breath and relax. The extra money has certainly helped you this last couple of years hasn't it?" Bat said.

"Of course but I never bargained for one of my agents getting shot to death."

"That was most unfortunate but look at it this way our plan will eliminate the problems tonight and after a while we'll get back to business as usual." Bat patted Wellston on the back as he grinned. Wellston sighed deeply as if resigned to the plan. "Now go with Moussa and take it one step at a time. Oh, and by the way you've been through so much here's a little extra this month for you."

Wellston opened the envelope and fanned the hundreds. His eyebrows rose. "Thank you, this'll help."

The three agents jumped into Hound Dog's Cadillac for the ride to Lansing. Hound Dog grinned.

"Wow, Dog. Smiling twice in one day," Ferguson said.

"Just plannin' ahead. No, sir, Mr. Wellston, I would never consort with a suspended employee, especially Mr. Ferguson," Hound Dog rattled off. "Lord, knows, sir, I was jus' drivin' round tonight and came across this man in trouble. I had no idea it was Mr. Ferguson when I got involved. Jus' being a good citizen," Pena said. "Don't that sound good."

"If our hunch is right, it'll explain why Wellston wanted me out of the way and why he wouldn't listen to the facts," Ferguson said.

"I gotta tell ya, Sean, I just don't know if Wellston has the balls for smuggling," Jessica said. "Something's not right."

"Guess we'll see," Ferguson said.

They arrived at the Capitol area after an hour's drive. The Treasury building was across the street from the Capitol; two of the four floors looked deserted. Lights burned on the second floor that housed the administration offices. The entire fourth floor was lit because it housed the computer operations, which ran twenty-four hours a day.

"Look's kinda dead, don't it," Hound Dog said.

The three checked in with state police security on the first floor and were escorted to the second floor where keycards were needed to gain access to the offices. It was an eerie sight to see the lights off and the building empty.

Chapter 29

A bell rang as the elevator arrived at the second floor of the Treasury building. Second floor, a pleasant voice announced. Ferguson wondered whom the voice belonged to or how a computer could speak in such a calming way. As the door opened, a gunshot stung the air. All four dropped to the floor like so many sacks of flour. The state trooper from security drew his 9mm Beretta and chambered a round.

"Stay down," he said. He was already on his handheld radio. "Jack, we got a situation on the second floor, in administration. Shot fired. Call it in," he said. They stayed low. All Ferguson could hear was the hum of a florescent light overhead. The trooper slid forward on his belly. His head bobbed out through the open door and back. He gulped and exhaled loudly. Sticking his head back out of the elevator far enough to look in both directions from the central bank of six elevators, all he could see were the six-foot high modular walls that created mazes throughout the floor.

The familiar ring of another elevator arriving split the air. Did the same voice announce the elevator or was it another?

"Doug, this is Jack, whaddya got?" The two troopers had to get control of the situation.

"Don't know yet. Heard the shot and nothin' else."

Now five were waiting for something to flush them from the elevators.

"Haven't seen or heard anyone," the trooper whispered to his partner in the other car. It was fifteen feet to the corner of the elevator corridor—in the open with no cover.

"Any of you guys carrying a weapon?"

"Got a thirty-eight," Hound Dog said. The other two shook their heads, no. "Ferguson, you come with me and Jack. Pena, you and Cooper stay here and hold the fort. The shot came from the administration offices, I think."

The trooper checked his grip on the gun he was holding and moved his fingers to improve it. Ferguson noted the sweat on the grip. The three stooped over and moved toward the offices on the right from the elevator. The loudness of the blast had disguised its origin. While his eyes darted from right to left, the trooper slid a magnetic access card across the brushed steel scanner. The security door to another hall where the offices were located clicked with an electronic burp.

The trooper breathed deeply to build up an oxygen supply before bursting through the door. He dived for carpet, his weapon off safety and ready to fire. The hall was deserted. The offices on the right side of the corridor were all dark, except for the beam of light that showed underneath two of the doors, one near the elevators and the other at the end of the hall. A light also emanated from an office another thirty feet down the hall.

"Shit," the trooper whispered. "If anyone's in any one of those offices and wants to take us out, it'd be like shooting ducks in a barrel." Twenty doors and Ferguson was sure he didn't want to see what was behind door number whatever, if a gunman was about.

He heard the faint sound of sirens in the distance, a lot of sirens. Relief would escape him, however, until he actually saw a lot of gunmetal blue and badges.

"Where to, now?" Ferguson said.

"Towards the light," Doug said. Ferguson noted the sweat forming on the trooper's upper lip. "Just twenty feet." The three bunched up in a line and waddled down the hall together, staying low.

"Just get outta this hall," Ferguson said. His heart was pounding, and he was sure everyone in the building could hear it. He grabbed his chest to quiet the pumping beast.

The three stopped just short of the first door where a light was on. The first trooper jumped across the doorway and turned the doorknob. He pushed the door open. It let out a squeak. The two troopers looked at each other with pained expressions.

"Damn it," Ferguson whispered. A deep breath and a dive through the door left Jack inside a reception area for the administrators. He fanned the room with the Beretta looking for a gunman. The lights were out except for the red glow of an exit lamp and the light from an inside office.

A counter located in front of them proclaimed the offices to be the home of the Administrator of Collection Division, William Daniels. The men moved silently to the door of the office. With guns drawn, both troopers peeked in to find a small black man sitting at the six foot oak desk with his feet up. A New York Yankees baseball cap covered his eyes. The trooper's hands shook as they tensed.

"Freeze," Jack screamed. When the man lurched, the executive chair he was sitting in shot out from under him and he fell to the floor. He quickly jumped up with eyes wide open.

"On the floor, face down," Doug ordered. The troopers stood in a classic shooting stance with legs bent at the knees and both hands on their weapons pointed straight ahead.

"I-I didn't do nothin'" the man screamed. "Don't shoot me.

"Shut up. Get down," Doug said as he waved his Beretta toward the floor.

The troopers couldn't help but notice the janitor's cart with a feather duster, broom, and a large barrel for trash.

"Where's your ID?" the trooper said. He patted the man down.

"M-my ID is on my shirt and my wallet's in my back pocket," the man said. He never blinked and his eyes looked like saucers.

After looking at the driver's license and Treasury identification, the trooper relaxed a bit.

"Sit and stay down against the windows," Jack said with relief in his voice.

The three men returned to the hall and looked to the other lighted office. A long sigh and Doug stepped into the hall again. In a few seconds they were in front of the door. This door was open, light spilled from inside. Ferguson recognized the office immediately as Steve Wellston's.

Inside the office it was as bright as day. After traversing the reception area, Doug gave the all-clear hand signal. Ferguson and Jack crossed the room cautiously, checking around the office to ensure no one had outflanked them. They stood and looked into the office of Steve Wellston.

The smell of cordite hit Ferguson immediately. It left no doubt where the gun

239

had been fired. The 12x15 office made from
modular walls had two doors and was plain
except for the state seal, plaques, awards,
and pictures of the occupant's passion, golf
courses. Ferguson looked at the picture he
always loved in the office, the tenth hole at
Augusta Country Club in Georgia. The wall
behind the desk was glass from top to bottom,
treated with a film so that people outside
were prevented from seeing inside.

Ferguson had never been in Wellston's
office at night, only during the day when the
capitol building stared back at whomever sat
across from Steve Wellston. Two doors, one on
either side of the office, led to an
administrative assistant's desk on one side
and a vacant office on the other side.
Jessica came up behind Ferguson.
"Reinforcements are here."

"Shit," Jessica said. Wellston's chair
had been turned toward the outside wall but a
large hole in the headrest gave a prelude to
what was on the other side. Someone was
sitting in Wellston's burgundy high-backed
leather chair. Blood was splattered on the
window and on the laminate covered walls.
They moved slowly around the chair, standing
immobile like stone monuments for a few
moments. Ferguson acted first. He moved
quickly to the chair but he could see there
was no hope.

"Aw, no, Steve." But Steve Wellston did
not hear him. Ferguson turned to his
comrades. "It's Wellston," Ferguson said.
"And he's holding a gun." The right hand was
wrapped around the handle of a 9mm Beretta.
Ferguson looked at his boss. A bullet had
penetrated the right side of his forehead,
traveled through the brain, and exited the

back of the head, taking a lot of the skull from just behind the ears. "Hollow point," Ferguson said.

"Damn. Guess he couldn't take the guilt after Kate died," Jessica said.

The agents looked around the office. Wellston's laptop was open in the middle of his desk. It was the only thing on the desk. The screen flickered as the flying Windows screensaver rushed at them. Ferguson tapped the keys and text instantly appeared on the screen. He gasped.

"It's a confession," Ferguson said. It says he was calling the shots in the smuggling ring when Kate was killed. "Oh my God." Ferguson composed himself and read aloud for everyone. "Janet, please forgive me. I can't live with myself knowing I caused the agent's death. God knows I never intended for it to happen. I thought I could stop the smuggling any time but the money was so easy. Please forgive..." Ferguson stared at the bottom of the screen.

The three stood in silence for a few minutes before the onslaught of police desecrated the solemn place.

"Damn," Ferguson said. The weight of what had happened was sinking in.

"Look, Boss," Hound Dog said. "I gotta say I think everything's cool. The guy was guilty, man. We got his ass cold. Kate never had a chance because of this asshole."

"Doesn't make it any easier, Dog," Ferguson said.

Within minutes the office was crawling with State Police. Much of the night was taken up with interviews and a thorough investigation of the scene. The crime lab people checked for prints, dusting everything

in sight.   Technicians clicked six-dozen
photographs from every conceivable angle, most
so gruesome they would make people turn away.

A thorough search of the building turned
up no one who wasn't authorized to be there.
The only exits were the bank of elevators or
the stairwells located on either end of the
building. The emergency exits were locked.
The only ways out were the emergency panic
bars on the doors that activated loud alarms
when opened. None had been touched.

State Treasurer, Ken Shapiro, arrived at
the offices at one in the morning, an hour
after the detectives, and immediately pulled
his agents into one of the empty offices.

"What happened guys?" Shapiro said.

"We were paged and told that Wellston
wanted to see us, pronto, in his office. Just
as we got off the elevator, we heard a gunshot
and when we got into the office, he was dead,"
Jessica said.

"Ferguson, what are you doing here?
You're still on suspension, if I'm not
mistaken," Shapiro said.

"I just came up because I was abducted
tonight after I talked to you and Wellston
told Pena he wanted me to come too."

"You were what?" Shapiro said eyes
widening.

"I was picked up tonight by two guys and
if it weren't for Hound Dog, I'd be toast
right now. He saved my life."

"This is unbelievable. At least Wellston
had some remorse for causing Kate's death. I
just hope he was alone in this thing."
Redness crept into Shapiro's face as he
talked. "You find anything in Wellston's
office after the suicide that might lead to

anyone else, because I want'em, every one of them?"

"Nothing but a short note to his wife, admitting to the smuggling and saying he was the cause of Kate's death," Ferguson said.

"Sean, I'm taking you off suspension. It's obvious why Wellston wanted you out of the picture. We need you back in the unit. I want to talk to you tomorrow afternoon. I'll be busy with legislators in the morning. Say two, in my office."

"I'll be there. Thank you, sir," Ferguson said.

"And Sean, I need to see you alone for a minute," Shapiro said. Ferguson and Shapiro walked toward the elevators.

"I think we need to keep a lid on this investigation. I'm glad we can put this to bed, even though Wellston was the man calling the shots. The bastard got what he deserves." The two men stopped and Shapiro put his hand on Ferguson's shoulder. "I hope we can put all this business behind us."

"Yes, sir." But something was already sticking in Ferguson's craw.

Chapter 30

By seven the morning after Wellston's death, Ferguson still had not slept. The State Police had called saying his Jeep had been found in Wixom with the keys in it so at least he would get his wheels back. He lay on the sofa at Jessica's staring at the ceiling, trying to make some sense of the previous night. He sat up, rubbed his bloodshot eyes, and rose quietly to make coffee. Would his life get back to normal now? As normal as can be expected, he thought. He wondered what Joanne and the girls were doing. He glanced at the wall clock. At 7:15 a.m. the girls would be jockeying for the first shower privilege. No, probably not. It took a cannon to wake Emily. Joanne would be making lunches. Peanut butter and jelly, the two constants in those lunches, would be slapped on the Wonder bread. Peanut butter on both halves of the bread would keep the bread from getting soggy. Did Joanne know that? Ferguson made the lunches when he could. Doubts crowded in. Would it ever be the same again? After sipping his first caffeine of the day, Ferguson grabbed the cordless phone and stepped into the den where he could have some privacy.

"Joanne?" he tentatively said when his wife answered the phone.

"Hello, Sean," she said, matter of factly.

"How are you?" he said.

"We're fine. And you?" she said.

Ferguson thought maybe the phone call was a mistake.

"Doin' okay. I just thought I'd call and let you know that Steve Wellston died last night." No response. "The Treasurer reinstated me. Steve was involved in the smuggling ring that caused Kate's death according to a note he left."

Ferguson hoped for a chink in the armor protecting Joanne's emotions. "You sure you're okay, Sean?" she said.

"As well as can be expected since I screwed up my life over the murders of two people I loved." Maybe not the best choice of words, he thought.

"And what about your daughters and me? Where do we fit into your life? Are you going to sacrifice the living for the dead?"

"I know it doesn't mean much, Joanne, but I know I've made mistakes but I just can't walk away from this. All I can say is I pray it's not too late for us." There was silence.

"We'll talk, Sean."

"That's all I ask," Ferguson said. He hung up the phone and lay down to rest.

His arrival at the office brought division employees to welcome him back. After a few backslaps and comments about his banishment, Ferguson retired to his cramped office and shut the door. Something just didn't sit right with him. He couldn't place it.

There was a knock at the door and Jessica popped her head in.

"What's up?"

"Something's wrong, Jess. I don't know what it is but something's not right about Steve's death. Can you think of anything we might have missed?"

"Nope. Not a thing. The sonofabitch got what's coming to him. Just drop it, Sean.

You know if I thought something was wrong, I'd call it," Jessica said.

"I know. Guess I'm looking for trouble. Thanks, Jess."

She left Ferguson to his thoughts.

What was it? What was bothering him? Ferguson doodled on the desk pad in front of him, making notes to no one. He punched the intercom button and Jessica returned.

"Come on in, Jess, and close the door," Ferguson said. Before Jessica could sit down Ferguson was talking. "He didn't do it. Wellston didn't kill himself."

Jessica was stunned. "How do you know that, Sean? We heard the shot. We smelled the cordite. Hell, half his head was gone. There wasn't anyone else on the floor, except for Rip Van Winkle, the cleaning guy. There wasn't any way anyone could get past us to get out of the building without an alarm sounding." Jessica rested. "So how can you say he was murdered?"

"Just bear with me, Jess," Ferguson said. He was in the mode. "How did Steve sign his name for as long as you knew him?"

"I don't know, S-T-E-V-E, I suppose," Jessica said.

"No, think about it."

"Oh yeah, he always left off the last E," Jessica said.

"Like he was always in a hurry."

"Exactly," Ferguson said.

"So what's your point," Jessica said.

"In Steve's note on the laptop, he typed his name with the E on the end. I've known him for fifteen years and he never used the letter."

"Maybe, it was a mistake; I mean, he wasn't himself," Jessica said.

246

"I don't think so. It also bothers me because Steve didn't have the guts to do it."

"But who then?" Jessica said.

"Dunno," Ferguson said. "But one thing's for sure. It's got to be someone who was tight with Wellston. The guy got out of the building without going down the elevators. He must have opened the emergency doors with a key or they'd have lit up the building like a Christmas tree."

"Hell there's at least a hundred people who have keys to that building," Jessica said.

"Yeah, but how many have the keys to the panic bars on the outside doors? Maybe ten people. Still too many to check out but it's a start."

"So what do you want us to do? I just got a call from Charley. He found a real pretty bug under your right fender. Said it was state of the art. Newest technology. He said they could tail you to hell and back," Jessica said. "He put one of his own homing devices somewhere else in your jeep so we can keep tabs on you, since you're so popular. He also put one on my Camaro."

"We need to keep this quiet," Ferguson said. "I'll brief Hound Dog about what we know. I think it's best if you two distance yourselves from me, for now. I'll shadow you and you do likewise. If we both have the GPS tracking capabilities maybe these guys will make a mistake. Make all calls on pay phones unless it's an emergency. The bad guys know I've got someone watchin' my back after last night and I'm concerned about you and the Dog."

After picking up his Jeep with big brother attached under the rear bumper,

Ferguson called the Treasurer on the private number in his office.

"Shapiro."

"Sir, this Sean Ferguson," he said.

"Sean, how are you? Everyone happy to put all this mess to bed?"

"That's why I called, sir. I don't think Wellston took his own life. I think he was murdered."

"W-what are you saying? We're not done with this? That we still have someone inside who's responsible? I can't believe that."

"Yes sir, that's exactly what I'm saying. Look, one of the techs at the state police lab found a homing device on my car. How many people have access to that technology? I now have one of our devices inside my Jeep and on Cooper's car so our people can track us. Steve spelled his name wrong on his note on the laptop. We're not out of this yet, I know it."

"Sean, meet me at my house tonight at 7:00 p.m. and bring Cooper. We better keep this quiet. I'll have the commander of the capitol security force there so we can discuss it. Don't say a word to anyone."

"Yes sir, We'll be there."

As he prepared to leave the office at 6:30p.m., Ferguson's phone rang. He snatched it up, thinking it might be Shapiro.

"Ferguson," he said.

"This is Jamal Ghaleed, Mr. Ferguson."

Ferguson tensed. "Yes, sir?"

"I am Michael's cousin. We found some papers at his house that may be of some help in catching the people responsible for his death."

"What are the papers?" Ferguson asked.

There are phone numbers in Dearborn and a note that he talked to people in Dearborn and the name Paul Hamood with other names I don't know. There is a letter from Hamood about his store."

"Jamal, can you fax me these documents now?" Ferguson asked, cutting the man off.

"Yes, I can. I just need to go up to my store. It would take about ten minutes to get there," Jamal said.

"Please do it, now. My number is 222-0978. I'll wait for your fax," Ferguson said.

Hanging up the phone, Ferguson hit the speed dial to call Jessica.

Chapter 31

Jessica's cell phone buzzed as she drove toward the Okemos exit on Interstate 96. She glanced at her watch knowing she was running a little late.

"Yeah, Sean. I'm on my way," Jessica said without waiting for a response.

"Jess, we got a break. Ghaleed's cousin Jamal called and is faxing evidence on Hamood. I can't leave until it comes. I need you to get to Shapiro's house. Tell him I've been delayed but I'll be there."

"I'll be there in ten minutes, Sean."

Jessica tromped on the accelerator and the Treasury surveillance Camaro lurched forward. Arriving at Treasurer Shapiro's house she tossed her cell phone on the passenger seat and jumped from the car trotting to the door of the tutor home. Shapiro opened the door while on a cordless phone and motioned Jessica to come in.

Putting his hand over the microphone on the phone he whispered to Jessica, "Wait out here, Ms. Cooper. I'll be done here in a minute. Thanks."

Jessica looked around the spacious foyer made homey by the two-dozen family pictures on the walls and the muted light of three table lamps scattered along the wainscoted walls. Colorful floral wallpaper provided a busy backdrop for the framed photographs. She started near the door, looking at a picture of Shapiro's father with John F Kennedy. Jessica recognized the man from his later years serving the state as a congressman in Washington.

Continuing down the row of various sized frames, she looked at other pictures with Shapiro himself shaking hands with politicians, some that Jess knew and some that she didn't. The last six or seven pictures showed the images of family properties and relatives. To pass the time she focused on the people in the photos until she reached the second photo from the end. Glancing at the photo, it took a few seconds for the writing and picture to register in her brain. What was it that triggered her brain? She stared at the picture as if waiting for it to talk to her.

"Holy shit. Why does that ring a bell?" she whispered to herself. It hit her like a ton of bricks. "No, It can't be. There must be some mistake," she whispered to herself. There certainly could be an explanation. But she knew she was right.

Pulling a small tablet from the breast pocket of her flannel shirt, she jotted down "Farhill Farm- Saline" just as it was printed on the picture. Ripping it from the tablet, Jessica shoved it into her breast pocket.

Spinning around she saw Shapiro end his call and put the phone on the desk as he moved toward her.

"I'm sorry, sir. Just got a call from dispatch. They need me right away but Sean Ferguson should be here momentarily." With a sweat bead forming on her brow she moved to the door as quickly as she could.

"Okay, Ms. Cooper. Is everything all right? You look nervous about something."

"I'm fine, sir. I-I'll be going now."

Jessica walked through the door and as it closed, sprinted to her car. Jamming the floor shifter into gear, she crammed the pedal down and the car screamed backwards onto the street. She felt for her cell phone but could not find it.

"Shit, don't tell me. Not the phone," Jessica said as she hurtled down Okemos road. She wouldn't even mind attracting a traffic cop right now. She had to talk to Ferguson.

The Camaro skidded sideways as she made the turn onto Okemos Road and headed south. As she neared Interstate 96, Jessica saw the Mobil gasoline station and roared into it. The tires screamed as she threw the shifter into park before she was stopped. Leaving the car running, she bolted into the station. Glancing at the clerk, she screamed, "Payphone?"

"In the back by the restrooms," the young man said. Passing the side door to the outside, she was already scrounging change from her pockets.

Jessica dropped two quarters into the phone and began punching numbers but before she could finish someone shoved something into her side so hard it took her breath away. Jessica turned to see a man with jet-black hair and a face that looked like the moonscape it had so many craters.

"Put the phone down, now, Ms. Cooper," Crater-face said, as his little smile turned to a sneer. The gun barrel pinched her side as it was pushed into ribs so hard she knew it would leave a bruise. "Now, walk right through this door and to the back of the station.

As they rounded the corner of the gas station, she saw the Lincoln Towncar. Crater-face tossed her the key. "Open the trunk."

Jessica did as she was told and just as it popped open she felt a stinging blow to her neck and she collapsed.

At 7:15 p.m. the fax still had not come and Ferguson had an uneasy feeling forming in his gut. He pulled Ghaleed's file for a home number. He fumbled with the phone as he urgently punched in the number. The telephone rang four times before being picked up.

"Mrs. Ghaleed, this is Sean Ferguson. Is Jamal there?"

"Mr. Ferguson, you have a lot of nerve calling me," Mrs. Ghaleed said. "And there is no Jamal here."

"Did he leave to go fax some papers?" Ferguson said as the words stuck in his throat.

"No. I don't know any Jamal," she said.

Ferguson's throat constricted and his chest felt as if a sledgehammer had landed. Ferguson hung up the phone. Why? Who called? Jessica! Oh my God! Ferguson hit the speed dial. "C'mon Jess. Answer dammit." But there was no answer. He clicked the phone off and hit Hound Dog's cell phone number.

After five rings the voicemail message came on. "This is Orlando Pena. I'm not..."

"Dammit!" Ferguson screamed. Ferguson fumbled with his phone as he hunted for Shapiro's home number in his wallet.

"She left about ten after seven, Sean," Shapiro said. "I was on the phone and she was waiting in my foyer. When I finished, she looked nervous and said she had to leave immediately and that you would be coming. What's going on?"

"I'll get back to you, sir. I think Cooper's in trouble. We have a homing device in her car so I'll try to find her," Ferguson said.

"I'll call the State Police Post for assistance and a statewide alert," Shapiro said.

Ferguson stopped on the Okemos Road exit about two miles from Shapiro's house and opened a briefcase with the tracking equipment. Jumping from the car he threw the antennae with the magnetic base on the roof of the car. Sliding back into the driver's seat, he switched the tracking equipment on and felt relief when he saw the blip on the screen indicating the device was working properly. His spirits lifted until he noticed that Jessica's car was not moving. He hit the speed dial for Jessica's phone. No answer.

Ferguson looked at the display and determined which direction he should go- south on Okemos Road.

Stomping on the gas pedal, Ferguson sped toward Okemos. As he came over a rise he saw a Mobil gasoline station and some activity near the door. A car sat near the door with its door open. As he neared, his heart soared at the sight of Jessica's Camaro. Pulling in, he found the engine running and the door left open. He sprang from his car and ran inside.

"Where is the woman who was driving that Camaro outside?" Ferguson screamed.

The attendant just shrugged and shook his head. "She came in and went right to the payphone in the back. The next thing I knew she was gone. I didn't know what to do so I called the police."

Ferguson ran to Jessica's car. The microphone had been ripped from the radio and flung into the back seat. Her cell phone was gone. He scrambled inside looking for anything that would give him an idea where she had gone.

A crumpled piece of paper lay on the floor on the passenger side of the car. In an instant Ferguson had it clutched in his hand, backing out of the car.

Running into the brightly lighted gasoline station, Ferguson screamed again. "Tell me the cars you saw come in here when the agent came in."

"I only saw the Camaro after she ran inside. I didn't see anything," the kid said, clearly nervous.

Ferguson's eyes darted left and right. "Anyone else see the car the woman got into. Please, anyone see anything."

No one saw anything. Dead end. Gone without a trace. He slammed the roof of the Camaro with his fist and staggered to his car. Slumping into the drivers seat, Ferguson suddenly felt totally helpless. Shoving his hand into the pocket of his jeans, he pulled the car keys out and the crumpled paper popped out and fell on the floor. Reaching down, he picked up the paper and tossed it in the ashtray.

After a few seconds he stared at the paper and slowly picked it up. Opening it, he read Farhill Farm- Saline area. He knew there was a post office box for Farhill from his visit to the post office but no address. There are dozens of farms out there in the county. Where in the hell was this one? Think Ferguson, he ordered.

Ferguson paged Hound Dog again without success. How do two agents get lost in a matter of an hour? It was now almost 9:00 p.m. and the darkness had settled in. Four police vehicles with lights flashing sat in

Rick J. Barrett

the gasoline station along with detective cars accomplishing nothing.

"This is all I've got Sarge," Ferguson said to the command officer in charge as he showed the paper. "I believe that Agent Cooper and maybe Pena are in grave danger but I have no idea where they've been taken."

Chapter 32

As Ferguson sat in his car praying
something would point them in the right
direction, thoughts he couldn't even face kept
popping into his head. It would tear out his
heart if something happened to Jessica and the
Hound. After fifteen minutes that felt like
hours, he stepped from the car and approached
the detective in charge.

"We gotta do something, Sarge. Have you
got anything?" Ferguson asked.

The man just shook his head back and
forth. "Sorry, Ferguson."

"I can't just sit around. I'm going down
to Ann Arbor. If I can roust someone from the
County Register of Deeds, maybe I can find out
where this Farhill Farm is," Ferguson said.
"I'll radio you if I find something."

Ferguson jumped into his car and pulled a
guide to Michigan government that listed all
eighty-three counties and the officials. What
did he expect to accomplish at this hour?
Where would they take his friends?

Throwing the car into gear he was on
Interstate 96 in minutes and pushing the Jeep
to ninety miles per hour- not even giving a
second thought to the speed limit.

Arriving in Ann Arbor just after ten
o'clock he grabbed the government directory
and went to the Ann Arbor police Department
downtown on Fifth and Huron. Running to the
desk he asked for the duty officer. A
Lieutenant Ward came to the desk.

Ferguson stuck his hand out.
"Lieutenant, my name is Sean Ferguson. I'm
with Treasury Fraud and two of my agents were
kidnapped earlier in Okemos. I have reason to

believe they are being taken to a farm in
Washtenaw County named Farhill. It's the only
lead I've got. State Police are attempting to
develop leads at the site of the kidnapping
but I felt I needed to be here."

"How can we help, Ferguson?"

"I need to find someone who knows where
this farm is. The only way I can think of is
to get someone from the Register of Deeds to
open the records tonight to do a search."

The lieutenant turned to his sergeant on
the desk. "We've got a list of home phones
for the county building don't we, Jim?"

In ten minutes they had the County Clerk
on his way to open the building that was
located only four blocks away.

"Thanks, Lieutenant. I'll be in touch
when I find what I'm looking for." Ferguson
ran out and jumped in his car for the short
ride.

While waiting, he pulled out his thirty-
eight and checked to make sure it was loaded.
He knew this might be the day he had to use it
to shoot someone.

Tom Fisk arrived to open the doors. With
suspenders holding up his dress slacks over a
t-shirt and his hair looking like it had spent
the last three days under a hat, Ferguson
appreciated the man's effort to get to his
office. The two men rushed to Fisk's office
on the second floor. The office had ten desks
arranged in two rows with in and out baskets
stacked full on every desk. Microfiche
viewers stood on three desks and card files
that must have been 100 years old lined one
wall. A counter ran twenty feet along another
wall. In a mixture of present and past, eight
computer stations and a server took up another
wall. The original plat books were stacked in

one corner and looked well used. Ferguson could relate to the stacks and stacks of paper. His desk could easily been put into this mix and no one would know he did anything different than the rest.

"If it's part of the records Mr. Ferguson, we'll find it," Fisk said.

But after thirty minutes of searching, they found nothing indicating a Farhill Farm in the records.

"I'm sorry Mr. Ferguson, I don't know where it's at," Fisk said.

Ferguson slammed one of the plat books closed. "It's okay, Mr. Fisk, it was a long shot anyway. I appreciate the effort." Ferguson turned to leave. Fisk turned out the lights and locked the door. Ferguson unlocked his car door and prepared to leave. He didn't have any idea where he would go but he had to go somewhere. Searching for his keys, he saw Fisk wave wildly as he ran toward Ferguson's car.

"I just thought of someone who might know something that will help you Mr. Ferguson. Heddy Frembes was the clerk around here for years and she grew up in Saline. Maybe, she'd be of some help," Fisk said. "She lives here in Ann Arbor now."

"Anything is worth a try," Ferguson said without much conviction.

Arriving at a senior apartment complex on the east side of Ann Arbor, Ferguson and Fisk found Frembes name on the marquee after getting past the guard. Ferguson pushed the button four or five times hoping Heddy was a light sleeper. Almost one in the morning, they were surprised to find her awake.

"Come on up, gentlemen, apartment seven-eighteen," Heddy said when she quickly answered the page.

Heddy could only be described as perky. To say someone is perky at eighty-two is a testimony to her spirit. Her hair was totally white but was obviously tended to on a regular basis by a hairdresser. She weighed only ninety pounds fully dressed but was about as toned as an old lady could get.

"Hi, Tommy. How are you these days? I think the last time I saw you was two years ago at that hoopla about the historical society," Heddy said.

Fisk looked a little embarrassed. "I'm sure you're right, Heddy."

"I'm a night owl gentlemen. Always have been. So what can I do for you at this late hour," she asked.

"Heddy, Mr. Ferguson is with the Treasury Department and he's trying to find a farm down Saline way called Farhill Farm. We've checked all the books and can't find any reference to Farhill Farm. Do you happen to know where it is?"

"Well, hell yes. I only lived a few miles from it back in 1934," she said confidently.

Ferguson immediately perked up and listened intently.

"It's about three miles south of Michigan Avenue west of town. Real pretty house with a bunch of gingerbread as I recall. Jamisons lived there," Heddy said.

Ferguson gave her a peck on the cheek and bolted for the door. "Thank you, Heddy," Ferguson said.

He was on the trail again but he had lost so much time. Would they still be alive? All he could do was get there as soon as possible and pray they were still alive. Glancing at his watch he was shocked to see that it had already been seven hours since they went missing.

The red phone rang in Bat's bedroom. At least he hadn't left for his office.

"Yes," Bat said as he picked up the receiver.

"This is Scarponi, boss. We got trouble down here. The Feds are all over us. They slapped me with a search warrant and know about the room in the back. There must be twenty of'em here and they are searching with a fine-tooth comb. What do I do?"

Bat sat bolt upright. "Damn, Scarponi. Protect the records and hopefully they won't find the other room. Call me when they're gone. Who's in charge?"

"Some guy named Moffat is pullin' the strings. He's the same guy I saw with Ferguson last week."

"I'll talk to you soon, Mr. Scarponi."

Bat pulled the phone out of the wall after hanging up. No, actually he wouldn't be talking to Scarponi again. He was so happy he had decided to recruit some new help some months ago- that explosives man. Bat dialed a cell phone number he had not used before.

"Hello," Boom Boom said.

"It is time to wake up, sir," Bat said.

"Yes."

"Take the package to Moussa's home at 856 Hendry in Ann Arbor. Hide it but not too well. Is that understood?"

"Yes, sir."

Chapter 33

Bat hit the speed dial to Moussa at the warehouse as he drove toward Lansing.

"Yeah."

Moussa, I can't get there right now and I want the agents out of the picture. Kill them as I would and dump their bodies. I don't care where but it has to be done now. They're too close."

"When will I see you," Moussa asked warily.

"I'll meet you at S&S in one week. Don't say anything to the others. Business as usual," Bat said before clicking off the phone. After stripping the phone of its directory of numbers, Bat opened the side window of the car and hurled it toward a wooded area adjoining the freeway.

Ferguson flew out of the parking lot at Heddy's apartment. Almost losing control on a turn, the car skidded as Ferguson punched the accelerator to regain control. As he neared the entrance to U.S. 23 to go south toward Michigan Avenue and Saline he grabbed the radio and called the State Police at the Brighton Post for help.

"Dispatch, this is Sean Ferguson with Treasury. I'm trying to find the agents who were kidnapped in Okemos and have a lead where they might be. I'm on my way and need backup now. Forsyth Road south off Michigan two miles west of Saline. Advise the Monroe Post and Washtenaw County Sheriff Department," Ferguson said breathlessly.

"Copy that, Agent Ferguson. Will send the troops."

Barreling toward Farhill Farm Ferguson could not help but wonder if he was too late to save his friends. "Please let them be alive."

The radio squawked. "Brighton Post to Ferguson. Troopers advise ETA in twenty minutes."

Shit, thought Ferguson, I'll be there in ten minutes.

His reaction was to bury the accelerator in the floor. Hurtling down Michigan, Ferguson tried to focus on the roads as they crossed until he found Forsyth Road. Stomping on the brake, the car fishtailed a bit and almost came to a complete stop right at the intersection. Ferguson turned the wheel left and hit the accelerator. He slowed as he went by mailbox after mailbox. Then he saw painted box- Farhill Farm. Stopping about a hundred feet from the drive, Ferguson took a deep breath to settle him.

He sat glancing at his watch before deciding that they would need some kind of reconnaissance before going in anyway so he might as well do it now.

Slipping out of his Jeep, Ferguson moved up the drive using the trees as cover. As he neared the clearing at the top of a rise he could see the white gingerbread on the house from the reflected moonlight just as Heddy has said. There were three cars parked near the barn and Ferguson recognized Hound Dog's Caddy as the one nearest the door.

So what's going on in there, you guys. Havin' a party or something, Ferguson wondered. Ferguson moved over to the side of the barn farthest from the house. Then he listened with his ear against the wall. He heard something but couldn't quite make it out. Then he clearly heard a scream. Was it Jessica?

He couldn't tell.

Glancing at his watch, Ferguson began to sweat. He griped his gun so tightly he thought it would be crushed. He shook his head. Where the hell were they, he thought. Almost nauseous from fear of waiting, Ferguson thought of a tune that stayed in the back of his mind. It whirled around in there. "Let's Get It On" by Marvin Gaye kept repeating until Ferguson made the decision.

Taking a deep breath, he bolted to the door and flung it open. He gasped and froze for what seemed like an eternity as he saw his two agents chained to horse stalls lying bloodied and limp as Moussa stood over them with a piece of pipe.

"You sonofabitch," Ferguson screamed as he came to his senses and fired his gun wide of his target.

Moussa dived for cover as he pulled his 45 from its holster and came up firing. The second shot hit Ferguson like a Mack truck in the left shoulder, spinning him around as the bullet plowed through him and exited out his back. As the pain invaded his brain he became disoriented and fell behind cases of cigarettes.

Oh, shit, it hurt, Ferguson thought and then his combat experience took over like autopilot. Shaking the cobwebs from his head he rolled and with his one good arm pulled himself away from the last place the man had seen him. Attempting to stem the flow of blood, Ferguson took a glove from his pocket and pushed it into the wound. White lights appeared as the excruciating pain racked him.

Got to move, he thought. He sat in an aisle about twenty feet long. If the man came around the corner on either end he would be mince meat. Ferguson slid on his side down the aisle as fast as he could and peering around the end of a case saw his chance to move toward a wall so he would only have to guard three sides. He stopped short when the man called.

"Ferguson, how nice of you to join us," Moussa said. "It saves me the trouble of looking for you. Now that I've taken care of the rest of your team, it was your turn anyway."

How did this man know them? Where did he get all the information? Was it really Wellston after all? He had to keep the man talking. He was on the other side of the warehouse now but Ferguson knew he would be coming. By giving Ferguson his whereabouts the man probably thought Ferguson would try and bolt for the door to live for another day and pick him off knowing his reflexes were slowed by the gunshot. The man obviously underestimated Ferguson's resolve. One of them would leave today in a body bag.

Leaning on a case of cigarettes, Ferguson strained to crouch to get the lay of the land. It looked like three rows of cigarettes, and then seven horse stalls. Ferguson was shocked by the extent of the construction that had been done inside. The whole front half of the barn was open and parked in the first three stalls were cars which no doubt were used for smuggling. Tiled floors throughout and fluorescent lights over the back half of the barn made it look like some industrial building. In fact, the only landmark that looked like a barn was the stall. Behind him,

Ferguson saw a long built-in area with
communication equipment blinking incessantly.

"Come on now, Ferguson," Moussa said,
"Give it up. You know the pain is just too
much. You've lost your whole team and your
friend from Vietnam. You don't want to
prolong the pain any longer, do you."

Oh, my God. How the hell does he know
about Billy? Ferguson thought. S&S is their
supplier. They own their own cigarette
wholesaler.

Ferguson took off one of his boots and
moved silently to the second row of cigarettes
near the back of the barn. He placed the boot
on its side so that anyone peering around the
corner would think he was there. He retreated
to the back corner of the room and behind what
looked like a makeshift closest for cleaning
materials and tools.

The pain threatened to consume him now
and Ferguson feared he would pass out. He
clutched the thirty-eight in his right hand
but the sweat and blood made it almost too
slippery to hold. His head slumped forward as
weakness and fatigue took him. He woke with a
start after hearing a scrapping noise along
the floor on the other side of the room.
Looking down at his shirt he saw the blood now
saturated the entire front of the garment.
Must be bleeding out, Ferguson thought.

The noise again- closer to the back of
the room. He was coming. Ferguson slunk back
into the closest as far as he dare without
knocking over buckets. Come on you bastard.
Take the bait.

Leaning over to look out of his hiding
place, Ferguson thought he saw a flash of
color. Was it the loss of blood or was the
man checking out his ruse? He held his breath

as he saw it again. The man slid around the
end of the last row as quiet as a mouse,
moving silently toward the boot. Ferguson
waited until the man was no more than fifteen
feet away and ready to pounce on his boot like
some cat after catnip. It was now or never.
Ferguson leaned falling out of his hiding
place with gun pointed at the man.

Surprised, Moussa attempted to raise his
weapon but Ferguson fired four rounds from his
own gun. Falling over on his left side the
pain was unbearable as the white lights
returned. The lights didn't dissipate this
time, though, and Ferguson's gun fell to the
floor as he went into the blinding light.

Chapter 34

The bright lights woke him but this time
it was a flashlight held by a doctor.
Ferguson's eyes darted wildly left and right
as he struggled to sit up. The pounding in
his head quashed that idea and he slumped back
onto the bed.

"Whoa, there partner, take it easy," the
doctor said. "You've been through the mill and
need rest. That was a mighty big hole in you
we had to patch up."

Joanne and the girls sprang to his side.
"Oh, Sean," Joanne said as she bent to kiss
him. Tears rolled down her face and she
cupped his hand in hers. "I'm so sorry."

"Joanne, I'm the one who should be sorry.
I've been away too long and you've borne the
brunt of my folly," Ferguson said.

Ferguson looked around his bed and felt
oddly at peace. The last thing he remembered
was firing his gun. "How did I get here?" he
said in a raspy voice.

"They brought you in last night after the
shootout," Joanne said. "They didn't know if
you would live or not you had lost so much
blood."

And then Ferguson remembered. "They
killed Jess and the Hound, Jo. I saw them
strung up in one of the stalls."

"No, no, Sean, they're okay. They were
knocked out and have a few broken bones but
they'll be fine. In fact, they're next door
waiting for you to wake up."

Ferguson blinked and rolled his head on
the pillow as the fuzziness started to fade
and his mind cleared. Ten minutes later
Jessica, sporting casts on her right arm and

leg, was pushed into the room in a wheelchair and Hound Dog with a cast on his left wrist, bandages on his head, and a mouthful of grinning teeth stepped in beside her.

Ferguson looked at Hound Dog. "Guess you're happy today."

"Guess I am," Hound Dog said as he started to laugh that deep baritone hoot.

"How you doin', Jess?" Ferguson asked.

"Just fine, for right now," she said, grinning at her boss.

Ken Shapiro came into the room. "Is anyone invited to this party?" he said grinning at his agents.

A look of terror contorted Jessica's face as all color drained from it.

"Yes, sir, anytime," Ferguson said.

"Sean, I want to offer my congratulations on breaking up what probably was the largest cigarettes smuggling operation ever in this state," Shapiro said. "We're still uncovering information but it was huge and stretched down to North Carolina." Moussa, the man you killed, appears to be the mastermind. We found papers in the barn that show these people might be tied to terrorism through Hamas or Hezbollah. The F.B.I. has them and will launch a full-scale investigation. They executed search warrants in North Carolina and at Moussa's home in Ann Arbor. A guy named Scarponi told us Moussa ran the show. We don't know all the stores involved but it's only a matter of time. What I can't believe is that they're using that farm for distribution. It was in our family for years until my uncle passed away twelve years ago. My cousins were living out of state and didn't want it so they sold it. I never dreamed it could be used for smuggling."

Rick J. Barrett

"So, we got them all?" Ferguson asked.

"We sure did. They found papers at Moussa's home for the farm that outlined the entire organization. Now, listen, you three. I want you to get rested up and we'll debrief in the next few days," Shapiro said as he shook hands all around and prepared to leave.

"As your doctor I concur with the need to get some rest. Everybody out while my patient gets some shuteye."

Ken Shapiro took the elevator down to the first floor of the University of Michigan Hospital in Ann Arbor, stepped outside and took a deep breath. It was a beautiful day and he thought maybe a walk in downtown Ann Arbor might do him some good. He was still eight or nine blocks from Main Street so he walked to his Lincoln Town Car in the lot to drive closer. Yes indeed, it was a glorious day.

About the Author

Rick Barrett is an avid reader who has taken his love of books to another level with the completion of the murder/ mystery, "Farhill Farm". He has used his experience as a Michigan Treasury Agent as a basis for the book. His nearly thirty years as a Warrant Officer working on collection and fraud cases have given him a unique perspective that comes through in the work. Cigarette smuggling, possible terrorist connections, and huge financial rewards combine for an intriguing story.

After attending Oakland University in Rochester, Michigan, Mr. Barrett began writing for his three young daughters while taking courses and attending seminars to hone his skill.

Printed in the United States
1366900005B/205-282

9 781410 775597